I0818002

The Vanquisher

Also by Zoe van Lingen

The Liberator Duology

The Liberator

The Vanquisher

Book 2

Zoe van Lingen

This is a work of fiction. Names, characters, places, and incidents either are the product of the author's imagination or are used fictitiously. Any resemblance to actual persons, living or dead, events, or locales is entirely coincidental.

zoevanlingen@gmail.com.

Cover design by Lena Yang

ISBN: 978-1-7776174-4-8

For everyone that's a hero to someone

Chapter 1

Jax knew where we could go. With no better options, Henry, Valerie and I followed him across the City. We kept our heads down and our hoods up to avoid drawing attention. There was no sense in making our location obvious to the Government.

Jax led us through part of the City I found familiar. It would've been quicker to take the road running down the side of the Apartment Districts, 1 through 12, but that was designated for vehicles and patrolled day and night by guards. One would've stopped us in seconds if we walked it, which was why we avoided it now as we had when we'd entered the City.

Jax led us southward, and we passed the streets I'd walked with my mom. The districts became foreign to me as we progressed. My former Apartment District was run down and neglected, but the horrid state of the final one we stepped into, visible even with the setting sun casting everything an orange hue, shocked me. The buildings' concrete walls were grimy with cracks running up their sides, and a layer of dirt coated the uneven asphalt. It crunched under my feet and sent clouds of dust into the air.

"We're almost there," Jax said as he pushed his hood off. There was tension in his shoulders that hadn't been present in the clearing.

"And just where is that?" Valerie asked. She kept her own hood up, though her blonde hair peeked out and hung down the front of her jacket.

We had left Charlie and the Colony fighters a few hours earlier. The extended time on our feet was draining on all of us, on top of the morning's battle. My adrenaline was gone, and the Leader's irate face as she plunged into the water lingered in my mind. It had left me shaken, but I couldn't dwell on what I'd done. Finding safety was my new priority.

"There," Jax said, pointing to a dilapidated building a hundred metres away.

"It has to be the worst building on the street," I muttered.

Henry, from his place beside me, squeezed my hand. He'd stayed next to me since we'd fetched Jax and fled. We hadn't discussed his father, or Malcolm's warning, but I knew a flurry of emotions must've swirled inside him. "At least we'll be inside before curfew," Henry said.

Jax nodded. It would be disastrous if a guard found us. Even with Max's support, I didn't want to risk being caught and arrested.

Our destination was in remarkably worse condition than the neighbouring structures, and I wasn't sure how it still stood or housed anyone. Jax opened the door with a loud and prolonged creak. The rusty hinges were in dire need of oil.

A gruff voice boomed from the darkness. "Who enters my building?"

I couldn't spot the speaker as the entry was shrouded in shadows. Jax stepped forward and flicked a light switch. Expecting bright light, I flung my arm over my eyes. Instead, a dim, flickering lightbulb cast a faint glow over the small foyer. An older man with greying hair, piercing brown eyes and dark skin, stood scowling in the hallway and blocking the staircase.

"We need somewhere to stay," Jax said. "Please, Mr. Irvine."

Mr. Irvine's eyes widened, and his eyebrows shot up. "Jax?" he asked, most of his hostility gone, though he had his arms crossed. "I never thought you'd show up here again."

I cut in before Jax, with his mouth open, could reply. "We had nowhere else to go." I was wary, but Mr. Irvine and Jax knew each other, so I tried to control my suspicion.

Mr. Irvine's eyes drifted onto me with recognition. "You're the girl from the video."

"Yes," I said, a bit shocked at his statement. "You watched it?"

He laughed. "Girl, you know when the screen turns on people drop everything to watch. A person can get into a lot of trouble if they don't."

I gaped, having not expected people to recognize me this easily. The day prior I'd been anonymous. This would make going out difficult.

"We weren't sure if it worked," Henry said, still holding my hand. "That's why Molly asked."

What Henry said was true, even with Jax's assurances that the video played as planned. We hadn't seen any signs of a reaction to my video, calling for support, as we'd crossed the City.

Mr. Irvine's eyes flicked across Henry before landing on Jax again. "You've got yourself a group of criminals for friends, Jax. I suppose you were behind the video." He narrowed his eyes, expecting Jax to deny it or cower in shame.

Jax kept his head high and maintained eye contact. "We only did what we had to. Will you help us or not?"

"All I can do is send you upstairs. I can't guarantee what happens when you get there." My Irvine stepped aside and waved us onward.

…

The interior of the building was in as bad a condition as the exterior. The stairs had cracks in them, and a thick layer of dust covered the banister. I gave it a wide berth to keep my hands and clothes clean.

"What floor are we going to?" Valerie asked from a couple stairs below me. It was the first thing she'd said since we entered the building.

"The fifth," Jax said.

Even though he was in front of me, and I couldn't see his face, I could tell something troubled him. His shoulders were tense and stiff, as if an enormous weight had settled on them. I opened my mouth to speak and thought better of it.

It didn't surprise me that this building lacked an elevator. Each landing we passed was as run-down and dirty as the last. When we reached the fifth floor, I was relieved, if only at leaving the staircase. The hallway was dimly lit, and dingy, red carpeting covered the floor. No one had cleaned it in a very long time, if ever. Jax strode down the hall with Valerie following. Henry and I brought up the rear.

"Do you think we're safe here?" I asked Henry, keeping my voice down.

"I don't know," he said, brushing his hair off his forehead with his free hand. "It's not like we have a better option."

"Jax seemed sure of it earlier," I said. "Now he seems tense."

Henry nodded as Jax stopped at a door, partway down the hallway.

Jax inhaled and turned to face us. "This is where I grew up. My parents still live here, and I don't know how they'll react."

Valerie gave him a lopsided smile. "Only one way to find out." She walked to the door, knocked twice, then stepped back and pushed Jax forward.

Jax turned to say something to Valerie when the door opened and a woman with age lines on her face and Jax's black hair and brown eyes peered out. She squinted like she couldn't believe what she saw. "Jax?"

Jax gulped. "Hi, Mom."

...

The inside of the apartment had paint peeling from the walls, though Jax's parents had tried to organize their things and remove the dirt. The apartment consisted of one large room with a small bathroom and kitchen on the left and a closed door straight ahead of the entrance. A pull-out, unholstered couch with blankets piled on one end sat in the middle of the room facing the right-hand wall where the news screen was.

A man, with a similar face shape to Jax's, sat on the couch. He lifted his head when we entered the room. "Jax? What are you doing here?"

"We need somewhere to stay," Jax mumbled, avoiding eye contact with the older man, presumably his dad.

"What happened to the Colony?" the man asked, his eyes creased. "Why did you leave?"

Jax opened his mouth and snapped it shut again. Sensing the conversation going nowhere, I sighed. Before I could speak, long blonde hair swished in the corner of my eye.

Valerie had taken a couple of steps forward and wore her most-charming smile. "It's my fault, Mr. Mori. I decided to overthrow the Leader, and we needed Jax's help."

I bristled at her words. It hadn't been a direct claim of credit, though she meant for her statement to be interpreted that way.

Henry bent to bring his mouth to my ear. "Relax. Val knows she's not in charge."

I nodded and, as my irritation settled, realized again how different Henry was from Gav, who would have brushed off my reaction. Gav had never known how to calm me the way Henry did.

"And who are you, dear?" Jax's mother asked, ignoring Henry and me. She stood with her arms crossed, one eyebrow cocked, and her attention on Valerie.

"Valerie Connor," Valerie answered, flicking her hair over her shoulder. "I'm a friend of Jax's. We met in the Colony."

Mrs. Mori lips parted, and Mr. Mori raised his eyebrows. Mrs. Mori walked a hesitant step forward and opened her mouth wider in preparation to speak.

"We attacked the Leader, and I killed her," I said. Attention shifted to me when I had been invisible seconds ago. "It didn't solve everything. We have enemies after us and nowhere else to go. Can we stay here or not?"

Mr. Mori burst into laughter and bent over with his hands on his knees. When his laughing fit subsided, he straightened up and smiled. "You're the girl I saw on the screen."

I jutted my chin out and stood tall. Why should I deny it? I had done it for the common person's benefit after all. "Yes."

"What you did was brave," Mr. Mori said. "Though, whether it was wise is to be seen. To answer your question, you may stay. We would rather have our son here than on the streets, unprotected."

Mrs. Mori bobbed her head. "Bring your things into the bedroom. We'll discuss sleeping arrangements."

Chapter 2

Against the bedroom's left-hand wall was a bed, wide enough to fit two people, made with a faded blue comforter and two flat pillows. Beside the bed was a worn, three-drawer dresser covered in chipped white paint. On the right-hand wall was a large closet. Across from the door, a small window framed in thin blue curtains displayed a metal fire escape ladder. It offered an easy exit, though I wasn't eager to use it.

Mrs. Mori turned to us as we set our bags on the bedroom's wooden floor. "You two girls can share the bed. Jax, you and…" she paused and turned to Henry, her eyes narrowed.

"Henry," he said, tightening his grasp on my hand. "Henry Connor."

Mrs. Mori's eyebrows shot up and her gaze flicked between Henry and his sister, no doubt noticing their resemblance and wondering about the privilege that had made it possible for them to have each other. I expected her to unleash a barrage of questions. Instead, she nodded, composed her face, and all signs of her shock disappeared. "Well, as I was saying, you two," she waved a finger between Jax and Henry. "Can sleep on the kitchen floor. It won't do to have the four of you share a room."

The tone of her voice made it clear this wasn't negotiable. I could see her point. Henry and I weren't married, or even in a Courtship; letting us share a room would break the law. Mrs. Mori didn't know us, aside from Jax, well enough to risk that.

"Okay," Jax said with a shrug. He walked to the closet, opened the door and pulled out a couple of thin sheets, one of which he tossed in Henry's direction. "We'll need these."

"Come along and give the girls some privacy," Mrs. Mori said as she ushered Jax and Henry back into the living room.

Henry shot me a glance as he dropped my hand and left. I tried to give him a reassuring smile as the door closed.

"Which side of the bed do you want?"

I blinked at Valerie, who stood at the foot of the bed. "I don't care."

She stared at me. "I know you'd rather share with Henry."

I tossed my head and closed my eyes, not denying her statement. We both knew it was true. "We can't. And really, I don't care. You can pick."

She shrugged, the motion bouncing her hair that spilled over her shoulders. "Alright."

I watched her empty her bag onto the far side of the bed. She'd placed herself closest to the fire escape. Perhaps she sought an easy exit, or she tried to be nice by shielding me from anyone that might try to break in through the window. Maybe it was a combination of both.

I threw my backpack on the near side of the bed, climbed up after it, sat crossed legged and unbraided my hair. When I tried to detangle it with my fingers, I missed a hairbrush. "How long do you think we'll be safe here?" I asked as I tugged out the remaining knots.

She collapsed onto the bed beside me. "I don't know if we're safe anywhere."

Her words weren't a surprise. There was an arrest warrant out for the four of us, and my image, along with my voice, had played on every screen in the City. It was a matter of time until someone discovered us, or turned us in. Where could we go? "We'll be careful until we come up with a better option."

"Is that want you want?" Valerie asked. "To hide?"

"Of course not." What had made her think that? I hadn't hidden when she'd asked me to lead the Rebel Cause, or when we'd attacked the tower. "I don't plan to let Ben win that easily. Plus, I still want to help Gav."

A smile blossomed on Valerie's face. "I don't want to hide either. We've come this far; we need to finish the job."

"We just need to figure out how."

...

It was difficult to sleep that first night in the Moris' apartment. It wasn't that the bed was uncomfortable, but that Henry wasn't nearby for the first time since we'd originally left the City. Every time I rolled over, I had to remind myself that the sleeping figure beside me was Valerie, who didn't want, and would react badly to, physical contact with me. The moonlight shone on her hair that wasn't under the blankets, making my sleep addled brain think it was Henry. I caught myself reaching a couple times and had to force my hands back to my sides.

After a spell of light sleep, sunlight streaming through the window woke me. When I opened my eyes, I realized I was alone. I flung the covers off and exited the bedroom.

In the apartment's main room, Jax and Henry sat side by side on the pull-out couch.

"Where's everyone else?" I asked, rubbing my eyes and stifling a yawn.

Why was I tired? I *had* slept. The previous day's events had exhausted me more than I'd realized.

"My parents went to work," Jax said. "And Valerie's in the bathroom."

"Are you hungry?" Henry asked. "I was going to wake you, but Val told me not to."

"A bit. Can we eat the food here?" It didn't seem right to eat the Moris' food when they obviously didn't have much money and we'd shown up unannounced. Overnight, they'd tripled their number of mouths to feed. Mom and I wouldn't have been able to afford that, and our home had been larger and in a nicer Apartment District.

"We have to," Jax said. "It isn't safe to leave, and we have no money. But my parents do. They live here by choice, not out of necessity."

I couldn't fathom that anyone would opt to live here. Yet, Jax wasn't a liar. Part of me wanted to believe him. "Why?"

"It's safer," Jax said. "They used to hack into the Government's databases and give information to the Rebel Cause. They're who taught me how to hack."

"They used to?" I asked. "Not anymore?"

Jax shook his head. "My parents stopped being active in the Rebel Cause when I was little, and we moved here. They thought it would stop the neighbours from snooping since they were garnering suspicion. After they taught me everything they knew, I left for the Colony. I wanted to help, and I couldn't do that here."

"You were brave," Henry said. "Unlike me."

"You are brave," Valerie said as she exited the bathroom. Her hair hung damp over her shoulders and down her back, and she wore a fresh pair of jeans and a t-shirt.

"I washed our clothes," she explained as she caught me staring at her clean outfit.

"I'm not as brave as I should be." Henry rose from the couch and closed the distance to me, taking my hands in his. "But I want to be." He dropped my hands, stepped back and ran his hand through his hair.

I missed the warmth of his touch and hugged my torso, needing something to do with my hands. "You don't need to change."

"Yeah," Valerie smirked. "Molly likes you already."

"I know," Henry said. "There's just something I need to do."

I froze, my mouth agape. What did he have to do? I couldn't imagine the answer. "What is it?"

Henry closed his eyes. When he reopened them, they shone with a ferocity I'd never seen from him before. "I need to confront my foster parents."

"Why?" Jax asked from his seat on the couch.

Valerie and I swiveled our heads to Jax, though it was Henry who spoke. "It's the only way to move on from my past."

"It's not safe," Jax said.

Jax had a point. We'd had just found a hiding place, and Henry wanted to leave. "You can't go alone. What if someone reports you?"

Henry smiled, the expression lighting the room up. "I don't want to go by myself. Will you come with me, Molly?"

"That is an even worse idea," Jax grumbled. "Molly's recognizable from the video."

I turned on Jax, ready to retort. There was no way I would let him stop me from supporting Henry. I needed something proactive to do, and Jax would not take it away.

"Oh, can it, Jax," Valerie snapped. "They'll be safe. And if my brother says he needs this, then I believe him."

"Good. Because we're going."

...

Henry had wanted to leave right away, but my rumbling stomach had other plans. I raided the fridge, still feeling apprehensive about eating the Moris' food, and stuffed some fruit and bread into my mouth. It wasn't the most cohesive meal, but it quieted my stomach. Afterwards, I retrieved my clothes from the bathroom, thankful Valerie had run them through the dryer, threw on a t-shirt and jeans and put on my jacket and my boots. It was lucky that Henry and I had grown up in the City; we were better equipped to blend in.

"Okay," I said upon exiting the bathroom. "I'm ready."

"You're sure about this?" Henry, wearing jeans and a black, denim jacket, asked as he took my hand.

The sparkle in his eyes made me yearn for the touch of his lips on mine. I swallowed. "Yes. I'd do anything for you."

"Then we'd better go before Valerie and Jax decide to stop us."

Neither of us feared Jax stopping us. If the showdown with the guards had revealed anything, it was that Jax wasn't a strong fighter. Valerie, however, was a force.

We left the apartment and retraced our steps to the staircase. Thankfully, we encountered no one as we made it downstairs and onto the street.

Taking a bus to Henry's old neighbourhood wasn't an option, both because we had no money and the risk of someone recognizing us was too great. We had pulled our jacket hoods up, but I didn't like the idea of close contact to strangers for a prolonged time. We went on foot; it wasn't a short walk but was less distance than we'd crossed the night prior. I didn't even feel tired as we neared a plain, concrete apartment building on a tidy street a couple blocks from my childhood home.

The building's interior was laid out identically to my old building, and I almost stopped at the third floor before I remembered where I was. Henry's foster parents lived on the seventh floor. He'd ridden the elevator when he'd lived here, which we couldn't do now. Even if no one spotted us in the lobby waiting for it, we couldn't be sure we wouldn't share it with another passenger and be left with no easy escape. So, we climbed to the seventh floor and turned down the hallway to apartment 702.

Chapter 3

Henry

Henry hadn't expected returning to his foster parents' apartment would be this difficult. He'd known it would be awkward, even a bit tense, but he hadn't anticipated this level of dread. It hit him like a tsunami when he and Molly reached the door.

He'd known since he left the City that he needed closure with his foster parents. Still, he couldn't do this alone. And he didn't want to. That's why he'd asked Molly to join him.

"You don't have to do this," Molly said. She always sounded confident, even when she didn't feel that way. Henry knew she doubted herself sometimes, yet she always pushed past it.

He shook his head and gulped. "Walking away won't help me move on." With a deep breath, he knocked on the door he used to unlock with a key.

…

Henry felt a degree of relief when his foster mom, Eleanor Newsome, opened the door. She squinted her small brown eyes; neither her face nor personality had ever been kind, yet he preferred her over her husband, Reginald. While she was cold and distant, Reginald was strict and intimidating.

"I didn't think you'd have the nerve to show your face here," Eleanor sneered.

"I have to talk to you and Reginald," Henry said. "May we come in?"

Eleanor shuffled back gestured for him and Molly to enter.

Henry stopped as he crossed the threshold and Eleanor shut the door. Reginald walked into the room from the hallway, not doubt coming to see who had knocked. Henry's heart pounded. He did his best to suppress his fear. This had been a mistake.

"You've come crawling back with a girl," Reginald jeered. He towered over both his wife and Henry and had the build of a man constantly ready for a fist fight – all muscle and short, cropped hair. "Surely you aren't deluded enough to come for our blessing. There must be something else you want. Spit it out boy. What is it?"

If Henry had been alone, he couldn't have formed coherent words. But Molly was with him, and she gave him courage. "No, I didn't come to get your blessing." It would have been a waste of time. "And I don't want anything from you. Not anymore." He had once wanted something from the Newsomes, what every child at the Foster Centre had yearned for: a loving family. They had never given it to him.

"I came to tell you that, no matter what you think, you don't control me anymore. I've found someone that loves me and makes me happy."

"You've always been brainless," Eleanor said, making Henry flinch despite himself. "But this is a level of daftness I didn't know was possible, even for you."

"The girl," Reginald spat, one of his giant fingers pointed at Molly's face. "Is not for you. You belong with Ben. It's not too late. Ben will take you back, and you will behave."

Reginald would do everything in his power to ensure Henry did just that. Nothing was too extreme if it brought Henry into line. He'd come here to get closure, which had been foolish. His life was slipping from his control all over again. The last time he'd felt this hopeless had been when the Newsomes had taken him in and laid down their long list of rules. Adapting to living with them had made the Foster Centre seem like a vacation.

Then Ben had approached his foster parents and made a deal. They'd bargained Henry away, and he'd agreed to it out of the attraction he felt to Ben. He'd also been desperate for freedom from their discipline, but he'd only traded their control for Ben's.

"How can you say that?" Molly unleashed her temper on Reginald. She had her fists balled at her sides and her feet planted, ready to pounce. This was a fight she wouldn't win, yet she would try for Henry's sake. "Henry isn't your puppet. You don't get to dictate his choices."

"He isn't competent enough to make decisions," Eleanor said. "We know what's best for him, and he will obey. He owes us that much."

Henry shrunk further inside himself with every word that Eleanor Newsome said. He'd felt whole and happy with Molly and Valerie. But maybe his foster mom was right, and he did owe them obedience.

"You're wrong," Molly spat through gritted teeth. She stood her ground, with her head high. Henry admired her courage. "He owes you nothing. If you ever loved him, you wouldn't demand this."

The Newsomes laughed. "Loved him? It isn't possible to love such a huge disappointment."

A disappointment. That's how they saw him. They didn't love him, and

Ben never had. Realizing that had made him believe he wasn't worthy of love. But two faces crept into his mind: Molly's and Valerie's. They loved him; he was certain of it.

He stole a glimpse of Molly's face. She'd pressed her lips into a thin line. Her nostrils flared, and fire blazed in her eyes. She was ready to come to his defense again. However, it was time to defend himself.

He reached out and clasped Molly's hand, knowing without looking exactly where it was. He still marveled at how naturally their hands fit together. "I'm sorry I wasn't what you wanted or expected," he told the Newsomes. "I tried to be. But I need to be myself. And you'll never see me again. I'll make sure of that."

Still clasping Molly's hand, Henry turned around and threw open the apartment door. Together, they fled down the stairs and didn't stop running until they stood on the street.

They were a few metres from the doors when Molly pulled him into a nearby, narrow alley, shrouded in shadow. None of the apartment windows or fire escapes faced that direction, granting them a measure of privacy.

Molly's lips met his. The kiss, like all of theirs, warmed his body. The fiery burn grew both more familiar and addictive each time. Every nerve in his being craved her touch. He wanted her hands on him, and he pulled her closer to run his hands through her hair. She broke the kiss before he could, leaving him dazed and disoriented. It was over too soon.

Henry collected himself just enough to see fear blossom in her eyes. Had he frightened her? He didn't think so. She grasped his arm and pressed him against the alley wall. Flattening herself next to him, she held a finger on her lips and gave a small shake of her head.

Determined to be brave, and curious to know what had frightened her, Henry leaned forward and craned his neck to see around the wall. He stayed long enough to spot a slim figure with hair black as night, skin pale as the moon, and blue eyes cold as ice, striding toward the Newsomes' apartment building. *Ben.*

Henry slid down the wall. A minute longer in his foster parents' apartment and they would've been caught. "They must've seen us coming and tipped him off."

An outstretched hand appeared in his face. He reached and accepted it, letting Molly pull him up. "That sound's right," she said. "They probably told him to come."

"Too bad for them that I'm not an object they can handover." The Newsomes thought of him as just that, which was their mistake. "We should get out of here before Ben finds us." He didn't want to face off with Ben that day. That confrontation could wait.

Molly nodded, her eyes shining against the alley's shadow. "Agreed."

Henry wanted to kiss her and shoved the urge away, knowing that too would have to wait. Instead, he contented himself with the warmth of her hand in his as they retraced the route to the Moris' apartment building. He would take any contact with Molly that she was willing to give him.

He'd acted on impulse and heartbreak when he'd kissed her in her dad's basement. She'd been Gavriel's girlfriend, but she had never looked at Gavriel the way she looked at Henry now. Nor had she told Gavriel she loved him.

It had taken him time to believe she loved him. At first, he'd thought she was using him as a crutch after Gavriel's kidnapping. Time had given each of them clarity and brought them together. Henry wanted to be with no one except Molly. The certainty he felt only grew as they went back to the Moris' apartment. He walked with her up the five flights of stairs and down the hall.

"What are we going to tell Valerie and Jax?" Molly asked.

Henry reached with his free hand and knocked on the apartment door. "The truth." He wouldn't hide it from his sister, and since Val trusted Jax, he would too.

...

"I can't believe they said that," Val said as she flung her arms around Henry when he and Molly finished relaying the events. Such a display of affection was rare for her.

"It's how they've always been," he said, shrugging as much as possible with Val's arms pinning his.

Val stepped back, her eyes shining from unshed tears. "I'm sorry. I should've tried harder to rescue you."

He shook his head. "You couldn't have stopped them taking me home." He didn't want Val to blame herself for something she hadn't caused. She'd only been eleven when the Newsomes had chosen him, still a child herself.

His sister frowned. "I should have tried."

"He's right," Jax said. "There's nothing you could've done."

Val's frown stayed, making it clear she disagreed. Henry knew of one thing he could do to ease her conscience, and he'd been planning it anyway. So, he asked her to join him on fire escape where they could talk in private.

She hugged him again, her face betraying her misery. He hugged her back for a few moments, broke it and braced his hands on the railing.

"I don't really want to discuss that more. It was just an excuse to get you alone."

"Why?" Her eyes, the same emerald as his, were on his face, and her fingers traced the railing bar.

"I need your help."

Chapter 4

Jax and I cooked supper while Henry and Valerie talked. I hadn't questioned why they needed privacy. Some conversations just required it.

"They really tried to hand him over to Ben?" Jax asked as he dumped a can of beans into the pot.

"Yes," I said, stirring with furious stokes and splashing water on my shirt. "They acted like he was an object they'd borrowed." It had made me appreciate my parents. They hadn't been perfect and had both kept their secrets, but they'd never tried to control me. These thoughts brought back my grief over losing my mom, which I unleashed on the soup.

Jax grabbed my arm and stilled it. "We want to eat the soup, not wash the kitchen with it."

I dropped the spoon with a huff, which sent more liquid splattering. "I know," I said, as I grabbed a nearby towel and wiped the spill. "Maybe you should stir."

Jax fished the spoon out of the pot and tossed it in the sink. He selected a clean one and stirred with calm, even strokes. I rolled my eyes and retrieved bowls from the cupboard. I needed something to do that wouldn't make a mess, or I would scream. There was no use in dwelling on the Newsomes.

They didn't know our location and couldn't send Ben after us. Knowing that didn't make it easier to forget what they'd attempted to do.

The apartment door opening snapped me out of my thoughts. I set down the final bowl with a thud as Mr. and Mrs. Mori walked in and hung their coats on the nearby hook. Mrs. Mori closed her eyes and sniffed. "Something smells delicious."

"Molly and I made soup," Jax said, approaching the table carrying the pot.

"Good, I'm starving," Valerie said as she and Henry exited the bedroom. Her normal, indifferent expression was back on her face. Whatever Henry had said to her must've cheered her up. This was good; Valerie needed to be at her best.

"Then come eat," I said as I filled a bowl with soup and grabbed a spoon.

Mr. and Mrs. Mori brought their bowls to the couch to give us a measure of privacy, and because there were only four chairs at the table.

I picked a chair at random and dipped my spoon into the soup. The broth, beans and canned vegetables reminded me of home and the meals my mom had made when we were low on rations. It also brought thoughts of Mrs. O'Kelly's snobby daughter cooking in the kitchen of my old apartment and eating off plates I'd used, if she hadn't thrown them out.

I expected to feel angry at this mental picture, but I was far from being the girl that had wanted to live there with Gav. That place was no longer my home, and, even if I returned, it would be a different place that would suffocate me in memories. It was time for me to move on as Henry had from his past. I emptied my bowl of soup, feeling more content that I had in a long while.

...

After the meal was over and the dishes were washed, the screen on the Moris' apartment wall came on. We all gathered around the couch and turned our attention to it, a habit ingrained in everyone who had ever lived in the City.

A wanted poster with my face on it occupied the centre of the screen. This couldn't be good. "Molly Birch," a grave voiceover said. "Is wanted for the most heinous crime possible in our beloved City. She led a treasonous attack on our Guard Corps, the protectors of our people, and on our Government."

My body went cold at the words, even as Jax's image replaced mine.

"Jax Mori is wanted for hacking into multiple electronic systems in the City, including the Car Gate, a guard uniform name tag, and the locking system of a Government building."

Jax tensed at the announcement as the wanted poster changed to Valerie. She got the briefest attention as the announcer charged her with treason and co-conspiracy.

The picture changed a final time to Henry. I reached for his hand and clutched it tight as the announcer stated the charges. "Henry Connor is wanted for helping runaways break out of the City, and Rebels break in, for impersonating a senior guard and for engaging in combat against his former comrades. Molly Birch and Henry Connor are believed to remain in the City, based on reports received today. Valerie Connor's and Jax Mori's locations are unknown. Citizens, if you spot any of these wanted criminals, notify the nearest guard or Government officer, by order of the Government." The screen went black.

"Jax," Mrs. Mori said, her face ashen. "You need to be careful. Maybe you should return to the Colony."

"No," he said.

"Jax—" Mr. Mori started.

"We'd never get to the Gate undetected," Henry said. "Let alone out of the City."

This might not be true, depending on which guards spotted us. But I added my agreement behind Henry's statement. We couldn't leave the City now, not with so much unfinished business. Even with the Newsomes reporting our presence, we needed to stay.

"They have a point, dear," Mr. Mori said. "They could get arrested, and we'd never see Jax again."

Mrs. Mori closed her eyes. When she reopened them, she sighed. "Stay here and stay inside. Don't let the neighbours spot you."

I shared a look with Valerie, Henry and Jax. There would be times we would need to go outside. However, if the only way for us to remain in the City was agreeing to remain within the walls of the Moris' apartment, so be it. I hoped the others saw it the same way.

"Okay," I said, willing my words to come across as sincere. "We can do that."

"Good," Mrs. Mori said, smiling. "It's what's best for keeping my son safe."

I admired Mrs. Mori for looking out for Jax, but keeping him safe wasn't best for everyone in the City. I kept this thought to myself, knowing it wouldn't change her mind.

...

That night, Valerie and I lay awake on the bed. Valerie rolled onto her side, propped her head on her arm and looked at me. "I'm glad you stood up for Henry. He needs people who care about him."

"He has us and Malcolm."

Valerie rolled onto her back; her blonde hair splayed under her shoulders. "I don't know how good it is that Dad showed up," she said, sounding younger than her nineteen years. "He abandoned us."

"I think he regrets it," I said, thinking about Malcolm's expression when Henry and Valerie met him in the woods. "He didn't do it to hurt you, just like my dad didn't leave me and my mom to hurt us."

"It's not the same," Valerie said. "You still had a parent."

I sighed and rolled over to face her. "And I'd do almost anything to get her back. I envy you. You can have him in your life, yet you're bitter about a decision he made fourteen years ago. Don't waste your chance."

I rose from the bed, walked to the window and climbed out to the fire escape. The cool night air hit my skin and made goose bumps rise on my arms. I let them hang by my sides. Compared to the warm air in the Colony, this was freezing; I had grown accustomed to the warmer weather south of the City. I stood there anyway, letting the chill wash my frustrations away and clear my head.

Just as I was ready to return indoors, Valerie climbed out, wearing a jacket and wrapping her arms around her torso to ward off the cold.

"You're right," she said. "I should be happy to have my dad back. I just have a hard time trusting people."

A let a smirk grow on my face. "I hadn't noticed."

She laughed. "I'm going to bed. Are you coming?"

"Sure."

...

After the Moris left for work the next morning, we all sat on the couch, the previous night's wanted ad at the forefront of our minds. We decided to lie low in the apartment for the time being, which felt like hiding.

"What are we going to do?" I asked, breaking the heavy silence that permeated the room.

Three heads swiveled in my direction, though no one spoke.

"Sitting in this apartment forever won't solve things," I continued, twirling a lock of my hair with my fingers out of restlessness and frustration.

"We have one piece of leverage," Jax said. "We could use it."

"That might be premature," Valerie said. "We'd have nothing left."

"I say we do it," I said, seeing how it could benefit our cause. No one outside the Guard Corps and Government knew what happened.

"I'm with Molly," Henry said.

Valerie frowned. "But—"

"You wanted her to lead, so let her do it. Sitting here won't accomplish anything. It'll only make people forget about our video."

Valerie sucked in a deep breath and let out a long exhale. "I'll consent to this, only because you all think it's a good idea. It had better work."

"Great," I said, glad that Valerie wasn't protesting. "What do you need for it, Jax?"

He grinned. "Just time and some cords from my bag. When are we doing this?"

"Why not now?" I asked. "We have nothing else to do."

Jax shrugged, "Okay." He entered the bedroom and emerged carrying his bag. Henry and Jax stored their things in the bedroom closet to keep anyone from tripping on them.

Jax crouched near the wall screen, produced a cord from his bag and connected it to his hacker's multitool and the screen. "I should edit the footage before I broadcast it across the City."

"Edit?" Henry asked. "Doesn't it show what we want?"

Jax shook his head, his black hair flapping over his ears. "It needs an intro and some context. People will be confused if we release it as is."

"You could record me for a voiceover," I said, thinking of the Government's wanted ad.

"No," Jax said. "That's too much focus on you. The Government will say it was a solo act and pile blame on you. Someone else should do it."

He and I both turned to Valerie and Henry. Valerie added her gaze on Henry, surprisingly not eager to take the lead.

"She's your girlfriend," Valerie told her brother, on catching Jax's and my bewildered expressions. "You should do it."

Henry walked over to Jax. "What do I need to do?"

"Just say what I tell you," Jax said. "First," he looked at me and Valerie. "You two should go in the bedroom. We need quiet."

"Come on," I said, grasping Valerie's arm and leading her toward the bedroom door. "Let's leave them to it."

Chapter 5

A couple hours passed before Henry came. Valerie and I had spent the time in silence, not wanting to interrupt the boys' progress. Valerie napped while I reorganized the contents of my bag and tried to tackle the tangles in my hair. I turned when the door creaked open.

Henry was leaning against the door jamb. "We just finished. I'm going to make lunch while Jax gets the broadcast set up."

"I'll help you," I said, getting off the bed. I was careful not to wake Valerie, who still lie sleeping, her features relaxed and peaceful.

When Henry and I stood in the main room, the bedroom door closed behind us, I spotted a small, white piece of paper on the floor near the entrance. My eyebrows wrinkled as I peered at it. "What is that?"

"I—" Henry sputtered. "I don't know."

"Someone slid it under the door a minute ago," Jax piped up from his position near the wall screen. He didn't glance at us when he spoke, instead kept his attention on his task. "I heard footsteps approach and stop at the door, then they went back the way they came from."

My curiosity grew by the second. Who would slide a note under the door? A select few people knew we were here. "And you didn't investigate?"

"No."

My feet carried me toward the paper, without my conscious input. I crouched and picked it up, turning it over in my hands. It was addressed to me and written with unfamiliar handwriting.

M.B.

Midnight. Apartment District 2, Third Street, empty lot. Come alone.

M.A.

M.A. I only knew one person with those initials. The question was how he found me and what he wanted. There was one way I could find out, and nothing would stop me from doing so.

"What does it say?" Jax asked.

"It's a message for me," I said, relaying to contents.

"You're going to go," Henry stated.

I put the note in my pocket. "Yes. It could be helpful."

"Or a trap," Jax said.

I thrust my hands in my pockets, careful not to crinkle the note. "I doubt it. If it is, it doesn't matter. I'm going."

"Are you sure it's safe to go alone?" Henry asked.

"Yes," I lied. "Besides, I have to; it's what the note says."

"What note?" Valerie asked from the bedroom door.

I fished the piece of paper out of my pocket and showed it to her. She scanned it, and a grin spread on her face. It wasn't the reaction I'd expected.

"You need to go. I'll cover for you and calm down the boys."

"Thanks," I said.

...

The Moris got home that afternoon before Jax finished hacking into the City's broadcast system. He was in the process, his multitool connected to the screen and the file loading, when his parents entered the apartment.

They came to a halt when they saw him crouched by the screen. "Jax!" Mrs. Mori exclaimed. "What are you doing?"

Henry, Valerie and I sat on the couch as Jax's head whipped around.

"Broadcasting," he said.

"You didn't make another ad, did you, son?" Mr. Mori asked, calmer than his wife.

"No."

"Then what—"

"You'll see in a second," Jax said, tapping the screen of his multitool.

The wall screen blinked on, and I glued my eyes to it. The memory of being in the tower ran through my mind, though I couldn't see myself on screen. The footage showed the Leader's chamber with the black-cloaked figure standing in the centre. Henry's voice narrated. I both heard and remembered the Leader's taunt and my reply. Then the fight began. It was surreal watching and remembering it at the same time. I saw glimpses of my arms and sometimes my legs. For the most part, I only heard Henry's voice mixed with my own and the Leader's and saw the cloaked figure lunge toward the camera.

Valerie and the Moris gasped as my onscreen arm ripped the Leader's mask off, revealing the angry, middle-aged woman underneath. The rest of the fight played out, ending with a rain of glass shards and Henry's voice proclaiming me as the Liberator, as a guard had done after the footage stopped.

Mr. and Mrs. Mori turned their heads to me, and I felt the weight of their eyes. "You were brave," Mr. Mori said. "Let's hope the general population doesn't despise you for what you did."

It hadn't felt brave at the time, nor sitting on the couch watching it. What I had done had been out of desperation and guilt. I still believed it had been the right action, but that didn't mean it was brave.

Before I answered Mr. Mori, screams broke out in the apartment building, coming from all directions.

Mrs. Mori shook her head and turned to her husband. "Come, dear. Let's go appease the neighbours," she said, ushering Mr. Mori out the door. As she crossed the threshold, she turned to us. "Stay here. And don't open the door."

…

Jax joined us on the couch, and the four of us sat listening to the screams. At first, I tried to tune them out, which was impossible. I let my ears absorb the noise, knowing I caused it. The more I listened, the more the sound changed. I sat up straight. "Do you hear that?"

"How can we not," Valerie deadpanned. "You'd have to be deaf not to."

"No," I said. "Someone's cheering."

"I hear it too," Henry said.

I closed my eyes and strained to focus through the racket. In the near distance, someone gave a joyous cheer, which morphed into a chant.

"All hail the Liberator!"

Other voices joined in and overtook the screams. The chant became its own overwhelming noise that I couldn't escape. Now everyone knew me. I hadn't thought much of the moniker when the guard had gifted it, and now I was stuck with it. At least it was a positive title.

"I guess some people liked it," Jax said.

"How long until the guards come to quell this?" Valerie asked her brother.

"I don't know," he said. "They're scattered around the City, which means a large group won't come, if any do."

The screen flicked back on with the Government's response. I gaped at what was on display, the chanting and screaming stopped and forgotten. Gav and Ben stood in front of a white wall, flanking a figure decked in familiar black gear, from the cloak and gloves to the mask with voice distorter. The sole difference was this version of the Leader was taller and stockier than the one I had pushed out a window. No one watching would spot it.

"Our Leader is alive and well," Ben told the camera, a smarmy smile on his face. "The video you witnessed was fabricated by our," he swept his hand over himself and Gav, "bitter and delusional exes, Henry Connor and Molly Birch, respectively."

Henry tensed. His breakup with Ben had been more fraught than mine with Gav. For my part, I felt for Gav. We hadn't ended things with any closure. And I still believed he could be saved from whatever brainwashing Carl Wessin and Ben had put him through. His frown and dead eyes doubled my conviction. I had to help him.

"This is bad," Henry groaned. "We gave Ben more fuel."

"Molly," Gav said, the strangled sound of his voice pulling my attention to the screen. This was a difficult video for him to make. "If you ever cared about me, you'll stop throwing this tantrum. Come back and we can regain what we had."

No, Gav, I thought. *We can't.* And I didn't want to.

Ben smirked. "If anyone knows the location of Molly Birch or her cohorts, tell the nearest guard or your district Government office. We're offering a two-thousand-dollar reward for each fugitive, no questions asked."

I thought I saw Gav wince as Ben announced the reward that would tempt a lot of people, but the expression was gone so fast I wasn't sure I hadn't imagined it. The screen went black when Ben finished speaking, which stopped me from further analysing Gav's face.

"They made that fast," Jax said,

"To discredit our video," Henry said. "Ben can be very convincing."

"Well," Valerie said, standing up and stretching her back. "It's our move now."

"This isn't a chess game," I said.

She frowned like I was testing her patience. "No, it's a man hunt that could escalate quickly. We need to prepare."

I crossed my arms over my chest. It wasn't like I was unaware of the situation. "Fine."

"Molly—" Henry started.

"No, I get it," I said. "It was just weird hearing what Gav said, and I need to clear my head."

The entire City now thought Gav and I had once been in a relationship, even though it had never been legal. He had conveniently left that part out. Maybe he had a plan, or maybe a deal with the Reviewer to let us marry if I went back to him. A couple months ago I would've snatched the chance to marry him, but that was the last thing I desired now. "I'm going to cook," I said, rising from the couch. "And I won't make a mess this time."

The Moris had vegetables in their fridge and rice in their pantry, so I made a stir fry. It was a simple meal to execute, and stirring the pan calmed my mind. I needed to help Gav move on, but that had to wait. I didn't know how long it would be before we were in the same place.

...

The four of us ate without the Moris, who hadn't returned. I worried but didn't think anything too terrible could've happened unless they ran into an overzealous guard. That scenario remained unlikely, and I tried to otherwise occupy my mind.

Henry and Jax insisted on cleaning the dishes, and Valerie whisked me off to the bedroom in the name of helping me get ready. I sat on the bed while she braided my hair.

"I just got the knots out from the last time," I grumbled.

"We can find a hairbrush," she said, ignoring my complaint. "Besides, this'll keep your hair out of your face in case something happens and you need to fight."

"It shouldn't come to that."

Her fingers stopped moving. "You never know."

"He won't ambush me. I'm sure of it."

"He might be followed," Valerie said, finishing my braid.

"You really need to work on your trust issues."

She laughed. "I don't want something to happen to you. For Henry's sake."

So, she did care. I smirked, knowing she couldn't see my face. "I'll be fine."

I rose from the bed and pulled on my boots and sturdy, black jacket. Paired with my black pants, the ensemble would help me blend into the shadows lining the streets.

The sun was setting, the sky visible through the window turning orange. I would wait until dusk to descend the fire escape. It was too risky to leave before, and I couldn't wait until dark and still make my meeting on time. I stood by the window and watched the orange part of the sky grow smaller until it turned to navy, then I eased the window open and placed my hands on the ledge. "Tell Henry I'll be back before sunrise."

Chapter 6

Henry

As Henry and Jax finished cleaning the kitchen, the Moris returned home. Mr. Mori had a small, folded piece of paper in his hand and smiled at Henry. He crossed the room and thrust it into Henry's hand. "Mr. Irvine said this is for you."

"From whom?" Henry asked. Who wanted to leave him a note and knew where he was?

"I don't know. He said a messenger dropped it off."

Henry unfolded and read the paper. It was typed, leaving no chance of recognizing the handwriting. Nonetheless, he knew the sender.

`H.`

`I don't wish to put you in further danger, but I believe I can be of assistance. Come tonight to Apartment District 11, corner of Fifth and Sixth Streets. I will await you there, and V., if she deigns to join you.`

`M.C.`

It seemed Henry had his own meeting to attend while Molly crossed the City. At least this would give him something useful to do instead of lying on the kitchen floor with Jax, kept awake with worry. "Thank you," he said, hoping Mr. Mori wouldn't ask about the contents. "How were the neighbours?"

"Some were happy," Mrs. Mori said with a shrug. "Others were horrified. A few children were frightened, which set off the screaming."

"That's understandable," Jax said.

Henry didn't understand how Jax was collected all the time. It was like nothing phased him. Did he even have nerves?

"Yes," Mr. Mori said. "Then the Government video sobered everyone. Now they don't know what to believe."

"Quite right, dear," Mrs. Mori said. "Where are the girls?"

"They went to bed," Jax lied.

"That's a good idea," Mrs. Mori said. "I think I'll do the same."

...

The Moris reclined on the pull-out bed, leaving Henry and Jax alone in the kitchen's dim light. Jax stretched his arms above his head and yawned. "One of us will need to stay awake to ensure they don't notice Molly is gone. Want to take turns?"

Henry shook his head and showed Jax the note. "I can't," he said, pulling on his jacket and tying his boots. "You'll have to cover for us."

Jax lay down with his jacket bunched under his head. "Hopefully, you'll get something useful from it."

Henry nodded and, satisfied that the Moris were asleep based on the sound of their breathing, crept to the bedroom and eased the door open. Inside, Valerie sat on the bed gazing out the window. She turned her head at the sound of the door closing behind Henry and narrowed her eyes. "What are you doing in here?"

"Get ready," he said, tossing her the note. "We have a meeting to get to."

She grabbed the note and read it. "I'll go because I don't think you should go alone."

Henry was unsure if this meant she didn't trust Malcolm or thought Henry needed protecting. It didn't matter that much.

Quicker than he'd expected, his sister had her jacket and boots on and climbed out the window. He went after her and eased the window closed. Valerie scaled down the fire escape ladder with nimble limbs and was waiting on the street as he finished his descent. She wore the hood of her jacket up, and he did the same to hide his blonde hair that would otherwise shine in the moonlight. Together, they ran to Apartment District 11.

...

It didn't take long to reach their intended district as they had begun their journey in Apartment District 12. Henry's thoughts wandered to Molly and her possible whereabouts. She had a longer distance to travel and was by herself. This made him uneasy, and he forced himself to focus. A clear mind was necessary to tackle this meeting.

He and Valerie slowed to a walk once they reached Apartment District 11. They concealed themselves in the shadows and read the street signs they passed. Henry could tell why the corner of Fifth and Sixth Streets was their meeting place. Fifth Street, which ran north-south as all odd numbered streets did, was commercial. None of the buildings had lights on, leaving the widely spaced streetlights and the moon as the sources of illumination. It was also currently not patrolled by a guard.

Sixth Street, as every even numbered street in the Apartment Districts did, ran east-west and perpendicular to the odd numbered streets. Having each district follow the same grid made navigating on foot simple and quick. Once they reached Sixth Street, it appeared to also have commercial buildings, at least on the part visible to him.

Malcolm leaned against the wall of a nearby building under a streetlight, his posture giving off the air of someone without a care in the world. He wore black pants and a dark grey blazer, and his uncovered blonde hair shone under the streetlight. Henry envied his nerve and wished he had the same confidence.

Malcolm stood straight as Henry and Valerie approached, the smile on his face reaching his eyes. "You came."

"We had to," Henry said, while Valerie lingered a few steps behind and kept silent.

"I thought you might be following Molly. Glad to see I was mistaken."

Valerie moved to Henry's side; her eyes narrowed. "How do you know about that?"

It's just like Val to be suspicious, Henry thought.

"All in due time, Valerie. Let's go inside before a guard comes by on patrol."

Valerie flashed Henry a look. It was clear she didn't trust their dad's words. But it wasn't safe to remain on the street.

"Okay," Henry told his dad. "Come on, Val."

His sister huffed as Malcolm led the way to building's entrance. He produced a key from his pocket, unlocked the door and gestured for Henry and Valerie to enter.

Henry stepped over the threshold, choosing to trust the man that had helped him and his friends before. There were no lights on inside the building. The moonlight shining through the windows was enough to display the sparsely furnished room. A massive, wide staircase, leading both up and down, stood on the centre-right of the wall ahead. Malcolm moved in that direction, and Henry followed, pleased to hear his sister's footsteps on the floor tiles behind him. She wouldn't let him continue alone.

At the staircase, Malcolm chose the side descending into darkness. Henry followed and was glad for the guard training exercise of maneuvering in dark spaces. Some of the skills instilled in him during training camp had proved useful in recent times, but he still wished he'd had the courage to refuse joining the Guard Corps in the first place.

On route to the basement, Henry heard his Valerie under her breath. He held back a chuckle, picturing her tripping on a stair.

At the bottom of the staircase stood an enormous, metal door the same size as an entire wall. Again, Malcolm produced a key from his pocket. This time he inserted it in the vertical slit between the door's two halves. With a hiss of pressure releasing, the halves slid apart. Henry felt no apprehension of going in after Malcolm. His sister, however, hesitated before stepping through. The doors shut behind her with a clang.

They stood in darkness in a windowless room. Malcolm flicked a nearby switch and lights in rows on the ceiling turned on. The effect was almost too bright, and Henry shielded his eyes with his hand. "Where are we?" he asked as his eyes adjusted to the harsh, white lighting.

"In a vault," Malcolm said. "The Rebel Cause claimed possession of the building years ago."

Henry surveyed the room. Smooth metal sheeting covered the walls, ceiling and floor. It was reminiscent of the Leader's tower, but the floors and ceilings there hadn't been covered in metal. There also hadn't been a couch and armchairs as there were here, situated on the edge of the light's reach.

"Why'd you lead us down here?" Valerie asked, standing with her arms crossed.

"Because no one will find us. The conversation we need to have requires privacy," Malcolm said.

"Does that mean you'll answer my question now?" Valerie asked.

Henry resisted the urge to sigh. He wished his sister would be less combative. It would make things simpler.

"I know Molly has a meeting tonight because Max told me."

"Why?" Valerie asked.

Malcolm paused. "Sit, and I'll tell you everything you want to know."

Henry sat beside his sister on the couch while Malcolm sat on an armchair opposite them.

"Max told me because we both have ties to the Rebel Cause, and the new Leader placed me in charge of the guards."

"Who's the new Leader?" Henry asked, already having an idea.

Malcolm exhaled. "Gavriel's father, Carl Wessin."

Henry's mouth fell open; and he snapped it shut. This confused him. He'd expected to hear Ben's father's name, not Gavriel's. "Not Bob Henson?"

Malcolm laughed. "He'd have to give up his position as the Reviewer, and no one can pry him from that. He loves flaunting direct and visible power and getting credit."

Like father, like son, Henry thought, though he had to admit Ben possessed more subtlety and ambition.

"What did you mean in your note?" Valerie asked, sounding a bit more at ease. "When you said you could help us."

"He's already helped," Henry said. "He just gave us intel."

"Yes," Malcolm said. "I intended to give information and to extend an offer of assistance, if you decide to exit the City, or to come back if you do leave."

"You mean?" Valerie asked, arching an eyebrow.

"I'll station friendly guards on your route and at the Gate. Max gave me the names of those who swore loyalty to Molly."

Henry shared a glance with his sister. "We might be leaving, but it's not confirmed."

His dad raised an eyebrow, so Henry divulged his plan. He hoped it didn't sound foolish. The only other person he'd told was Valerie.

"I hope that goes the way you want," Malcolm said, fishing in his blazer pocket and producing a small, flat, rectangular, black box with two buttons on its side. He tossed it to Henry. "Take this. Send me a message when you finalize your plan, and I'll shuffle the guards."

"Thank you," Henry said, tucking the device into his jacket pocket. He made a mental note to ask Jax what it was. It seemed electronic, and was some sort of messaging device, which meant Jax probably knew.

"One more question," Valerie asked. "What do the Leader, Gavriel and Ben want? You must know."

Malcolm's eyes landed on Valerie. "Gavriel blames Henry for his breakup with Molly. He wants her back and for her to abandon the Rebel Cause, though he believes she's too caught up in it to do so. Carl is after power; he's always been ambitious. As for Ben, revenge fuels him; the desire for that and his rage radiate off him whenever he's not in front of a camera. He hasn't revealed his end goal, though I suspect it's an ambitious one."

"That sounds like Ben," Henry said, choosing to focus on his ex rather than his former best friend. Gavriel's anger toward him and pining for Molly were too painful to think about. "He'd only share his plan if he thought it helped him."

"You did well to dump him," Malcolm said.

"I still want to punch him in the face," Valerie said.

"Val," Henry said, giving her a glare. Now was not the time for her to act like his protector. He felt his dad's eyes on him and turned his face straight ahead again.

Malcolm had leaned forward and frowned. "It's nice to see you've taken to the role of older sister, Valerie." He rose and brushed his hands along his pants, though they weren't wrinkled or dirty. "You two should head back before it gets too late." With that, he walked back to the vault door, key in hand.

Henry sprung to his feet and darted after him. "Wait! I have a question." Valerie couldn't be the only one to ask their dad multiple questions.

Malcolm inserted the key and didn't glance at Henry. "What is it?"

"How did you know where to send the note?"

"I assure you, you're safe, Henry," Malcolm said as the doors opened with another hiss. "Let's just say two former members of the Rebel Cause sent out a notice."

The Moris.

"I almost forgot," Malcolm said, keeping his voice low to keep Valerie from overhearing as she walked to the door. "I have something for you." He dug into his pocket and produced a small box, which he offered to Henry. "It belonged to your mom. I've kept it hidden long enough, and I thought you might find use for it."

Henry took the box and moved to open the lid.

Malcolm placed his hand over Henry's. "Open it later. Right now, you should go with your sister. A guard will come soon." Malcolm dropped his hand and shooed Henry and Valerie out.

Henry stuffed the box in his pocket and left with Valerie. They climbed the dark stairs to the dim, moonlit building's main floor, exited and retreated to Apartment District 12. While they climbed the fire escape ladder to the Moris' apartment, Henry processed what had transpired that night. The events doubled his certainty about what he needed to do. He stripped his jacket off, wadded it under his head and fell asleep on the kitchen floor, next to an already sleeping Jax, with his plan in his mind and a grin on his face.

Chapter 7

I got down the metal fire escape ladder faster than I thought was possible and jumped to the ground from a few rungs up. When my boots hit the pavement, I sprinted. I ran through alleys and darkened streets undetected. The streets seemed free of guards, making me wonder if my contact had something to do with it.

The Apartment Districts got cleaner and less run down the closer they were to the rich Quarters bordering the coast. I slowed my pace after a few, unable to maintain it. My legs tired, but I forced myself to keep moving.

The night sky was black as ink by the time I reached Apartment District 2. I was glad there were no clouds, as the moon served as my source of illumination. Streetlights, even in this posh district, were sparse.

I stepped onto Third Street and walked. It was residential, which put me on edge. There was no telling who might be watching out a window. As I progressed, the buildings thinned, and the meeting place revealed itself: a large empty lot between two buildings. Neither had windows facing it.

I crossed the street and walked toward the open space. There was no nearby streetlight, and the buildings obstructed the moonlight. I hoped the ground was level and I wouldn't trip over my own feet.

"You're here," Max said as he stepped from the shadows.

"Am I late? I don't know what time it is."

"No, you're fine. Come this way; it isn't safe to stay out here." He turned and retreated in the direction from which he'd come. Seeing no other option, I followed.

...

Max led the way to a shorter building at the back of the lot. He pushed the door open, I steeled my nerves and entered after him into a building well-lit with bright lights dotting the ceiling at even intervals. The walls had faded beige paint on them with no windows to interrupt it. A large, thin rug covered the grey tiled floor, and a beige couch and matching chairs in the centre of the room framed a small, metal coffee table.

"What is this place?"

"A safe house run by the Rebel Cause."

"Is anyone else here?" I scanned the space like I could find the answer in this room.

"Not that I know of," Max said with a shrug. "Take a seat."

His answer did little to reassure me, but I had other questions. And the only way to get answers was to humour him. So, I sat on the couch.

"You must be thirsty," he said. "Wait here."

I sighed as he left the room. He came back a minute later, carrying a glass filled with clear liquid. I tracked it as he neared and proffered it to me. Was it water or something else? The guards were under the Government's control, regardless of the pledge some had given me. I couldn't be certain he hadn't arranged this meeting to do away with me.

"It's just water," he said, his brown eyes warm and inviting. "If I wanted you dead,

I wouldn't have risked my life for you."

"Why did you? You said it was the right thing, but there must be more too it." Had it been a ploy to get me to let down my defenses? Or was he genuine about trying to help?

"You're Jack's daughter." That was a sentence I'd heard too many times in the Colony. He stated it like it was an obvious reason for helping me, while the Colonists had said it like they owed me because of my association to my dad.

I crossed my arms and stared into his eyes. *He had better not be another of Dad's hero worshippers.* "How'd you know that?"

"You look like him. It wasn't hard to figure out, even if he hadn't asked me to watch out for you."

I should have guessed. My dad seemed to have influence over every part of the Rebel Cause, which was ironic as he wouldn't claim leadership for himself. "He told you to meet with me."

Max's eyes widened. "No. There's been no word from him since your return to the City."

This was unexpected. If dad hadn't told him, who had? It made me wonder, so I asked.

"Two old friends sent a message."

I was certain of whom he meant, as there were only two people who could have done it. I accepted the offered glass and downed a gulp of water, not realizing how thirsty I was until the liquid hit my throat. In moments, I drained the entire glass. "I assume you have something to discuss."

"I do," Max said as he sat next to me. He turned his head to maintain eye contact. "You should leave the City. It isn't safe for you here."

Here was someone else who wanted me to hide. "I'd be useless in the Colony. I need to stay."

"The Government knew you were coming," Max said. "The Leader planned to make an example of arresting whoever entered their chamber and instructed the guards to leave the door ajar. You thwarted them, and the video you released has furthered the Government's anger."

"Gav didn't leave it open?" I had assumed someone on my side had aided my entry. Had I been mistaken? Was Gav that lost?

"No. Your ex is not on your side. He is angry and will not risk himself for your cause when he does not believe in it."

Gav. It was difficult to come to terms with him being against me. "Did he tell them we were coming?" If the answer was yes, I wasn't sure I could stand it. Maybe I deserved it; we would have betrayed each other then.

"No. He was adamant that you wouldn't choose to lead such a, and I quote, 'trivial and unnecessary movement'. I assume your signal from the abandoned house gave it away."

I didn't feel relieved. How could I when Gav had belittled an important cause and underestimated me? Had he really assumed I'd hide in the Colony while others put themselves at risk? It didn't matter; this information changed nothing.

"I can't give up," I told Max, meeting his seriousness with my own. "There's too much at stake." In truth, running away to save myself felt selfish and cowardly. I wasn't that girl anymore. And this had become my problem to solve. Leaving the people to their own devices would crush me.

A smile crept onto Max's face, and his eyes bored into me. "I never said you had to give up. But you cannot accomplish much with the threat of hostile guards lurking on the streets outside your window. There are limits to the protection I can give you."

My face heated, and I struggled to remain calm as I turned my face away. He'd lit a match and set me aflame. How dare he treat me like a helpless child? "I don't need your protection."

"Is that so?" The weight of his eyes lingered on my face. He was unperturbed at my outburst. "I'm glad I went to the effort of saving you when you didn't need me."

I fumed, but he was right. Without his help, I would've been arrested before I ever left the City. My temper fizzled out as the rational part of my brain took over. "Alright, maybe I do need your help."

"You can't save anyone if you're in jail. I'm not telling you to do anything or saying you need to leave forever. I'm just advising that leaving might give you an advantage."

"What kind of advantage?" Hiding was a step back in my mind, not a way to accomplish anything.

Max reclined against the couch cushions. "The Government won't be happy about you and your friends escaping arrest again. You'll force them to send someone after you and waste resources. They'll never leave their tower to do it themselves."

I exhaled in a huff. There was a logic to this. "You have a point, but I can't commit to anything. I'd have to discuss it, and I can't see Valerie and Jax agreeing."

"Of course," he said.

I leaned forward placed my palms on the couch to propel myself up. It was a waste of my time to come this way just to be told to leave. "Is that all you wanted to say?"

"I also thought you might want some information."

This piqued my interest, and I settled on the cushions again. "What kind of information?"

"Come, and you'll find out."

...

I went with him down the dark, dim hallway to a narrow, spiral staircase made of concrete. We climbed up to the next story, and he veered down another beige painted hall. I scrambled to catch up and spotted him opening a metal door on the left. He waited, holding it open, for me. When I reached the door, he gestured for me to enter first. Trusting his intentions, I walked in.

As I stepped inside, I gasped. Shelves covered the walls, each covered in books. A metal table with chairs on either side sat in the middle of the room. Strewn papers covered its top. The only place where I'd ever seen this many books was my old school's library.

"What is all this?" I asked.

"A sample of documents the Rebel Cause has compiled over the years. You should have no trouble finding dirt on the Government in here."

"These are all Government documents?" There wasn't enough time to go through everything.

Max shrugged. "The majority are. I can't say there aren't files on other topics mixed in."

If he was unsure what was in the room, I'd never find anything useful. I stood near the centre of the room and spun around, scanning the shelves up and down. A large book with a worn, red cover caught my eye. I plucked it from the shelf.

Once it was in my grasp, I blew the dust off the cover. It had no title, which didn't matter. Who would label a tome filled with smuggled Government secrets? Surely the pages inside would divulge the topic. I plopped it down on the tabletop, sat on the nearest chair and flipped to a random page.

The contents weren't easy to decipher at a quick glance. A part of my mind screamed the book could be useful, and I didn't want to leave it here. I closed the cover and clutched it tight. "I'm taking this with me," I told Max, who stood nearby facing the shelves.

He reached up and selected another tome. His eyes stayed on the shelf. "It won't do you any good if you leave it here."

He tucked his chosen book in the crook of his left arm. I watched as he walked, following the shelves, and selected more. When his arms were full, he deposited the pile on the table, sending up a cloud of dust that made us cough. "You might as well take these," he said, once the dust settled and we both stopped coughing.

I waved my hand in front of my face to disperse the few remaining dust particles. "I can't carry all that."

Max laughed. The sound was infectious, and I joined in. The sight of his hair and shirt speckled with dust made the situation more comical. I imagined I was just as dust-covered, which would take some explaining back at the Moris' apartment. I shook my hair and brushed off my shoulders, sending another cloud of dust into the air. This time I scooted my chair back and covered my face with my hands.

When I lowered my hands, Max was wiping his grimy face with his hand. "I'll bag them for you. There are spare backpacks in the supply closet."

He walked out of the room, leaving me with the small pile of books.

I slouched on my chair and stared at them. There was no simple explanation for their appearance that Valerie and the boys would believe, let alone the Moris. There had to be a hiding place somewhere in the apartment.

Before I could puzzle out a plan, Max returned with a black backpack. The colour choice was obvious; it was easier to conceal in the dark of night when most people would try to flee the City undetected. That was also relevant for my run home.

While Max was filling the backpack with books, I noticed he had put a jacket on top of his dusty shirt. "Are you going somewhere?" I asked as he added the last tome and zipped the backpack.

"I'm escorting you back."

I froze. This was not a good idea. Explaining the books was one problem. But what excuse could I give for him? "What?"

"You don't have time to go by foot. Sunrise is in a couple hours. And we can't risk those books getting in the wrong hands."

"You're driving me?" This plan made me uncomfortable but getting noticed after sunrise was worse.

Max nodded. Seeing no other way, I rose from my chair and grabbed the backpack from him. I slid my arms into the straps and tightened them to fit my frame. I might have been willing to accept a ride, but I could insist on carrying the cargo. "Let's go."

Chapter 8

Max led the way downstairs, veered toward a door on the opposite side of the building from where we'd entered and grabbed a set of keys off a hook on the wall. Once outside, we stood on a small, secluded patch of asphalt with a couple vehicles parked on it.

Max approached the nearest vehicle: a black pickup truck. He inserted the key into the door, unlocked it, climbed onto the seat and called to me. "Get in."

I jogged over to the passenger's side door, removed the backpack as I sat and placed it on my lap. We fastened our seatbelts, and he inserted the key into the ignition. The truck was off the asphalt by the time Max spoke again.

"Pull your hood up," he said, his eyes not leaving the road.

I did as instructed, though I hoped we wouldn't encounter anyone.

Max drove through the district, and I glanced out the window. Even in darkness, I could see how well-kept the buildings and streets were compared to the district I'd grown up in and especially to the Moris'.

The few guards standing on street corners made no move to stop our truck. "Relax," Max said when we passed the first guard. "This is identical to a Government issued guard truck. They'd have to stop us and scan the plate to realize it's not one of theirs."

"And if they decide to do that, what's the plan?" I asked. Relying on other guards not stopping us didn't strike me as a reliable course of action.

"I'll say I'm bringing you in, and they'll probably let us go."

Probably. It wasn't reassuring, and it depended on whether the guard who stopped us was loyal to me or the Government. It still felt surreal that part of the Guard Corps had sworn loyalty to me. A couple days wasn't enough to get used to that. I wasn't sure I believed it, and there were other issues on my mind.

"Besides," Max said. "A lot of guards are busy giving people warnings for acting on your video."

"What?" My heart dropped. I didn't want anyone getting in trouble because of me. The blame for that would lie heavy on my shoulders. Was I strong enough to bear it?

"Some landlords reported riots in their hallways and foyers. As far as I know, no citizens rioted outside or impacted businesses. And Government buildings are secure for now."

I hunched in my seat; my arms crossed around the backpack. "I guess the video had an impact."

Max was silent. He seemed unlikely to reply, so I resumed my window gazing. "You need to be careful," he said, keeping his voice quiet when he broke his silence. "A lot of people could wind up in trouble for thinking they're helping your cause when they have no direction."

How can I give them direction, I thought, *when I'm not sure they should be involved.*

...

Max drove on, and I kept up my sightseeing. I was watching for guards that might stop us, but I also wanted a view I didn't get on my previous trips through the City. We drove the road lining the western side of each district, the one reserved for vehicles. All the buildings backing onto the road were made of concrete, which should have meant they were identical. But the condition of each told a story. The nicer, cleaner buildings with smooth, crack-free, white walls spoke of a relative wealth; not as much as the stand-a-lone houses in the rich Quarters, just enough that the inhabitants probably didn't go hungry. The farther south we got, the dingier the buildings were. A heaviness settled on me as I saw the stained buildings with cracks running up their grey walls. The splits seemed cosmetic. How long until they became a hazard?

Someone had to help, though it felt like too great a task to take on. I couldn't do it alone. Luckily, I didn't have to. This comforted me as the truck kept moving. We passed my former district, and I was glad we didn't drive down my old street. I assumed the things Dad and I had left behind had been thrown out, which didn't matter; I wasn't attached to some furniture and dishes. Besides, none of what we'd left had been of any value.

The rest of the districts passed by in increasing levels of disrepair. After a while, I tired of the view and reclined my seat, deciding instead to gaze at the truck's ceiling. The smooth and steady motion of the truck threatened to lull me to sleep. I blinked, desperate to stay awake.

It felt both like forever and no time at all before we turned into Apartment District 12. I sat upright and adjusted the backpack on my lap. In moments, I would have to climb the fire escape ladder, which was a task requiring alertness. Falling from the ladder would be a pathetic end.

Max steered the truck toward the Moris' apartment building. He stopped a couple streets away and removed the keys from the ignition. I hefted the backpack of books and secured it on my back as I exited. To my dismay, Max got out and stood on the street. "I'm coming with you."

"Why?"

"I have my reasons. And you have valuable cargo that needs protecting."

I rolled my eyes. Of course he cared about the books. It made sense; we couldn't let Government-loyal guards get their hands on them. "Fine," I said, walking in the direction of the Moris' building.

His footsteps fell into sync with mine. I kept my hood pulled up as we walked, mindful that a guard was on patrol nearby. Even with Max present, I didn't fancy my chances if an unfriendly guard spotted me.

It took us longer than I'd expected to reach the Moris' street, weighted down as I was by the books. *They'd better be useful.* If not, I'd curse Max for persuading me to take them. I was glad when we stepped onto the correct street; it meant I could soon dump the books onto the bedroom's floor and collapse on the bed. That is if Max didn't insist on staying. Sleep would be impossible with him in the room.

We trudged down the street, careful to stay out of sight. The sky was lightening, though no hint of the sun was visible. It still made me nervous. Curfew ended at sunrise, meaning we had a short window to make it inside before people trickled onto the street.

We had made it halfway when a guard stepped onto the street from a perpendicular one, his flashlight arcing back and forth as he walked toward us. Within seconds, it would shine on us.

My breath caught in my throat and my feet froze in place. Strong hands, Max's I assumed, grabbed my jacket and yanked me sideways. I shook myself out of the daze my head was in and ran with Max. We hid behind the dumpster in a nearby alley. My heart pounded as the guard made slow progress down the street, sweeping his flashlight as he walked. I crouched lower and held my breath as the beam swung to our hiding spot and lingered for what felt like an eternity. When the guard moved on, Max held me back with a shake of his head and a hand on my arm. I understood his meaning; we had to wait until the guard was out of earshot.

When the guard was gone a couple minutes, Max determined it was safe, and we resumed our trek to the street behind the Moris' apartment. We stood, side by side, at the base of the metal ladder I was certain led to the correct apartment.

"Go ahead," Max said. "I'll climb after you."

With a sigh, I placed my hands on the ladder's rungs and climbed. It had been easier to scale down it than to pull myself up carrying a heavy weight. Before Henry's training sessions, I wouldn't've been able to.

My legs wobbled as I disembarked the ladder and stood on the small landing, panting from the exertion. Mere seconds later Max joined me. He wasn't the slightest bit winded, though he hadn't carried anything.

"I could have carried the books, you know," he whispered with a knowing smirk.

I swatted him on the arm once my breathing returned to its normal rate. "I handled it."

"True enough," Max said.

I closed my eyes. "Let's get inside already."

I slid the window up until it was open enough to climb through. Pushing on the windowsill with my hands, I hefted my body up and swung my legs over. The backpack barely fit through the gap, and I was happy to learn, as my feet hit the bedroom floor and I slid my arms from the straps, it hadn't snagged; the windowsill had brushed most of the dust off my shirt. and I was in the correct apartment. There was my bag across the room and Valerie's on the floor between the bed and window. The bed was empty. I had expected Valerie to be sleeping, but she must've gone to a different room.

I turned to wave Max after me and saw that he was already climbing through the window with practised ease. I wondered how many times he'd done this before and why. Once he was in the room, he eased the window closed.

I exhaled and walked around the bed to my side, carrying the books snug to my chest. Crouching, I slid the backpack under the bed, far enough that no one walking into the room should spot it, but close enough for me to grab.

Max stood a metre away, his eyes on where I had stowed the books. "You don't want your friends' help going through them?"

"I haven't decided what to tell them," I said as I sat on the bed and brushed the remaining dust off my clothes. Every part of me craved sleep, but I forced myself to resist until Max was gone at least.

He chuckled. "You'll have to figure it out. Someone is sure to come in here at some point, considering someone else sleeps here."

He'd spotted Valerie's bag. I nodded, knowing that the time for explaining was fast approaching, which didn't make it easier. "If you have any ideas, I'm interested," I said around a yawn, turning my head in his direction and forcing my sleepy eyes to focus.

"Well, you could—"

I frowned, curious as to why he stopped midsentence, when my ears registered what he must have heard seconds before: footsteps nearing the other side of the door. Before Max or I could react, the doorknob turned and the door itself swung open, revealing a figure with blinking, tired eyes and sleep-tousled, blonde hair that shone golden in the dawn light streaming through the window.

"Molly?" Valerie asked. "Are you in here?"

Chapter 9

Henry

Voices coming from the bedroom woke Henry. Careful not to wake Jax or the Moris, he got to his feet and approached the door, the box in his jacket pocket forgotten. The door was ajar, so he widened the opening and stepped into the room.

Valerie stood near the door, her attention on a man hovering at the foot of the bed where Molly sat with a faint smear of dust on her clothes and hair. She gave Henry a weak smile, appearing on the verge of falling asleep. It did little to disperse the unexpected jealousy he felt toward the stranger.

"Henry," Molly said. "I'm glad you're here. I don't want to tell this story more than once. Where's Jax?"

"Asleep."

Molly sighed. "Can you wake him up?"

Henry frowned. "I'd rather just tell him later." He didn't like his chances of waking Jax without his parents hearing, or of Jax having an amenable reaction.

"Just leave him," Valerie said, her eyes still glued to the stranger's face, studying him. "We don't have much time before the Moris wake up."

"Alright," Molly said, the tone of her voice implying she was too exhausted to argue. "Where should we start, Max?"

"From the beginning," the stranger, whose name was Max apparently, said.

Molly swatted Max's arm and rolled her eyes. "You're no help."

Henry was confused by her closeness with Max, though his voice was familiar. He couldn't place where or when he'd heard it and didn't get a chance to question Molly about it as she dove into her account of the night's events. As she spoke, Valerie climbed onto her side of the bed, her eyes still on Max and a coy smile on her mouth. She brushed her hair behind her shoulders and leaned closer as if enraptured by the stranger.

Molly waved Henry over with a flick of her hand. He sat on the bed, and she held his hand, her thumb tracing circles over his palm. She kept relaying her tale, and Henry tried to focus. It was difficult when her body was close to him and the urge to hold her was strong. He'd worried about her while he was with Malcolm, and on the way home afterward. For once, his worry had been entirely selfish; he hadn't wanted to lose her. But the only thing close to dangerous that had happened had been her close call with the guard finishing his patrol.

Henry knew from his few night patrol experiences that this close to dawn the guards were eager to return home to sleep. Their attention was rarely where it should be at that hour, and Molly hadn't been in real danger. Besides, she'd had a guard with her who was skilled at saving her. That made Henry jealous, especially since all he'd done was pile more trouble on her life.

In her tale, Molly had said, with obvious reluctance, that Max wanted her to leave the City. It didn't take a perceptive genius to realize she didn't like that. Henry didn't blame her; he would've been upset if Malcolm had summoned him only to tell him to leave and hide because he was in danger. This lessoned his jealousy a degree, but it lingered.

"That isn't the whole story," Max said when Molly finished her tale.

Molly sighed and dropped Henry's hand. She got off the bed and knelt on the floor. Henry watched her lean forward and pull out a black backpack. She hefted it onto the bed, its weight causing a dip in the mattress.

"Max thinks these might have useful information," she said as she unzipped the backpack, tipped it upside down and dumped out a pile of dusty books. They were old and worn with yellowed pages and no titles on their covers.

"You carried these?" Henry asked.

"Why were they under the bed?" Valerie asked, tearing her eyes off Max's face long enough to peer at them.

"Yes, I carried them," Molly said, sounding proud of the fact. "And because I don't know what to do with them."

"You should be careful," Max said, his own eyes on the books. "Limit whom you let see them."

"That's why they were under the bed," Molly snapped.

Valerie grabbed the book nearest to her and flipped through its pages. "There was no point in hiding them from us. But I agree that we shouldn't let the Moris see them."

Henry plucked a book off the top of the pile. It was heavy, not because it was large in terms of page size, but it was thick. What secrets did they hide?

Molly pushed the books to the middle of the bed, leaving space on the edge that she occupied by flopping down on her back. "Everyone out," she commanded as she shielded her eyes from the sun streaming in through the window with her hand. "The Moris will be awake soon, and I'm exhausted."

Valerie sighed, placed her book down and rose from the bed. Henry dropped the book he held and got to his feet. Molly grabbed his wrist. She yanked on his arm, pulling him down to her eye line.

"Come back when the Moris leave." It was an order not a request. Henry didn't mind. He wanted time near and with her. She released his arm, and he stood up again.

Henry walked to the bedroom door, while Max headed to the window and Valerie trailed the guard. Henry shook his head as he walked into the apartment's main room and lay down on the kitchen floor, his jacket as his pillow. Apparently, his sister was the one pining after Max. He had no business dictating who she was romantic with, and he didn't mind if his sister had a crush anyway. As long as Molly wasn't catching feelings for the older guard, he'd stay out of it.

Valerie exited the bedroom, yawning as she stretched her arms above her head. Henry sat up and watched her walk to the fridge and pour two glasses of apple juice. She came and crouched by Henry, offering him one of the glasses with an outstretched arm.

Henry accepted it and drank the juice. Small gestures like that were how Valerie showed that she cared. He liked having her around, though it made him wish their childhoods had been different. It would've been nice to have grown up with Valerie and Malcolm. And maybe his sister would've been comfortable saying how she felt instead of hinting at it through gestures. As he pondered his family situation, the Moris stirred and rose from the couch. Jax rolled over and woke with a start when his face hit the tile floor.

"About time," Valerie said.

"You could've woken me up," Jax mumbled as he sat up and yawned. "What did I miss?"

"I'll tell you later," Valerie said.

Jax frowned and scrunched his eyebrows. "Okay."

Mrs. Mori went into the bathroom while Mr. Mori brewed a pot of coffee. Henry never cared for the drink, finding it too bitter, not that he'd tried it before living with Ben; the Newsomes hadn't allowed him too. When the coffee was ready, Mr. Mori filled two mugs and asked if anyone else wanted some. Only Jax accepted his offer.

Jax sat at the table stirring a heaping spoonful of sweetener into his. Sugar was an expense most people could afford only in small quantities, so artificial sweeteners were common and popular substitutes. Ben had always bought real sugar, just because he could. It was another way he flaunted his wealth.

Mrs. Mori exited the bathroom, wearing a fresh outfit and her hair immaculately styled, sweetened her cup of coffee and put two bagels in the toaster while Mr. Mori spent his turn in the bathroom. "Promise me you'll stay safe today, Jax," she said. "There's no telling what'll happen after last night."

Jax nodded as he sipped his coffee. "We'll stay here and keep the door locked. Don't worry, Mom."

"Good," Mrs. Mori said, busying herself with gathering her and her husband's bagged lunches from the fridge. When the toaster popped, she spread peanut butter on the bagel halves and passed two to her husband as he came from the bathroom wearing a clean, yet worn, grey two-piece suit.

"Stay safe, kids," Mr. Mori said, ruffling Jax's hair before he steered his wife to the door, each of them carrying their breakfast, lunch and work bag.

"We will, Dad," Jax said as he smoothed his hair, and his parents exited the apartment and locked the door.

"I'm hungry," Valerie said, rising from the floor and walking toward the fridge. "You guys want anything?"

"Some toast," Jax said, going to join Valerie. "I can get it."

"I'll eat later." Henry had something to do first. And he was already entering the bedroom before he heard his sister's reply.

...

Henry eased the door shut behind him. "Molly, are you awake?"

She mumbled a reply that he couldn't decipher. He approached the bed and found her sprawled under the blanket with the books scattered beside her. He lifted the backpack from the foot of the bed, where she must've thrown or kicked it, and stacked the books inside. When all the books were in it, he zipped it and placed it under the bed where she'd stowed it before. If he could help make her sleeping space more comfortable, he would. Besides, she couldn't complain about storing the books where she'd placed them herself.

With that task done, and space cleared for him, Henry climbed on the bed and reclined next to Molly. He'd missed being this close to her. He brushed her hair from her face, being as gentle as he could to not disturb her rest.

"You came," she said, her voice heavy from sleep. She didn't open her eyes.

"You told me to."

With her eyes still closed, she beckoned him to come closer. "Hold me. Please, Henry."

Without hesitation, Henry lay under the blanket and slid his arm under her torso. There were few requests of hers that he would refuse. This wasn't one of them. He did this with eagerness, the act fulfilling his own desire as much as hers.

She rolled her body, pressing her back into his chest, as he draped his free arm over her. "I love you," she said in the final moments before she fell asleep, and her breathing slowed into an even rhythm.

"I love you too," Henry said with a kiss on her forehead. Even in slumber, part of her might have heard him. He hoped so. Because he did love Molly with every atom in his being.

She'd always been beautiful in his eyes, since the day in the school hallway when he'd first spotted her weighted down with an armload of textbooks. She'd been smaller then, with only her face and chestnut hair peeking out above the stack of books. Now her beauty was magnified in sleep, her features relaxed and peaceful.

Henry studied her features and tried to memorize them. He wanted nothing to separate him and Molly. If something, or someone, did, he'd need an accurate image of her in his memory to keep his sanity. But she was much more than a pretty girl. He also tried to commit to memory her bravery, strength and kindness.

He rested his head on the pillow; her head was on his arm and her hair brushed his chin. He sighed. They hadn't shared a bed since leaving the Colony. The house they'd occupied had been small, but he missed it. It had been their own space and offered privacy. Here, his sister was on the other side of the door, and they couldn't sleep in the same bed.

That didn't matter, not when he was finally alone with Molly, and they were safe from immediate danger. He adjusted his arms around her and settled into the mattress. He'd gotten a decent amount of sleep after his meeting with Malcolm, but the bed was comfier and warmer than sleeping on the kitchen floor, and his eyelids grew heavy. He pulled the blanket up over his shoulders, careful to keep it off Molly's face and let himself drift to sleep, the girl he loved safe in his arms.

Chapter 10

When I woke, early afternoon sunlight streamed through the curtains, and I had vague memories of Henry joining me in bed. I knew it wasn't my imagination because his arms were still around me. And the blanket, which had been waist high, now covered our bodies. The combined warmth of Henry's body and the blanket soothed me, but my stomach told me it was time to eat. "Henry?" I asked as I wiggled around in his arms.

He blinked, his eyebrows creasing. "What's wrong?"

"I'm hungry."

His face relaxed as he laughed and sat up, sliding his arm out from under me. "Okay. Let's get something to eat."

I nodded as I freed myself from the covers. My hair was still braided, and I supposed my clothes weren't too wrinkled or dirty. I had gotten most of the dust off. After kicking everyone out, I had managed to take my boots and jacket off; I went and grabbed them from the floor at foot of the bed. I tossed my jacket onto the bed and pulled my boots on. Going shoeless around the apartment left my feet frozen.

I stood and saw Henry looking at me with a gleam in his eyes. He was trying hard to keep his face neutral. I craned my neck to get a glimpse of my outfit. It was fine to my eyes. "Why are you staring at me? Am I a mess?"

Henry shook his head. "You're beautiful."

"You haven't answered my question."

He shrugged. "Sorry. I didn't mean to stare."

This felt like a lie, or at least like it wasn't the whole truth. I didn't press the issue. If he had a secret, I was certain he had a good reason. And my stomach rumbled again, demanding food. "Okay," I said as I opened the door and stepped into the main room.

...

Henry and I made peanut butter and jam sandwiches and sat at the table to eat. I inhaled mine to satisfy the growing hunger pain in my stomach. In my peripheral vision, I kept catching Henry gazing at me. He moved his eyes away whenever I tried to look at his face. It was strange. It felt like he was studying me like I was a rare species of house plant.

Desperate for escape, I washed my plate in the sink and approached Valerie on the couch. She sat with an old magazine, presumably Mrs. Mori's, open on her lap.

"Do you know why Henry's acting weird?" I asked, keeping my voice low. He was still across the room, washing his own plate.

She didn't move her eyes off the magazine page. "Weird in what way?"

"He keeps looking at me."

"He loves you. He's allowed to look at you."

"But—"

She tore her eyes from the magazine, closed it and set it on the couch. "I think being cooped up is driving us all crazy, and you need a distraction. How about I help go through the books Max gave you?"

I sighed, knowing it was a task someone needed accomplish and one I needed to oversee. I also realized I wouldn't get any more details out of her. "Fine."

"Great," she said, with a too-cheerful grin. "Jax can keep Henry occupied."

I turned my head to Jax who leaned against the wall by the screen, holding his hacker's tool. The sight didn't give me confidence that he'd keep Henry busy. But Henry didn't need a babysitter.

Valerie shooed me into the bedroom. "Molly and I are going through the books," she explained to the boys and closed the door behind us before I could hear their replies.

"Do you have any of that stationery left?" she asked. "It would help if we wrote down anything important that we find."

"Yeah, I do," I said as I retrieved my backpack. "It's in here." I unzipped the front pocket and pulled out the remaining sheets of paper from the stationery shop I'd bought with Jax. They had only sold packs, and I'd just needed one sheet to write my dad a note, which ended up being unnecessary. I stuck my hand in the pocket and grasped the pen hiding at the bottom. "I only have one pen though."

"We can share," Valerie said as she sat crossed legged on the bed. "As long as we don't lose it or run out of ink."

I pulled the backpack of books from its hiding spot, though I couldn't remember putting them there before I feel asleep, unzipped it and dumped the contents onto the bed. Hopefully, Max wouldn't be angry at my not-so-delicate treatment of the books. Not that they were being well treated before when they sat on shelves collecting dust, and I wasn't trying to destroy them. I just had no patience to remove them one by one. I made myself space on the bed and, with my feet tucked under me and my flask nearby, I chose a book at random and flipped open its cover.

Valerie asked, "What's Max's name short for? Do you know?"

"I have no idea. The tag on his uniform only said Max."

"Huh," Valerie said. "It must be short for something. No one names their kid just Max."

I looked up from the page I hadn't been reading and saw Valerie's eyes on me. She wasn't even holding a book. I closed mine and adjusted my position to face her and quirked an eyebrow.

"I bet it's something like Maximillian. He has the looks to pull off something distinguished like that."

"Why do you care?" This was out of character for her. She was usually task focused, not distracted by a stranger she met hours before. "I thought we were supposed to be going through the books."

"I don't care," she said. It was an obvious lie based on the tone of her voice and the blush on her face.

"You're attracted to him," I said, cluing in. If I thought about it, I could see why she might be. He was handsome and nice enough.

"I—" she sputtered then sighed, loud and frustrated. "I mean, he is cute."

I chuckled. "You barely know him."

"I didn't say I'm in love with him. Just that he's cute. And I wouldn't mind spending time with him."

Seeing that we wouldn't get anything productive done in the immediate future, I flopped onto my back and turned my head toward her. "Have you dated anyone?" I asked. I knew few details of her personal life, which was something I intended to remedy.

She laughed, as if the idea of her dating was a joke. "Kaydon scared off anyone I might be interested in. He's shadowed me for years. I've ignored his advances."

She wasn't oblivious to his crush. This was a surprise, considering her behaviour around him when I'd been in the Colony, and I felt a bit sympathetic toward Kaydon. "You never told him you didn't feel the same way?" The Valerie I'd come to know wasn't cold enough to lead someone on.

She stayed silent a long moment before she answered, her voice a degree louder than a whisper when she did speak. "I tried. I said the words, and he never listened. He said it didn't matter if I didn't love him because I'd learn to in time. He said I couldn't choose anyone else because it would crush him."

My sympathy vanished, and I sat upright. "That's horrible. He can't trap you like that."

Her voice grew with conviction and volume. "Not anymore he can't. I was going to make him ride with Charlie even if Juna hadn't. I needed space."

I nodded. "That's understandable. It does makes me wonder what he's up to now though."

She rolled her eyes. "Probably in the house with Juna pining over me and fretting. I'm not lucky enough for him to have moved on."

The mental picture of Kaydon alone with Juna and his unrequited crush made me break into unrestrained laughter. I figured Juna would've tired of him by now, leaving him alone with his feelings and self pity.

Then another possibility came to my mind, one less humorous. "You don't think he's cooped up on a watch tower keeping an eye out for you?" I asked, remembering when I had first reached the Colony and Kaydon had been in a panic because Valerie was late.

She groaned, her face in her hands. "If he is, then at least he isn't driving Juna insane."

"So, you don't want to go back. Like Max said I should."

She turned toward me. "He might have a point. Besides, the Moris won't let us go anywhere. We can't do much from here."

"I know. I don't think I could've gotten away with going to meet Max if you hadn't been here to cover for me."

"About that," Valerie said, averting her eyes. "Henry got a note from Malcolm, and we went to meet him."

"What did he want?"

"He said the new Leader, Carl Wessin, put him in charge of the guards. And that he can help us get out of the City if we plan to. He also knew about your meeting with Max."

My body turned cold and heavy, like a car was resting on my shoulders. I had expected Bob Henson to take the Leader's job, or some random Inner Circle member I'd never heard of. For it to be the man that had issued our arrest warrants was worse than I had imagined. "Gav's dad is the new Leader?"

"Yes."

Nothing good could come from this. Having only met Carl Wessin once, I wasn't eager to be reacquainted. The man was emotionless and calculating, and Gav was under his influence. Max must've spoken the truth when he said Gav wasn't on my side. He'd never choose me or the Rebel Cause over his family.

"That makes it more important for us to find something useful in these books," I said, gesturing to the tomes spread across the bed with a wave of my hand. We needed something big.

"Alright," Valerie said. "We can do it."

Getting her to start was easier than I had expected. And once she delved in, she became laser focused on the task, as was her usual method.

I reopened the book on my lap and flipped through its pages. It wasn't that interesting at first as it appeared to be mundane lists of arrests and sentences for petty crimes. The crime making the most appearances on the list was food theft. This wasn't a shock; everyone in the City lived on rations that could be added to if you had money. The poor were starving. I almost gave up on the book, and was about to toss it aside, when the last page I flipped to, near the back of the book, displayed a different list.

I grabbed the pen and a piece of stationery and marked down the book's cover colour, as that was the only distinguishing feature, and the page number. "Valerie," I called, and then again with a louder voice.

Her head snapped up. "What?"

"Read this," I held the book open and turned it to show her.

Her eyebrows shot up and her lips parted, forming a small circle. "Seems like we're off to a good start."

It was, but I feared the public's reaction to the information. Who would want to find out the unfortunate fate their relative sentenced to life in prison had suffered? The Government must've banned visits to keep this secret. Even under dire threat, the information would've made its way out otherwise.

"Oh no," Valerie gasped, pressing the open pages of her book against her torso to conceal them from me.

"What is it?" I needed to know what she had found. She closed her eyes and scrunched up her face; clearly the page's contents weren't pleasant. But the point of this exercise was to find that type of information.

I pried the book from her hands. She offered little resistance, like she realized struggling would delay the inevitable. Flipping the book around, I glanced at the open page. Another list, this time cataloging prices. It was what was being sold that was disturbing.

With a heavy heart, I documented it on the sheet of stationery. We needed every useful piece of information we could get, no matter how horrible. And this stood a chance of impacting more people than the information about prisoners.

"We don't need to show Henry," I said, knowing where her emotions laid. Mine were in a similar spot; we both cared for him and knew this piece of information would upset him. A quiet thought voiced itself in my head. *It would also upset Gav.* I closed my mind to it. Now wasn't the time to think about him.

"It's not right to keep it secret from him. He deserves to know."

I nodded, a lump forming in my throat and a knot in the pit of my stomach. "Alright, we can take a break and tell him now."

She voiced her agreement, and we both rose from the bed. I clutched the book and together we exited the bedroom to find Henry.

Chapter 11

When we stepped in the hall Jax was on us. "You're done already?" he asked, not-so-subtly disguising his panic.

"We have something to show Henry," I said, attempting to side-step Jax, who moved to block my path.

"He's busy," Jax said. "You can't—"

"It's okay, Jax," Henry called. "Let them come in."

Jax stepped aside, and I walked to Henry, holding the book aloft. A delicious smell I wafted through the air the closer I got to the kitchen. Garlic maybe? I tried to clear my head and focus on the book.

"We found something you should read," I said, holding up the page to his eye line.

He scanned it and ran his hand through his golden locks as he exhaled. "No wonder the Newsomes were so disappointed."

I analyzed his face, but he didn't appear upset. "You aren't angry?"

The corner of his mouth tipped up. "No. It actually explains a lot. But I'm trying to move on. I wasted enough years being hurt and manipulated by them, and they were never my family."

"You're taking it better than I would have," I said, admiring his strength.

"Gavriel wouldn't take it well either," Henry said, a flash of regret appearing on his face. "I'm sure he doesn't know."

"No," I said. "Probably not."

The smile on Henry's face grew, and his eyes were on me again. "Are you hungry? I know we ate a couple hours ago, but I thought we could have an early meal, before the Moris come home."

"Why?" He was up to something. What was it?

"You're saying you don't want a private meal with me?" He held a hand to his chest and pretended to be wounded.

"What about Valerie and Jax?"

Henry's eyes twinkled, and he lowered his hand. "They'll eat later. Jax said he doesn't mind, and my sister will understand." He offered me his hand, with his palm up, clearly expecting me to take it.

I interlaced my fingers with his. Touching him felt as natural as breathing. Holding Gav's hand had been different, like two puzzle pieces that seem like they should fit together but one is wrong when you try to connect them.

Henry led me to the kitchen table. Someone had folded a piece of purple fabric into an intricate rose and placed it on the centre of the tabletop. As I eyed it, Henry dropped my hand and pulled out one of the chairs. I sat, growing more curious by the minute.

"I can move it in myself."

He laughed, sounding more carefree than I had ever heard him. "I know." And he let me do it.

As I moved my chair in, Henry set a glass in front of me. It held a yellow liquid with bubbles suspended throughout it. He put an identical glass at the place setting across the table.

I raised mine and drank a small sip, surprised at the tingle on my tongue. It tasted like apple juice, but I couldn't figure out why it was bubbly.

"Mrs. Mori said we could drink her carbonated juice. I asked her when I saw it in the fridge. She thought you'd like it," he said.

"This wasn't a spontaneous plan?" I swirled the glass and drank another sip. *He must be up to something big.* He'd never put much planning into gestures before. They had always seemed spur of the moment. Maybe that was intentional.

"No," he said, his attention on me more than his apple juice. "I wanted to surprise you with something special."

I decided to enjoy the experience of him doing something for me. If the meal was the secret that he'd hidden that morning, I didn't mind. It at least meant I didn't have to cook, and I couldn't create another mess. "What did you make?"

"I wish I'd had access to fresher ingredients," he said, not giving my question a direct answer. "Since we can't go anywhere, I made do with what was here."

He walked to the oven and removed a baking sheet and a pan. I couldn't tell what was on either, so I forced myself to be patient and let Henry carry out his surprise. He brought over two plates, set one in front of me and the other across the table as he sat.

I studied mine: roasted carrots and a circle of baked polenta covered with mushrooms and a beige sauce. The scent I'd noticed earlier came from the food. I pierced a small bite with my fork and placed it in my mouth. The taste was even better than the smell: creamy, rich and spiced. I moaned, unable to help myself.

"You like it?" Henry asked, his own food untouched.

I nodded, as I swallowed. "What's the sauce made of?"

"Cashews. It was difficult to make without a blender. I didn't want you to hear the noise."

"You put a lot of effort into this." Why? What made him plan this?

He blushed as he ate a bite. I grinned, pleased that I could make his cheeks pink. I wanted him to be happy.

We ate the rest of the meal, discussing the other information I'd found in the books. It wasn't the most pleasant topic, but we had little else new in our lives, and this was important. I didn't bring up his meeting with Malcolm, trusting him to tell me when he was ready.

After every drop of food on our plates was gone, Henry deposited the dishes in the sink. He went to the fridge and removed something that he concealed behind his back as he crouched and reached into his jacket pocket with his free hand.

I turned to watch him, not knowing what was going on. As I rotated, I noticed Jax and Valerie weren't in the room. We were alone, though I assumed they'd only gone into the bedroom. Where else was there? They hadn't walked past us to go into the bathroom. As I puzzled over their disappearance, Henry approached me.

…

When Henry reached my chair, he knelt on one knee and my heart sped up. He moved his hand from his back and offered what he held to me. I peered at it and could make it out despite my pounding heart threatening to blur my vision. On a small plate was a large sugar cookie decorated with icing that wasn't purely decorative. Someone, Henry I assumed, had written a message on top in purple: *Will you marry me?*

I flung my hand over my mouth as my eyes watered. They weren't full blown tears, and I wasn't sad. Happy crying was something I hadn't done before. Who knew it felt both wonderful and strange?

Henry gulped with nerves evident on his face. He glanced at the black box in his other hand and offered it to me. "My dad gave me this tonight. Valerie and I went to meet him." He averted his eyes as he said this, clearly worried I'd be upset that he saw his own father. "It was my mom's. I haven't opened it; I wanted to wait for you."

I moved my hand from my mouth and lifted the box from his palm. It was velvety soft and higher quality than anything my parents could've afforded, making me wonder what it contained. "You're sure you want me to have it?" I didn't feel worthy of something this expensive.

He dipped his head once. "Yes."

I threw my arms around him, trying to keep most of my weight off him and not crush the cookie. "I love you, Henry Connor. And yes, I'll marry you. I would've said yes even without the fancy box."

Henry set the cookie on the table, scooped me into his arms and sat on the floor cradling me on his lap. "It's yours regardless. Open it."

I removed the lid and gasped. Inside, in a satin lining, was a gold ring with a large red gemstone on top framed by smaller, clear gems. Circling the ring was a matching gold bracelet with red and clear gemstones spaced around it in even intervals. "It's beautiful. Do you know what the stones are?"

"Even with as little knowledge as I have of my parents, I imagine they're rubies and diamonds."

I'd forgotten his parents had been wealthy. It made me feel inadequate.

"I've never seen real diamonds before. My mom's ring was silver with a pink quartz stone."

"My dad thought I could find use for this when he gave it to me. I'm certain he meant giving it to you." He plucked the ring from its nestling place and slid it on my left ring finger.

It was a bit loose, but it stayed in place when I waved my hand around. I offered him my right wrist when he reached for the bracelet and undid the clasp. He wrapped the dainty gold chain around my wrist and fastened it. It was a perfect fit. Did that mean I deserved to wear it? Loving Henry should have made me worthy.

His fingers lingered on my skin, tracing my wrist. "Gold suits you," he said. "But you should know, I was going to propose even before my dad gave me the box."

I craned my neck to view his face. There was more vulnerability and hope on it than I could remember seeing. Our lips met. Like each of our kisses, the contact sent sparks through my body, like tiny fireworks shooting from my nerves. I craved it, like an addict yearning for a drug fix; it made me feel on fire and alive. And that fiery passion was the best sensation I'd ever experienced. Kissing Gav had never felt like this.

The sound of someone squealing entered my ears, killing the moment and ending our kiss too early for my liking. Henry and I untangled our bodies, and he helped me up from the floor.

Valerie threw her arms around me. "You said yes, didn't you?"

Obviously, Henry had told his sister, and probably Jax, his plan. "I did," I said, pulling back from the hug and thrusting my hand in her face to show off my ring.

"Wow," she said. "Where'd you get that, Henry?"

He blushed again, the pink hue of his cheeks making him more attractive. "From Dad. He said it was Mom's."

"It came with this," I said, raising my right arm to display the bracelet. "I've never had anything this expensive."

"Both are gorgeous," Valerie said, without a hint of jealousy or resentment in her voice.

"You aren't upset that I gave them to Molly instead of you?" Henry asked.

Valerie shook her head. "No. Molly should have them. She'll be family soon enough."

It hit me then that Henry and I wouldn't have a typical path to marriage. There was no chance of us having a Courtship; our application would never be accepted even if we filed one. I had no word for what we were. The only path to marriage I knew was through a Courtship. Valerie was right regardless. Henry and I would marry, and she'd be my sister-in-law, which was something few people in the City had. One problem remained; we couldn't wed in the City. I sighed. "Max will be happy. I have a reason to leave now."

"Dad will help us. He gave me something to message him with, if Jax can figure out how to use it." Henry went to his backpack and produced a small, flat, rectangular box with rounded corners and edges.

"It's a phone," Valerie said.

Henry and I both stared at her. Phones weren't common in the City, and the ones I'd seen in school and Government buildings hadn't been as small or mobile; to prevent their theft, they'd had a limited range from their charging base and were much bigger and bulkier. This was easily concealable.

"Charlie has one," she said. "He showed it to me."

"You know how to work it? Why didn't you tell me when Dad gave it to me?" Henry asked, holding it out to her.

She shrugged. "I know the basics. And it wasn't important then. We had other things to discuss with Dad." She grabbed the phone and pressed a button on its side and frowned. "It needs sunlight to charge. I'll go put it on the windowsill."

Once again, Henry and I were alone. I yearned to resume our make out session, but the Moris would be back soon, and we had plans to make. "Are you okay with leaving the City again?"

"I want to marry you, Molly. I know it can't happen here. And home for me is wherever you and Val are."

"When we come back," I said, averting my eyes and refusing to include the if. "No one will recognize our marriage as legal."

"As long as our friends and families accept it, that's all that matters to me."

I ran my finger along my bracelet, following the smooth design all the way around. "It doesn't feel like enough. It won't stop Ben or Gav."

Henry held my hands in his as we stood face-to-face, our foreheads touching. "Nothing will stop their quests for revenge, but that shouldn't impact our relationship."

"You're right." Other people's opinions couldn't dictate my choices. Why would I let them now?

Chapter 12

Henry

Henry had come a long way since his breakup with Ben. Back then, even though it was only a couple months ago, he hadn't had the courage to go after things he wanted. That night at the Gate changed him. He'd chosen his friend, and more importantly, Molly, over Ben. It was something he still didn't regret, even now that Gavriel hated him.

After hopefully soothing Molly's concerns about Ben and Gavriel, Henry cleaned up the mess he'd made in the kitchen and pocketed the cookie. He didn't want the Moris to find evidence of his proposal when they came home. Even with their connection to the Rebel Cause, he wasn't he could trust them. Jax would have to give them some excuse, so they'd let him leave. The truth didn't seem like the best option.

"Let me help," his sister said, standing beside him and holding a dishtowel. "Molly's showing Jax her jewelry."

"You don't have to."

She chortled. "I want to talk to you. I'm not going to just stand here and babble while you work."

"Alright," he said, passing her the wet plate he'd just rinsed. If this was another way for his sister to show her affection, he'd take it.

She dried the plate and set it in the open cabinet. "I hope Molly isn't rushing you into anything."

As if Molly could do that when he was the one overeager to marry her. He'd leave that night if it was possible. "She's not rushing me," he said, passing his sister the next plate to dry. "If anything, I'm rushing her. It wasn't that long ago that she was planning to marry Gavriel."

"She doesn't love him," Valerie said like it were a fact everyone knew.

Henry stopped scrubbing the glass he was holding. "How would you know?"

"I see the way she looks at you. It's not an expression she could fake."

"What expression is it?" He resumed cleaning the glass. It gave him somewhere other than Valerie's face to place his attention. He'd looked at Molly more than he probably should've and was familiar with her expressions, but he wanted to hear his sister's take.

"One that says she loves you and that she's happy. It's the same expression Mom and Dad had in the photos he showed us when we were little. I'm sure you were too young to remember."

Henry remembered nothing of living with Valerie and their dad. And the lack of memories made him feel empty. A chunk of his life was missing. "I don't even remember arriving at the Foster Centre. The first clear memory I have is from when I was six. Gavriel and I snuck some extra food into our beds to eat at night, and he accepted all the blame for it."

"You miss him, don't you?" Valerie asked.

Henry nodded. "He's a different person now. He hates me."

"Molly seems set on helping him."

Molly and Henry had agreed on helping Gavriel. They both felt they owed him that much. Henry just wasn't sure how they'd accomplish it. "It's the right thing to do." Whether or not Gavriel was still his friend, Henry had a debt to repay.

"If you say so." She dried the last glass Henry gave her as the apartment door opened, and the Moris walked in.

…

Luckily, Jax exited the bedroom before his parents entered. Henry hadn't wanted to explain to the Moris why their son was alone with Molly, even though the reason was innocent.

Molly herself exited the bedroom when the Moris arrived. She was wearing a fresh outfit, and her ring was missing from her finger and her bracelet was absent from her wrist. Henry understood why; explaining their appearance to the Moris wouldn't be easy. What believable excuse could she give without risking the truth? It didn't make him less pained, or it easier to tear his eyes away from where her jewelry had been.

"What did you kids get up to today?" Mrs. Mori asked as her husband went into the kitchen.

Henry shared a look with the others. His mind spun, trying to come up with a convincing story, but Molly beat him to it.

"Packing," she lied. "We've decided you were right. It's best if we leave the City."

Mrs. Mori's eyebrows shot up. "Have you now?"

"We've intruded on you long enough," Valerie said, piling on her charm. Henry knew this was a difficult act for her as she didn't appreciate being called a kid when she'd been independent for seven years. "It's only right that we let you have your space again."

Molly and Jax nodded.

Mrs. Mori narrowed her eyes. "What brought this on?"

"Staying cooped up in the apartment is driving us crazy and putting you and Dad at risk, Mom," Jax said. "Plus, there isn't enough space."

Mrs. Mori heaved a sigh. "As long as you're safe, Jax. I couldn't bear it if something happened."

"We'll be safe," Henry said and decided to take a small risk. "My dad will help us."

Mrs. Mori breathed in and closed her eyes. When she exhaled and opened her eyes, she spoke. "When are you leaving?"

"As soon as we hear back from my dad." Hopefully, the phone was charged by now, and Malcolm would answer when they sent a message. The earlier they could leave, the better.

"Keep us posted," Mrs. Mori said, walking off to join her husband in the kitchen.

...

"Why did you tell her that?" Valerie asked Molly in a whisper, her arms crossed over her chest. "We could've snuck out of here."

"You three maybe," Jax said. "If I left without notice, she'd send a search party. We wouldn't get far. And if I just left a note, she would've been devastated."

Henry knew what Jax said was true, based on seeing how Mrs. Mori fretted over her son. Henry had never had that kind of relationship. Eleanor Newsome wasn't the caring type, and he'd never known his biological mom. And he wouldn't have a mother-in-law either. Molly still grieved for her mom but relating was difficult for Henry. How could he mourn someone he didn't remember?

"Fine," Valerie said. "We still have to be discreet and careful though."

"You're forgetting that Henry and I left the City before, just as you and Jax did," Molly said, the challenge in her eyes matching Valerie's.

"Discreet isn't the word I'd use to describe that," Henry muttered, remembering the sirens, the dilapidated shack and Max's flashlight. "Especially since Ben trailed us and summoned the guards, and I set off the alarm."

Molly flashed a wicked grin, like he'd bolstered her point. "Exactly. It can only go better this time."

"One problem," Jax said. "I can't open the Gate from this side."

"I can," Henry said. He'd left his old uniform at his father's abandoned house, but his tools were still packed in his bag. They were too valuable to part with, and too dangerous to let fall into the wrong hands. He'd buried them at the bottom of his overstuffed bag. They only reminded him of a life he'd never wanted.

"That's settled then," Valerie said. "I'll go get the phone, and you can message Dad." She disappeared into the bedroom, returned moments later and thrust the phone into Henry's hand.

It felt cold and smooth, a texture he hadn't expected. The Newsomes had a phone in their apartment. It was thicker, larger and rougher than the one Malcolm had given him and didn't come off its base on a table. Henry had seen them turn it on and heard them talk into it and voices answering them. He'd never been allowed to use it or to speak when they used it. It hadn't been portable like the one Malcolm had given him.

He tapped the shiny side, figuring it must be the display screen, and the phone lit up. On its surface, he saw the word 'messages' and tapped it with his finger. The screen changed, turning to white and a single word appeared: 'Dad'. Assuming his strategy was correct, Henry pressed the word and the screen changed again to a white box with rows of letters laid out underneath.

Henry, cautiously at first, but with growing confidence and speed, tapped out a message to Malcolm, pressing the send button when he finished. He wasn't sure it had worked until a minute later a message appeared under the one he'd sent.

"What did he say?" Jax asked, trying to peer at the screen.

Henry tilted the phone to give Jax a better view of the message: '**Your ride will be there tonight. One hour after curfew. Be safe.**' He'd gotten his wish; they were leaving that night.

Jax's eyes widened. "A ride?"

Henry shrugged and pocketed the phone. "Apparently."

"It better not be Charlie's truck," Molly said. "I can't take that again."

Henry agreed. His two rides in the truck had been nerve-wracking. Molly had been beside him both times, but the first had been torture being pressed against her and unable to take comfort from it. He'd had to keep himself from touching her. Even now, with her as his future wife, he didn't want to crawl into the truck's hidden compartment.

"Nothing we can do if that's what our ride is," Valerie said. "Let's go pack." She walked to the bedroom, and Molly trailed behind, flashing Henry an apologetic grin as she went.

Jax retrieved his bag and Henry's, knelt in the main room and stuffed his with items Henry guessed were hacking tools. Henry knew Jax hadn't brought much else from the Colony, only a couple changes of clothes and a toothbrush.

Jax's life was in the Colony, and his parents allowed it.

Henry felt a bit jealous that Jax knew his parents and had their love and support. He wanted a relationship with his own dad, which wasn't easy when Malcolm was part of the Government. It was difficult not to wonder how things might've been different if Malcolm had turned down the Inner Circle job offer. Henry didn't want to resent his father for it, but a part of him did.

He entered the bathroom to fetch the toothbrushes, and on his return offered Jax's to him. Henry packed his own with his few other belongings. Reluctantly, he moved his old guard's tools to the top of his bag, thinking he might need them and hoping he wouldn't. He kept the phone in his jacket pocket, the one without the cookie, and pulled the garment on. After tying his bootlaces, he went to the girls with their toothbrushes in his grasp.

In the bedroom, Valerie sat on the bed folding her clothes. Molly sat beside her, cramming her belongings into her bag. She still had stationery, some of which was written on, that she was trying to slide into her bag's pocket without wrinkling it.

Henry passed each of the girls their toothbrush and lingered near Molly. "Can I help?"

"It had extra room before," she grumbled.

"I told you to fold your clothes," Valerie said, placing her neat pile of clothes and toothbrush into her bag with room to spare.

Henry sat on the bed and picked up some of Molly's clothes to smooth. "Val's right. They'll fit better."

Molly's shoulders slumped, and she sighed.

"I'll do it, and you can pack them," Henry said.

Molly tossed her head, her braided hair swinging side to side. She picked up her bag and dumped it upside down, spilling books onto the bed. "Not my greatest idea. I tried to pack the books in here. I don't know how I'm going to carry two bags."

"You'll manage," Henry said, still folding Molly's clothes. "Your stuff isn't going to fit in the same bag anyway." She'd never let anyone carry her stuff or the books, so he didn't offer.

Molly slid the books back into their own backpack and put her folded clothes into her bag. "Thank you," she told Henry, placing her hand over his own.

It was then, gazing down at her warm hand, that Henry saw his mother's ring on her finger. She wore her jacket now, and the bracelet peeked out from under the cuff. It made him happy seeing her wear the jewelry and validated his belief that she hadn't accepted them out of pity. He wanted to kiss her, but his sister was in the room, and soon they'd be leaving with Jax. Kissing would have to wait.

"I'm going to go grab something to eat with Jax before we leave," Valerie said, reading the room and making a hasty exit.

"I hope you aren't upset because I took the jewelry off," Molly said, a faint blush on her cheeks, her eyes on the bedsheets and her hands clasped in her lap. She didn't blush often, and Henry thought it was from embarrassment this time.

"I'm not upset. How could I be? We can't tell the world we're going to marry."

She lifted her face to meet his eyes, her own wide, vulnerable and burning with a determined fire. "I wish we could. I want everyone to know you're mine."

Chapter 13

Henry's lips were on mine as the words left my mouth. The impact sent me backward onto the bed, his body atop mine. I looped my hands arms around his neck as he balanced his weight on his forearms. Familiar electricity surged through my veins, and my entire body screamed for more.

Henry pushed himself up. "I told myself I'd wait to do that," he said, the weight of his emerald eyes on me. They were like gemstones, as spectacular as the rubies in my jewelry.

"I'm glad you didn't wait," I said, resisting the urge to pull him to me. It was hard to restrain myself when all I wanted was to touch him. "But I get it. We don't have a ton of privacy here."

He nodded and stood. In seconds he'd crossed the room to the window. "It's almost curfew. The sun's going down."

I pivoted to get a view of the sky. Deep, orange light shone through the windowpanes, sharpening Henry's features and enhancing the gold of his hair. He was like a living statue, something prized for its beauty. I tore my eyes away to keep from starting a new make out session. It was lucky I did as the door opened and Jax walked in carrying his bag followed by Valerie carrying food.

So much for having some privacy. "Why aren't you eating in the kitchen?" I asked, eyeing the sandwiches and fruit Valerie carried.

"Tell her, Jax," Valerie spat through gritted teeth as she glared at him.

"I told my parents we're leaving tonight, and my mom broke out in tears. It got awkward."

"Awkward doesn't begin to describe it," Valerie said as she sat on the bed, threw a sandwich down and bit into the other.

Henry turned from the window. "Think she'll send someone after us?"

"She won't," Jax said, dropping his bag on the bed and reaching for the sandwich Valerie had dropped. "She did this last time I left."

"How'd your dad take the news?" I asked.

Jax swallowed a bite. "He understands."

"You're lucky," Henry said. "I've only seen my father twice that I can remember."

"I know," Jax said. "It's not easy to leave, but I have to. Just like last time. And they realize it's the best way for me to stay safe." He resumed eating after delivering this speech. I didn't know how he stayed calm about everything.

One thing I shared with Valerie and Henry was an absentee father. I supposed I was fortunate to have always known who mine was. He hadn't lived with me but had contacted both Mom and me. That was better than wondering about his identity. And I didn't resent him, like Valerie, and sometimes Henry, appeared to resent Malcolm. It was odd too that our dads were old friends. I had a hard time picturing it since they came from such different upbringings.

"I'm not sure I would've left with Gav if my mom was still alive," I said, my eyes on the blanket. "It would've been too painful." In truth I had fled with Gav hoping to cling to one part of my life. The Government and Mrs.

O'Kelly had stripped everything else away, and the abundance of loss all at once had overwhelmed me. My desperation had driven and fueled me to flee; I hadn't realized it would lead to something more important than my own problems.

"No use in reminiscing," Valerie said, having finished her sandwich, her eyes on the sky. "The sun's down, so we have an hour."

Henry smirked. "You just don't want to talk about Dad."

I thought I saw pain and anger flash across Valerie's face, but she suppressed her emotions, making me doubt I had seen her reaction. "I have nothing to say about him right now," she said, the tone of her voice and her crossed arms making it clear she thought the discussion was over.

"Fine," I said. "What should we talk about?"

"I have something we should discuss," Jax stated. "I found something useful in one of the books when you and Henry were… busy."

I reached for and grabbed the backpack of books and pulled it to me. "Did you mark it down?" I asked as I unzipped the pocket storing the stationery and pulled the sheets out.

"Yes. You might not like the information though." He shifted his weight from one foot to the other and back again and kept his eyes off me.

I froze, pages of paper in my grasp. Obviously, it was another unpleasant piece of information, which is what we sought, but it had Jax nervous, and he acted like it would affect me in particular. It must've been terrible.

With a deep breath, I flipped through the pages searching for unfamiliar handwriting. Most of the notes were in my script, and a couple were in Valerie's. After a lot of searching, I found an item in handwriting I didn't recognize and assumed it must be Jax's.

I read the entry and dove into the backpack for the corresponding book. When the small, blue-covered tome was in my clutches, I flipped it open and scanned the page numbers until I reached the one Jax had noted.

I had to force myself to read the entire page. It had seemed suspicious to me that Mom had deteriorated so fast after her arrival to the End Camp, but I'd had no reason to think she'd died of anything other than her illness. Not until now. "It makes sense," I said, my voice less hollow than I had expected. "I'm sure the Government finds it cheaper and more efficient than feeding and caring for the patients long term."

Jax blinked, like he was surprised by my reaction. "You aren't upset?"

"Of course I am. But we can use this information to prevent it from happening to someone else. That's the point, isn't it?"

Jax looked at Valerie, his eyebrows pinched together. "She took that better than you said she would."

Valerie swatted him on the arm. "I said it wasn't something you should blurt to her because it would be upsetting."

"I thought you said—" Jax started.

"Guys. It doesn't matter who said what earlier." I slid the stationery and book back in the backpack, zipped the pockets closed and rose from the bed. My personal bag fit comfortably on my back, and I cradled the book pack against my torso as I crossed the room to the window, put my bags on the floor and stood beside Henry, thankful that Valerie and Jax had ceased their bickering.

Henry's fingers brushed my arm as we gazed out the window. The sun had vanished for the night, leaving the sky dark blue. The moon and stars were out, adding to the illumination from the streetlights. Whatever our ride was, I hoped it would be prompt. I needed to leave this apartment; it was stifling me.

I spent the remnants of the hour watching the street, turning my head from one direction to the other every so often, ensuring I didn't miss any incoming vehicle that might stop near our fire escape.

As I watched for our ride, a dark figure moved toward us. I almost didn't notice as they were lurking in the shadows near the buildings. But they had one piece of bad luck and their reflexes were a tad too slow to counter it. A light went on in a building diagonal from the Moris'. The approaching person was almost past the window when the light hit their red hair peeking out from under a black hat. It only lasted a moment, which was enough for me to spot them. I tracked the figure – an easier task now that I was aware of their presence – all the way to the bottom of the fire escape that led to the window I was peeking out of.

I dropped into a crouch, waving Henry back, and craned my neck above the windowsill to get as much of a view as I could. The person, a girl about a year or so older than me, climbed the fire escape ladder with practiced ease. Ignoring the lump that formed in my throat, I hoped, knowing it was pointless, that she wouldn't stop at the Moris' landing.

"There's a girl climbing the fire escape," I whispered as loudly as I dared. Three heads swiveled in my direction, but Henry then craned his neck to peer out the window from the side.

"With our luck, she's coming here," Jax said.

My fears and Jax's statement proved true as the girl disembarked at the landing outside our window. I got to my feet, not wanting to face this threat from the floor. The girl stood on the landing, leaning against the railing with her hands in the pockets of her black, denim jacket.

Someone would spot her standing there before too long. *If I don't get rid of her, we'll miss our ride.* I shoved the window up and swung my leg over the edge, ignoring the others' protests. As I brought my other leg over and turned to close the window, I saw Henry following me. He dropped to his feet and closed the window behind him, giving me a curt nod. Knowing he wouldn't go back inside, not matter what I said, I rounded on the girl. "Who are you? And what do you want?"

She laughed, the sound carrying in the air. "I have a message for you. You are Molly Birch, right?"

I stared her down, refusing to let her dictate the conversation. "What is it?"

She grinned, like a predator ready to kill after it's had its fun. "Be careful, Little Sapling. You're on the path to doom, and when it comes, you'll be uprooted and left to rot."

I didn't know the meaning of this message, but it felt like an insult. How dare this strange girl track me down to deliver threats. Did Ben or Gav send her? I lunged at her, but Henry's arms wrapped around my torso and kept me back. Flailing my arms, I restrained myself from screaming, a small part of my mind recognizing it wasn't a good idea to draw attention.

"You're trying to scare us off?" Henry asked, still holding me, my feet dangling above the metal platform. "Why?"

The girl shrugged. "Not me in specific. I'm only the messenger. The Little Sapling might have the Rebel Cause on her side, but they're a bunch of Colony sympathizers and cowards. The Devout see your antics as detrimental."

Who were the Devout? I'd never heard of them, but I hadn't of the Inner

Circle either before Malcolm's warning. Henry's arms loosened around my torso, and my feet touched the landing again. I wiggled my way free and stepped toward the girl, bringing my face centimetres from hers. She didn't flinch. "My antics, as you call them, are me doing what's right. Whoever the Devout are can just stay out of my way. I don't see them trying to fix things."

"You don't understand, Little Sapling. There is nothing to fix because of the Devout."

This girl was delusional if she couldn't admit there were problems in the City. "Stop calling me that."

She met my eyes, her own twinkling with mischief and amusement. This was entertainment to her. "It's just a play on your name. No need to throw a tantrum."

"I think Molly's reaction was justified," Henry said, glaring at the girl. "I'm not sure I'd be that tame."

The girl laughed again. "You're only angry because I spoke the truth about your sister. If she wasn't a coward, she would have led, not persuaded someone to do it for her."

Henry pounced at the girl, but her reflexes were quick now, making me think she'd wanted me to spot her on the street. She ducked under Henry's arm and sidestepped him. When she straightened up, a smile pulled at her lips.

"This was more fun than I expected," she said. "But your ride's here."

I moved my eyes to the street, which a black van with tinted windows crept down with dimmed headlights. It stopped below the fire escape ladder, waiting for us. I opened the window and climbed back in the apartment to grab my bags and hoisted Henry's out with them. "Our ride is here," I told

Valerie and Jax. "And it's not Charlie's truck."

Chapter 14

Once Valerie and Jax exited the window with their bags, we descended the ladder. I had slung the book backpack's strap over my left arm and had to keep adjusting it to stop it from sliding off. The mystery girl had gone first, her lithe body speeding down the rungs. She waited on the street while we finished climbing down.

Valerie and Jax stared at her, both quizzical and suspicious. Why was she hanging around? The sound of the driver's door opening tore my attention away from her. Footsteps on the asphalt followed, and Max rounded the side of the truck.

"Sage Parker," he said. "What are you doing here?"

The girl, Sage, stood straight smirked. "Devout business. Not that you need to know."

"Oh really?" he asked, cocking an eyebrow.

"You two know each other?" I asked. There was no telling if this was good or bad.

"The Devout know everything," Sage said, with the assurance and belief of a brainwashed cult member.

Max rolled his eyes. "Stop spreading lies, Sage. Go back to your headquarters before I drive you there myself."

Sage gave a shrug and a small salute as she turned and stalked down the street. She vanished into the shadows, and I tried to forget her presence.

"The Devout are a Government backed organization," Max said. "They buy excess and unsold goods from shop owners and suppliers and sell them for inflated prices. They also deal with information from anyone for the right price."

"Seems like they found some information on us," I said. It was just perfect that I had a Government approved group after me on top of an arrest warrant.

Max snorted. "Aside from the videos, hardly."

"That sounds accurate," Henry said. "Nothing she said about us hasn't been advertised by our videos or the Government's."

Valerie scrunched her eyebrows together and frowned. "What did she say?"

"She gave me a message," I said, relaying it to the best of my memory. "And she called the Rebel Cause supporters cowards."

Valerie bristled.

"I'm sure the Devout aren't happy with your recent publicity," Max said. "The Rebel Cause threatens their operation and profits."

"Just want I need, more unhappy enemies," I muttered.

"Ones with ties to the Government," Jax added.

Valerie elbowed him. "Can we get going? Standing on the street doesn't feel safe."

Max approached the back of the van and threw open its doors, revealing a small storage space. "Put your things in here."

Valerie, Jax and Henry deposited their bags, and I added my personal bag to the pile. I hesitated before placing the book backpack, both eager and wary of having it out of my sight. After deliberating, I set it on the floor and walked away. There was no need to cradle the books on my lap. I could trust Max.

Max had opened the side door of the van while we stowed our things, revealing a row of seats. I counted three, while there were four of us. While I pondered the dilemma, Max opened the passenger door. "One of you will have to sit here," he said. "Maybe—"

"I'll do it," Valerie said, with obvious eagerness. "Molly and Henry can sit together while Jax naps." She gave Jax a pointed stare as she spoke. I wasn't sure he'd get the hint.

"Fine by me," Max said. "Hop in."

Valerie climbed onto the passenger seat faster than the rest of us could move. I grinned at Henry. "I'll take the middle seat."

He nodded in response, and we filed in the van after Jax. The interior was uninterrupted black. A soft, sturdy fabric covered the seats, though the sides, floor and roof had a coarser material on them. Max revved the engine, and we drove off with a screech of tires.

From my vantage point, I could see Valerie twisted on her seat to face Max. Her hand rested on the middle storage console, mere centimetres from his thigh. I averted my eyes and watched the view from the window beside Henry. I reached for Henry's hand and held it, and Max drove south on the road reserved for vehicles, heading toward the Gate. We passed some parked guard vans, none of which stopped us. I squeezed my eyes shut and ducked as we passed the first.

"Stay calm, Molly," Henry said. "This is a guard van. They have no reason to stop us."

"Your boyfriend's right," Max said, his eyes meeting mine through the rear-view mirror. "Guards often move in vans like this at night. In daylight there's too much traffic."

That explained why I'd never seen a vehicle like this when I'd lived in the City. It also brought a question I had to ask. "Did you steal this, Max?"

He laughed. "No. I got permission to take it. It's an old van, and they were going to retire it. I simply suggested to Malcolm I might have a use for it."

Of course, Malcolm had known. He'd told Henry a ride was coming, and we'd all pictured Charlie's truck. The idea that Henry's dad would've arranged that was almost comical in hindsight.

"How far are you taking us?" Valerie asked.

"To the Colony," Max said.

"You're not dropping us off somewhere?" I found it difficult to believe the van would remain safe and undetected the entirety of that distance.

"I promised Jack I'd watch out for you, and that includes getting you safely to the Colony."

I leaned back on my seat. Malcolm might have organized our ride, but my dad was the reason we'd have it for the duration of our journey. It still made me uncomfortable when people did or said things simply because of whose daughter I was.

As I mulled this over, we approached the Car Gate. The last time I'd exited through it had been terrifying and adrenaline filled. I was glad I didn't have to run this time as the Gate opened in silence and closed behind us when it scanned the night access pass on the van's windshield. I let out my held breath. As far as our enemies knew, we were still in the City.

The trip through the Outskirts was almost enjoyable this time. Max steered the van down the centre road, leaving us in plain sight and away from my dad's house. It wasn't that I was eager to stay there again, but I would've appreciated seeing it.

Valerie chatted away to Max, who gave polite responses and sometimes glanced in her direction. I hope he would be kind. She deserved that after Kaydon's interference whenever a boy showed interest in her. That didn't mean I wanted to hear their conversation.

I leaned my head on Henry's shoulder as Jax peered out the van's window on his side. Henry's fingers found the tie binding my braid and tugged it free. He ran his fingers through my hair, working out the tangles. His touch lingered, finding my scalp and beginning to massage.

I twined my arms around his shoulders, turning my body sideways. Our seatbelts stopped us from getting too close. That was for the best as we weren't exactly in a private setting, and the others would likely protest if we started to make out.

The gentle motion of the van threatened to put me to sleep, and my eyes grew heavier with each passing moment. I gave in, dropped my arms and let my body go slack against Henry as he moved his arms to my sides and wrapped me in a hug. Just as I dozed off, the truck stopped, and Max muttered under his breath. I sat up, rubbing my eyes. "We're not there already, are we?" Even at a higher speed than Charlie's truck, it wasn't possible.

"No." Max dug in his pocket and pulled out a small piece of paper. From my vantage point, I couldn't determine the words written on it. "We're being stopped at the checkpoint."

"Stopped?" Jax asked. "By whom?"

"Outskirts guards," Max said. He opened the door and exited the van.

I couldn't see him, or the guards he mentioned, so I wiggled out of Henry's arms, unbuckled my seatbelt and climbed onto the front seat. "Did you see them, Valerie?"

"Yup," she replied. "They waved a yellow flag on a pole to stop us."

"Sounds like what happened when we were in Charlie's truck," Henry said. "Someone stopped us then too."

Hiding in the truck's compartment as Charlie uncovered the platform above our heads replayed in my mind, and I felt the same fear as I had then. Yet this time it was less about my own safety. "I hope they don't find the books."

Luck was on my side for once as Max returned to the van. I scurried back to my place as he opened the door and sat. He turned the key, put the van in drive and we resumed our journey. I hadn't realized my heart had sped up until the apprehension passed and it slowed to its normal pace. "What happened?"

"It's a standard checkpoint," he said. "They used to let guard vans go through without stopping, but since your return to the City, they check everyone coming and going. I showed them my credentials, and they didn't inspect the trunk. It helped that they were loyal to you."

I froze. Even if that was true, I wasn't sure it was a good idea to announce our trip or me being there. "How do you know? Did you tell them I'm in the truck?" There was no guarantee that a guard wouldn't turn on me under the right circumstances.

"I saw their names on the station list in Malcolm's office when I acquired the truck. And I didn't give you away. There is too much risk in that."

My body sagged in relief. I'd known I could trust him.

"Are we past the Outskirts now?" Henry asked.

"Almost," Max replied. "We'll be in the Colony in no time. You four should try to rest."

Jax voiced his agreement and fell into an immediate sleep, his breathing even and deep. Valerie denied being tired and offered to help Max navigate with the excuse that he'd never visited the Colony. This was her way of arranging some semi-private time with him.

Henry opened his arms for me. I settled into them, like metal drawn to a magnet. I expected sleep to come fast, considering how tired I'd been minutes ago, but it didn't. The tires on the road were silent, and that lack of noise was eerie. Their gentle, uninterrupted motion was no longer soothing. Henry, sensing my insomnia, rubbed my shoulders, easing the knots that I hadn't been aware of.

"Are you tired?" I asked him in a whisper.

"A bit," he said, keeping his voice low. Neither of us were keen about Valerie knowing we were awake. But she must've expected as she said nothing personal to Max. The only words I heard her utter were assurances that we were on course to the Colony.

I adjusted my body, trying, despite the seatbelt, to find a comfortable position. Henry's arm shifted as I moved, adapting to my needs. I didn't think he realized he did it; the gesture felt as natural and effortless as breathing.

Over his shoulder, I had a glimpse of the sky. It was a cloudless night, and the stars were out in their splendor. I tried to find a constellation I knew, but none were recognizable. The sight was still beautiful, though not as much as the boy holding me in his arms. Even in the darkness inside the van, Henry was radiant. Tearing my eyes from the window, I drank in the sight of him. Every angle pleased my eye. Gav was cute in his own way, but he hadn't made me want what I yearned for when I saw Henry.

Those urges needed to wait. I contented myself with being held and closed my eyes. Sleep evaded me for a while longer, until the feeling of Henry's body against mine lulled me into slumber. The sky was pre-dawn indigo when I woke with a lurch forward and a harsh stop of the truck. We had arrived at the Colony fence.

Chapter 15

Henry

Henry remained awake after Molly drifted to sleep. He wasn't tired, not after the nap he'd taken with Molly. But his sister thought he was sleeping, or didn't care, as she kept her attention on Max.

"Open the console," Max instructed Valerie.

Henry saw his sister lift the lid then insert her hand in the open gap. She pulled out a folded piece of paper, which she hastened to smooth. "What is it?" she asked.

"Don't know," Max answered. "It's from Malcolm."

The part of Valerie's body that Henry could see went rigid. Henry yearned to read the paper, but he kept his mouth shut. It hadn't been handed to him anyway.

Valerie broke free of her frozen state and extended her hand, holding the paper, in Max's direction. "Give it to Henry."

Max shook his head. "He told me to give it to you."

Valerie slumped forward. "I don't know why he's sending me letters. He knows I remember what he did."

Henry knew his sister harboured ill feelings toward their dad, yet she clung to her grudge when Malcolm was trying to make amends. Couldn't she see that their dad was trying to change?

"Perhaps what you remember isn't as accurate as you believe," Max said.

Valerie's voice broke when she replied. "You're saying he didn't fake his death and abandon us? He left me at home with Henry until the foster agents brought us to the Centre and dragged us apart. I spent fourteen years separated from my brother because of him."

Henry bit his tongue to keep from speaking and closed his eyes. He hated hearing his sister upset, and he couldn't let her know he'd heard. Molly and Jax slumbered, and he hoped their even breathing would mask his.

"Read the note," Max said. "It might have answers."

"I'm not sure I believe that," she said. "But I'll read it anyway."

"Good."

They lapsed into silence and Henry tried to will himself to sleep. He succeeded at some point because the next thing he knew, his sister was whispering his name. Cracking his eyes open, he sat up and dislodged his arms from around Molly. Thankfully, she stayed asleep, even as he propped her against the seat.

"Valerie?" Henry asked, around a yawn. Why was she waking him up? A glance out the window told him they weren't in the Colony, though the van wasn't moving, and Max was sleeping on the driver's seat.

Valerie peered at Henry from the passenger seat, her body twisted to face him and bent at the waist. "Come outside with me."

To Henry, his sister's face was uncanny. It was a feminine version of his own, and sometimes it unsettled him how many features they shared. "Why?"

"I have something to show you."

Henry unbuckled his seatbelt and reached for the door. When he opened it, he stepped outside, and the cool air made goosebumps rise on his arms. His sister came beside him, one arm crossed against her torso, the other in her pocket.

She produced a folded piece of paper – Henry assumed it was the same one Max had given her – and proffered it to him. "Read this," she said as his fingers closed around the paper. "Dad wrote it mostly to me, but he added a note for you."

"And you want me to read my note?" This confused Henry. His sister didn't share personal things often.

"You can read all of it. He wouldn't mind, and neither will I. In fact, I think he meant for us to read it together."

Henry braced himself and read. The letter was handwritten, unlike the previous correspondences Malcolm had sent. What was so important that he'd risk an enemy recognizing his handwriting? The only way to find out was to read, so Henry did.

To my children,

Valerie, I'm sorry. I know you blame and resent me. I understand why, and you have every right to. You must know, there are things I couldn't tell you at five years old and haven't had the opportunity to since. It was never my intention to have you separated from Henry. I was naïve to think it wouldn't happen.

If there had been a way for me to stay with both of you, I would've seized it. Sadly, it wasn't a possibility. After your mom died, in my grief and desperation, I lost the security we'd been privileged to have. We were bankrupt, and the only lifeline I had was given to me by an old friend of my family.

I hesitated to accept their offer, as I'd always differed from their opinion of our Government, especially after meeting your mom. She was the one who introduced me to Molly's parents.

Jack was making his own sacrifices and convinced me to join the Government. He'd reasoned I could do good from the inside, which was another naivety. Neither of us knew how difficult being separated from our families would be. We both learned.

I couldn't take you or Henry with me. It was imperative that, in the Government's eyes, I separated myself from your mom, due to her connection to the Rebel Cause, and, by association, both of you. They would've taken you from me, and I shudder to think of the horrible fates you would have suffered. Giving you up to the Foster Centre was the most difficult and painful thing I've ever done, but it allowed you to survive. I don't assume this letter will make you forgive me. It's an explanation I owe you regardless.

Your father, Malcolm Connor.

Below the letter to Valerie, as she'd said, was a shorter note addressed to Henry. He gulped and read on.

Henry, my son. I'll spare you a letter of explanations. You are more forgiving than your sister, much like your mom was. Instead, I'll tell you one thing I believe will help you and Molly. The names of the Inner Circle Members: Bob Henson, Annette Henson, Carli Fare and Scarlet Everbee. Carl Wessin's position is vacant, though his rumoured replacement is someone with whom Molly should be familiar: Humphrey Walston. I expect he will accept the position in the coming days.

Best of luck, your father.

Malcom was correct; Henry was more forgiving than Valerie. He didn't resent his dad, though maybe he would have if he'd been able to remember life before the Foster Centre. Having finished reading, he shot Valerie a glimpse. "Can I keep this? Molly and Jax need to see the last part."

"Go ahead," Valerie said with a shrug. "We should go wake up Max though if we want to reach the Colony before sun-up."

Henry gave his agreement and climbed back in the van as his sister mounted the passenger seat and shook Max until he woke.

"Guess my nap's over," Max said. He turned the key and the van's engine roared to life.

There was something Henry needed to do before going back to sleep. He reached over and shook Jax awake, careful not to disturb Molly. When Jax blinked, Henry pulled his proposal cookie from his pocket. "Can you take a picture of this?"

Jax nodded in his sleepy haze, took the cookie and pulled his multitool out of his pocket. He put the cookie on the space between him and Molly, positioned his device over it and tapped the screen. "Done. Can I go back to sleep now?"

Henry nodded as he re-pocketed the cookie. "Go ahead." He was tired himself, but he'd wanted to preserve the souvenir from his proposal while it was still intact. Later, he'd break it in half and give Molly a piece. For now, he returned to his slumber. When he woke, they were pulling up to the Colony's northern gate and the sky was ink blue. The stars had faded, but the sun hadn't yet appeared.

Molly was awake and watching out the window over Henry's shoulder. She smiled when she noticed he no longer slept. "We're here. I didn't think I'd see it again." She sounded wistful almost, like she'd missed the place.

Henry had enjoyed being in the Colony with Molly, but he would go anywhere with her. He'd follow her to the hottest, most barren wasteland if it was the sole way to be with her. "I know. I didn't think so either."

"You two are too sentimental," Jax said. "This is home for me, and I don't get all emotional over it."

Jax didn't seem to get emotional about anything. Henry didn't envy him. It seemed like a muted and dull way to live.

"Wait a second," Molly said. "Where are Valerie and Max?"

The alarm in Molly's voice made Henry notice that the front seats were empty, and both doors were open. He didn't have long to ponder the reason why as Max came back, closed both doors and drove forward. "Good to see you're all awake," he said as they passed under the watchtower and stopped on the other side.

Henry heard the gate close behind them and saw Valerie hop onto her seat, panting and out of breath. She must've climbed the fence to open the gate. Perhaps Max had given her a boost, explaining why they had both left.

After Valerie buckled her seatbelt, the van carried them down the slope to the concentric circles of buildings. Henry remembered trekking down on foot and how curious he'd been to find what lay at the bottom. The circles of houses didn't surprise him this time; their destination did. Instead of going to the house he'd shared with Molly, Valerie directed Max to the house she and Jax had shared with Kaydon and Juna. Max followed her instructions and stopped mere metres from the door.

The sun hadn't risen, which meant Kaydon and Juna were preparing to sleep for the day. As the van stopped, Max and Valerie exited. Molly shared a look with Henry, and he shrugged as Jax stepped out of the van. It wasn't a huge deal if they had to walk to their own house. They'd done it before.

Henry opened the door on his side of the van and offered Molly his arm. She rested her hand on it, the touch of her fingers igniting sparks on his skin, even through his jacket. When their feet contacted the ground, the warm air hit his face. It had been easy to forget how hot it was in the Colony, even though he'd lived there five days prior. None of their group had expected to return this soon.

"Get your stuff," Valerie said. "You two are staying here."

"Why?" Molly asked.

Henry knew how much she'd liked having their own place. He'd been fond of it too. "There isn't enough space."

His sister laughed. "Kaydon and Juna will move into your old house."

"They won't like that," Jax said.

"I don't care," Valerie snapped. "They *have* to."

The house's front door flung open, framing Kaydon in the pre-dawn light. "Val, you're back. I knew I heard your voice."

A wide, forced grin appeared on Valerie's face, though the expression wasn't happy. "Yes, Kaydon I am. Where's Juna?"

Kaydon ignored her question, fixing his gaze on Max, who leaned against the van's door watching the situation unfolding before him. "Who's he?"

One side of Max's mouth tipped up. He didn't speak.

"That doesn't concern you," Valerie said. "Take me to Juna."

"But—" Kaydon began.

"Now!" Valerie ordered.

Henry wasn't used to this side of his sister. He was still stunned from her outburst as Kaydon shook his head and led Valerie into the house.

"I tried to tell her," Jax said as he pulled his bag from the van's trunk.

Molly was beside him, bent over and reaching for her personal bag and the backpack of books. She grabbed a strap from each bag and pulled. Henry thought it was lucky that nothing ripped as the bags slid along the van's floor. Once they reached the edge, she hefted her belongings onto her back and scooped the books into her arms.

Henry approached the van in search of his own items. As he neared, Molly turned, and his mother's bracelet on her exposed wrist glinted in the day's first rays of sun. She was always beautiful, but the pink light of the early-morning sun softened her features. Henry could barely manage the walk past her to reach for and retrieve his bag. With his things back in his possession, he reached for the van's doors, intending to close them.

"Leave them," Max said. "I need to grab my stuff."

"You're staying?" Molly asked, sounding annoyed but also like she'd expected this outcome.

Max smirked. "You aren't getting rid of me. It's not safe to leave you here alone."

She huffed. "Let me guess. This is because of your promise to my dad."

"You got it."

"Fine," she said as she spun around and walked to the house.

Henry jogged after her and caught up, not as weighted down as she was. He grasped her arm, and her feet stopped moving. Her neck turned, and their eyes met. Henry needed every part of his willpower to sustain his self control. Oh, how he wanted to kiss her. Her ease at showing her emotions made him admire her more. "Don't be angry. Having him around might be helpful."

She shook her head, her brown hair swaying back and forth. "I'm not angry. It's just weird being treated differently because of my dad."

"I imagine it would be," he said, removing his hand from her arm.

"You don't though," she said. "It's one of the things I like about you. You see me as me, not as Jack's daughter."

Henry didn't know her dad well, having met him a couple of times. He'd only ever known Molly as herself, though for years she'd been Gavriel's girlfriend, not his. Still, he'd seen how brave and kind she was. "You're at your best when you're being yourself."

Her smile widened and her pupils dilated. He was about to lean toward her mouth, when the house's door opened, and angry footsteps broke the moment. He and Molly both turned to the noise. Juna and Kaydon were carrying their belongings. Juna was unperturbed, while Kaydon wore an expression that Henry would call irritation at best. Together they headed down the street, in the general direction of his and Molly's former home.

Valerie exited the house and snatched her bag. "Let's get inside before the heat comes."

Chapter 16

Whatever Valerie had told Kaydon and Juna to make them leave had put Kaydon in a bad mood. I could tell by his body language and facial expression as he stomped down the street. Valerie acted like it hadn't happened as we filed inside. The situation left me uneasy.

"You two can share a room," she said, wagging a finger between me and Henry. "Unless you want to stay separate until the wedding."

Max arched an eyebrow. "Wedding?"

Henry elbowed his sister in the ribs.

She stepped back and rubbed her side. "He's staying here. He'll find out anyway."

Valerie had a point. Though I hadn't wanted him to find out by her blurting it. "We'll share a room," I said. "Just point out which one."

"Second on the right," she said.

I pushed past the group and veered toward the door, trusting Henry would follow me. And he did. He was there before I needed to search for him. He opened the door and held it for me to enter.

Inside the room were two wooden framed beds, each with a matching dresser and nightstand. It was devoid of decorations, leaving me no clues about whom the former occupants were. I dropped my backpacks onto the nearest bed and sat beside them, letting myself fall backward and recline. "I'm glad I don't have to lug the books around anymore. My arms are sore."

"Worse than in training?" Henry asked as he sat on the other bed.

"You didn't make me carry heavy things," I said.

"Maybe I should have. Obviously, I didn't prepare you enough."

"I think I've got my practice in."

Henry rose from the bed and crossed the room to mine. He sat beside me and massaged my forearms. "I would've carried something for you. If you'd wanted me to."

He would have, as would have Max. Yet, it was something I needed to do for myself. I couldn't find the words to express why. Fortunately, I didn't need to.

"Don't worry. I know you have reasons for doing it yourself. I just want you to know you can ask for my help if you want it. Or need it."

Henry was always willing to help, and I wished he could. The burden I carried would've been easier to bear if I'd shared it with him. It also would've been the most selfish thing imaginable. I slipped my arms from his grasp and twined them behind his torso. Bending my elbows, I brought his face to mine until our lips almost, but not quite, touched. "I know. But there are some things no one can help me with."

"Well, there's one thing I know can help with." He pulled out of my embrace and sat up.

What was he talking about?

Sticking his hand in his pocket, he pulled out a folded piece of paper. "Max gave this to Val from Dad. The end has a note for me with information he thinks can help us."

I pushed myself to sitting as he unfolded the paper, and my curiosity overpowered my desire for him. He held the paper so I could see it, and I read it. My mouth opened and I stifled a gasp. "Humphrey Walston. He's Government-loyal."

The sight of his name on paper brought me back to the time he'd lived in my apartment and followed me everywhere. I'd been glad when he left, and I wasn't eager for our reunion. He wasn't the most empathetic person, though no one was worse in that regard than Ben.

"I assume he must be to have a shot at the position," Henry said. "How much do you know about him?"

"Not a lot," I said. "Only that he doesn't have a permanent address and is the snobbiest person ever. He didn't talk about his personal life."

"Snobbier than your former neighbour?" Henry asked, a twinkle in his eye.

I chuckled. "I think he has Mrs. O'Kelly beat."

"I trust your conclusion," Henry said. "You know them both more than I do."

"The problem is, neither of us know anything about the other members, aside from Bob Henson." The other names on the note were all foreign to me, though I assumed Annette was Ben's mom. How was this information going to help?

Henry smiled. "We still have the advantage of knowing their names. My dad took a big risk in writing them down."

It amazed me sometimes how trusting Henry was of Malcolm when his sister wasn't. Their age difference must have played a factor as Valerie held memories from the time Malcolm was present in their lives and saw his actions as a betrayal. It was also weird that my parents had been friends with the Connors. "I wish there was a way to use that info."

"That's something we can worry about on another day." Henry held my hands and positioned himself to face me. "You know every Colonist will find out about our wedding."

I groaned. "There's not way to avoid that, is there?"

He lifted an eyebrow and frowned. "It sounds like you want it kept secret."

I shook my head. There was nothing I wanted more than to announce our relationship. If only there wasn't a list of reasons not to. "I don't want a bunch of people fawning over me because of it. People here act weird already because of my dad."

Henry laughed, soft and carefree. I loved being one of the few people he felt relaxed with. He'd spent too many years trying to make everyone else happy at his expense. "We can let them help, as long as though don't try to control the event."

I dipped my head. "Agreed."

...

Henry and I had just rearranged the furniture when someone stomped down the hall, exited the main door and slammed it. Our room didn't have a window facing the street, so I was unable to see them. Whoever it was had to be upset.

I fled the house, ignoring Henry's questions. Once out in the street, early morning light hit my eyes, and I squinted. Precious time ticked away before I spotted two fresh sets of boot prints leading to the Market. I ran in that direction, acting on instinct more than logic.

As I neared, voices became clear and I saw a flash of familiar, long, blonde hair. Valerie was here, and she must've had company. I ducked behind the nearest stall in the vacant Market that gave me a view of Valerie with her back facing me.

"First you disappear, then you kick me out, and now you won't tell me who the stranger with you is?" Kaydon asked. "You owe me answers, Valerie. I demand them."

I kept my head over the top of the booth, just enough to peek over. Kaydon glowered at Valerie, his complete attention on her.

"Kaydon," Valerie said, somehow keeping her voice calm. "Listen to me. You and Juna had to move out. I need my brother with me, and that means Molly too."

Kaydon snorted. "You don't even know them. I'm the one you've lived with for years. The one who loves you and has backed you up, and you're shoving me aside for your hero's daughter, a stranger and your look-a-like who doesn't even remember you?"

How could be talk about me, Max and Henry like that? I flinched, and Valerie formed fists at her side as Kaydon finished.

"Kaydon!" she yelled, loud enough to be heard down the street. "You don't get it. For years, I've told you I don't love you. You never listened to me!"

"Oh, I did listen. It's just that you'll learn to love me back. You have to."

"That's not how it works! You can't force me to develop feelings for you."

"It's the stranger, isn't it?" Kaydon asked, an ominous and wild glint in his eye. "You like him. Don't worry, I'll take care of him, and things can return to normal."

Valerie let out a sound like a scream mixed with a roar and charged Kaydon, toppling him to the ground. She hit him with repeated blows from her fists. He didn't try to defend himself, choosing instead to roll out from under her when she finished.

"You'll regret this, Valerie Connor," he spat as he stood and sneered at her on her knees as she panted.

He stalked from the Market before she could respond. I planned to sneak back to the house, but the sound of her crying stopped me. Pushing aside the awkwardness, I strode from my hiding place and knelt beside her. She needed someone that cared. And, right then, it had to be me. "Valerie?"

She wiped her face with the back of her hand and sniffled. "What are you doing here?"

"I heard someone run outside and slam the door."

"You followed me."

"Someone had to make sure there wasn't trouble. Next time I can let you run off to danger by yourself."

"I'm glad Henry likes you," she said as she stood, dusted off her clothes and wiped the tears from her face. "You're good for him."

"Thanks," I said, scrambling to stand up. "I'm glad I have your approval."

"Don't let it go to your head." She walked out of the Market and toward the house, and I hurried to catch up. "We shouldn't tell the others about this."

"But Henry—"

"This was just Kaydon being upset because I kicked him out," Valerie said with a wave of dismissal. "He'll get over it."

"Regardless, they need to know," I said, fixing her with a stare. "You should tell them. If you don't, I will."

She chewed her lip and exhaled. "It's going to worry them over nothing."

"Secrets don't protect people." They hadn't protected me when my parents kept my mom's illness and my dad's smuggling hidden. And they didn't stay secret forever. "It'll turn out worse when they find out later."

"Fine," she huffed as we reached the door. "I'll tell them now."

She marched inside and barged into the kitchen. "Meeting in the kitchen!"

I covered my ears as she yelled into me when I stepped into the room. Jax was the first to come, with Max trailing behind. Henry came after, a quizzical expression on his face as he stopped at my side.

"Don't worry," I told him. "My hearing is coming back."

Valerie flashed me a small smile and dove into relaying her confrontation with Kaydon. To my relief, she didn't spare any details. I didn't want to fill in gaps later. She told the events, and I stayed silent, having nothing of substance to add.

"Kaydon's always had a crush on you," Jax said once Valerie finished. "Sounds like he snapped."

"None of you should tell him anything," Max said. "He's not trustworthy."

Valerie gave a bark of a laugh. "I won't tell him anything. Especially not after this morning."

Kaydon had always acted odd to me, though I'd never been able to pinpoint what was off. And I wasn't about to divulge our plan to him. "Fine by me."

Jax and Henry added their assent, and Max bobbed his head. We were all satisfied with our agreement and went our separate ways to wait out the day's heat. Henry and I returned to our new bedroom together and collapsed on the beds we'd pushed together. He pulled the cookie from his pocket, broke it in half and offered one of the pieces to me. I was sad to see it go, but we couldn't preserve it forever, and he told me Jax had taken a picture. We nibbled it while he held me. His arms felt like the safest place in the world, and I fell asleep wrapped up in them when the cookie was gone. It was twilight when I woke again, alone in the room.

Chapter 17

Sitting up in bed, I tried to push back my panic. Henry had left the room; that didn't mean he'd fled the house or the Colony. I got to my feet and searched the rooms. Jax and Max were in the kitchen eating bowls of stew. Spinning on my heel, I returned to the hall, and headed for the main room where Valerie had presented us to Jax, Juna and Kaydon all those weeks ago. I opened the door. Inside, Valerie and Henry sat on the couch, and Henry slipped a piece of paper behind his back as I entered.

He smiled. "You're awake."

"Yeah," I said, eyeing where he'd hidden the paper. "What are you two doing?"

Henry bit his lip and glanced at his sister. Something was making him nervous. I wanted to know what.

"Wedding stuff," Valerie said, with a flick of her hand. "It's a good thing you came. Henry needs space, and we have to go dress shopping."

"Space for what?" I asked, moving my eyes between them. They were up to something, and I hated not knowing.

"Just something he needs to do," Valerie said as she stood and walked to me. She put her hand on my arm and steered me out of the room.

I was in my room putting on my jacket and boots, per Valerie's instructions, before I could process what was happening. "You really want to go dress shopping?" I hadn't worn a dress in a long time, and Valerie didn't strike me as the type to ever wear one.

"You can't get married in your normal clothes. You need a dress."

"I guess," I said with a shrug. "I haven't thought about it."

"Of course not," she soothed. "He proposed yesterday."

It had happened so fast, and I had no idea how to prepare for a wedding. If we'd been a normal City couple, he would've worn his guard uniform and I would've donned a simple, white dress. The local Government official from one of our Apartment Districts would've presided over the ceremony, making it an affair steeped in formalities and legalities. The idea of a Colony wedding free from the restrictions imposed on couples in the City both excited and terrified me. "I don't know how to have a Colony wedding. I assume it's not like a City wedding."

Valerie led me out of the house and toward the Market. "It can be whatever you want. Though you shouldn't go too casual, or no one will take it seriously."

"So, fancy and personalized?"

"Exactly," she beamed. "First decision: the dress. We'll pick out fabric and have it made for you."

I'd never worn clothes that weren't manufactured in the Outskirts. Having a custom-made dress was a strange concept. "Why can't I just pick an already made one?"

"Because none of the ready-made clothes here are suitable for a wedding dress. It's easier to get fabric that stores can't or don't want to use anymore instead of full wedding dresses. Usually, it's not in season according to the rich, but it's still fancier than anything the average citizen owns," Valerie said as we stopped at her intended vendor.

A woman, about thirty in age, dressed in a pink and white flowered, short sleeve dress with glittering bangle bracelets on her left wrist stood behind the booth. Her face lit up as Valerie and I stopped at her stall. "Valerie Connor. You're never visited my wares. Has Kaydon worn you down?"

"Actually," I said, stepping forward. "I'm the one getting married. Not Valerie."

The woman's eyes widened. "Molly Birch. Who's your lucky, future spouse?"

"She's marrying my brother," Valerie said. "We need fabric for her dress. Do you have anything good, Marisa?"

Marisa clapped and bounced on her heels. "Anything for Molly Birch. Come, come closer."

Valerie gave me a little shove, and I stumbled forward. "Wait a minute," I said. "I don't want special treatment just because you have some sort of hero worship toward my dad."

Marisa's brown eyes twinkled. "My goodness. I forgot you stayed in the City after the battle."

"What does that have to do with anything?" It was bad enough when people treated me weird because of my name. Now they were doing it because I hadn't been present for a couple days, which was somehow worse.

She beamed, like a kid excited to share a secret. "You earned a hero's reputation of your own for what you did. Now come with me, and I'll show you the good stuff." She exited the back of the booth and moved in the direction of the Market exit. Valerie rushed after her, and I, with a sigh, followed suit.

"Where are we going, Marisa?" Valerie asked as we caught up.

"You didn't think I kept my best merchandise at my booth, did you?" she asked, as she brushed her long, brown curls over her shoulder. "It's much too valuable to keep at my stall where anyone might take or ruin it."

She veered right at the Market entrance and strode down the street. We trailed her to a small house with yellow curtains hanging in the front window. Inside, patterned tapestries plastered the walls. Printed fabrics rested on every surface and piece of furniture in the room and a giant, patterned rug covered every centimetre of the floor. It was like an overstocked fabric store.

Marisa walked down the centre of the main room and gestured to the table. "Sit and tell me what kind of dress you want."

I lowered myself onto the cushion atop the nearest stool, while Valerie sat on the one beside me. "I don't know. I haven't had time to worry about that."

"You must have a preference," Marisa said, sitting across from me and peering at my face, like she was studying a book.

"I—"

"What were you going to wear when you thought you'd marry Gavriel?" Valerie asked.

"This isn't your first time planning a wedding?" Marisa asked, eyebrows raised.

"It is," I shook my head. Gav and I hadn't gotten to the planning phase. "Gav and I submitted a Courtship application in the City that got denied. And I always figured I'd wear whatever dress my parents could afford."

"Oh, you poor thing," Marisa cooed. "I'll help you select something you'll feel beautiful in." She scooped the pile of fabrics off the table and carried them across the room. Picking up a different bundle, she returned and splayed them across the table's metal top. "Something in here should be suitable."

I reached for the fabrics and rested my hand atop the various pieces. The smooth and soft textiles were a change from my normal clothes. As I perused the pile, a swatch of pale purple peeking out from the bottom of the heap drew my attention. I grasped it and pried it free. It was as light as air, though not sheer.

"Ah. The fabric has called you." Marisa plucked it from my grasp, pushed the other fabrics to the side and placed the purple piece in the newly cleared space. "It's perfect for a wedding dress. But we need more. Please," she made a sweeping gesture with her hand. "Select again."

I searched the pile again, finding nothing that attracted my eye. "I don't think I can. The purple is pretty, but I don't see anything else I like."

She scooped the fabrics up in one motion and deposited them with the original batch that had covered the table. Turning around, she beckoned me over. "Perhaps if you peruse, something will catch your eye."

I examined the piles of fabrics all around me as Valerie stayed seated on her stool. I had never seen this many fabrics, not that I'd visited many textile stores in the City. Mom hadn't been a talented sewer, and I'd never learned.

"Narrowing down your options may help. Sparkles or lace?" she asked, holding up two different pieces.

"Neither." The sparkly fabric was too shiny, and the lace too itchy and old fashioned. I didn't picture myself wearing either.

"Excellent. That narrows it down. Come this way." Marisa moved to a different section of the room, and I followed her. Valerie rose from the table and joined us.

"Now for the colour," Marisa said. "Do you want to use traditional white with the purple? Or would you prefer a completely coloured gown?"

"White." If I was going to be a bride, I wanted to honour at least one tradition.

"Then you should go through these," Marisa instructed, pointing to a stack of white and ivory fabrics.

I rifled through them, held some up with the purple and settled on two pieces that I thought would compliment each other and the purple. Marisa added another piece, this time gauzy, to make a veil. "What do you think?" I asked Valerie, holding up my selections.

She shrugged. "It's hard to tell when they're just pieces of cloth. Henry will think you're beautiful in it regardless."

Marisa turned to Valerie. "Are you the bride's attendant? Or the groom's?"

Valerie averted her eyes, ashamed to admit what I'd already assumed. "I'll be Henry's."

"Very well," Marisa said. "Molly, you can take your pieces and return with your attendant to choose their outfit's material."

Wedding planning was getting overwhelming fast. I had no idea who I would have as my attendant. It was a detail I'd never figured out when I'd planned to marry Gav either. Friends weren't something I'd had a lot of. "I guess I'll see you shortly then," I managed to say. "Thank you, Marisa."

She nodded and smiled as she shooed Valerie and I out of her house. I cradled my bundle of textiles in my arms, careful not to drop or wrinkle them. "Where are we headed now?"

"To Katie's. If her mama is feeling better, she'll sew your dress. She used to do it for weddings in the City."

"And if she isn't better?" I asked. The frail woman I'd seen at Katie's house hadn't been able to sit up, let alone sew a wedding dress.

"We'll find a plan B," Valerie said as we walked to Katie's home. "There must be another sewer that's willing to help."

"I hope so." When I'd said yes to Henry's proposal, I hadn't thought about all the details that needed planning. In truth, I'd never thought about them with Gav either. Marrying Gav had seemed like an eventual inevitability. With my inexperience, I'd assumed someone else would take care of the details.

Now I'd have to choose everything, though other people would do the creating. It still didn't seem fair, as we walked up to Katie's door and knocked, that I was the only one doing the decision making. I resolved, as Katie opened her door, to convince Henry to help when I returned home. It wouldn't be a difficult ask, and he'd agree to it. That's what I told myself anyway, as Valerie and I stepped inside.

Chapter 18

Henry

Henry waited until Molly fell asleep before creeping out of the room. He sought his sister and her advice. In the room with the screen, where Valerie had introduced him and Molly to Jax, Juna and Kaydon, he found her. She lay on the couch, a blanket covering her body up to her chin.

"Val?" he called as he shut the door.

She sat up and rubbed her eyes. "What's wrong?"

"Can we talk?" Asking for help was something new for him. The Newsomes hadn't been the helpful sort; they'd always left him to his own devices. But planning a wedding, especially his wedding, was out of his skill set. The only person he could ask for help from was his sister. Molly had enough to deal with.

"Come sit," Valerie sat, giving the couch cushion a pat. "I'm always here when you need me. That's what family does."

"I wouldn't know," he admitted as he sat beside his sister.

She gave him a sad smile and rested her hand on his knee. "What do you want to talk about?"

Henry sighed. "I don't know anything about planning a wedding."

"I've been to a few Colony weddings," Valerie said. "I'll take Molly to

Marisa, the fabric vendor, to get dress supplies. And you can write your vows."

"I didn't write them when Ben and I had a Courtship," he said. "Ben said we'd just use the standard ones the official provides. What do I say?"

"Start by forgetting about your rotten ex," Valerie said. "Think about Molly. Say what she means to you and what you're promising her."

Valerie rose from the couch and approached the desk. She rifled through one of its drawers and produced a pad of paper and a pen. Returning to the couch, she placed the items in Henry's lap. "If it helps, you can start by listing your ideas. Try summarising her best attributes."

Henry chewed his lip. How could he summarize the best parts of Molly into a few sentences? He started by listing her qualities that he admired, and sometimes envied: her bravery, kindness and desire for justice. As for the promises, that was the easier part. Wording them in a romantic way he could say to an audience was more of a challenge.

No one had paid him much attention growing up, aside from Gavriel. Even Ben had ignored him when he wasn't bossing Henry around. This left him uncomfortable in front of a crowd with the attention on him. At least Molly would share it. She seemed unaffected by crowds and eyes on her, and Henry, once again, envied her courage. "How's this?" he asked Valerie when he'd completed a draft of his ideas.

Valerie snatched the paper and examined it. "Not bad for a start, though it's a bit much. You should trim it down, put it in a better order and into full sentences."

Henry reclaimed the paper, flipped it over and tried to organize the things he wanted to say into a somewhat logical sequence with complete ideas. Much more time than he'd expected must have passed because Molly burst into the room, and the sky visible through the window had turned dark.

He grinned at her and hid the paper behind his back. She couldn't see his attempt at vow writing. It was too embarrassing. He was glad for his sister as she ushered Molly out to dress shop, and he resumed his composing.

When he got his vows somewhere he could be satisfied with, he hid them in the desk drawer and went to the kitchen. It was empty, though evidence of Jax and Max having been present was in the sink. He opened the fridge, scanned the contents and decided on leftover pasta. Figuring he could eat it cold, he didn't bother heating it, scooped some into a bowl and then to his mouth.

When the food was gone, and he'd washed his plate, the front door opened and closed. It would be mere moments before Molly and Valerie found him. He heard his sister in the hall making her excuses to leave Molly.

He waited, expecting Molly to enter the kitchen. First her footsteps went into their bedroom. A minute later she reopened the door and approached the kitchen, her footsteps growing louder. He leaned against the counter, his legs crossed at the ankle, as she walked in and settled her eyes on him. "How was dress shopping?"

"Weird," she said going to the fridge and taking out some cut-up fruit, which she popped in her mouth with no hesitation. "Turns out someone has to sew it for me. Katie's mama isn't up to it, so Katie is going to ask around."

"It'll be custom made for you?" He liked the idea of Molly in something unique. She needed something special, not a copy of a dress poor City girls wore.

"Yes," she said. "I picked out the material. Marisa is a fabric hoarder; her house is stuffed with it."

He couldn't stop himself from laughing as he pictured it.

Molly smiled, though it only lasted a few moments until her face turned serious again. "I have to go back with Katie. She said she'd be my attendant, and now she needs a dress too. Wedding planning is stressing me out, and there's still a lot to do."

"I'm sorry," he said. "Tell me how I can help, and I'll do it."

Her face lit up, and she flung herself at him. He half expected a kiss, but she wrapped her arms around his torso and squeezed. "I was trying to figure out how to ask you," she said breaking the embrace. "I guess I worried for nothing."

"All you had to do was ask." There was nothing she could ask from him that he wouldn't do. "I'd never say no. Besides, it's my fault you're under this stress."

"Does this mean you'll come with me tomorrow to find a decorator for the Market and create a design?"

"Yes. It's my wedding too. I'd like to have some input." The idea of leaving everything to her and then just showing up to the ceremony didn't sit right with him. It's what Ben had wanted him to do, which felt too hands-off.

"Great," Molly said, as the first hints of sunrise shone through the kitchen window. "Just be prepared for a fancy event. Valerie thinks most of the Colonists will come and that we have to go all out."

"As long as I get to marry you," Henry said, gazing at Molly's dawn-lit face. "It doesn't matter who comes."

"You'd marry me if I wore this?" Molly asked, indicating her jeans and faded t-shirt. She widened her eyes and bit her lip.

"Yes," he said. "Valerie would have a fit though, and it isn't even her wedding."

Molly laughed so hard she doubled over and used a minute to catch her breath. Her eyes twinkled and glistened when she straightened up. "Your sister has strong opinions. And one of them is that our wedding needs to be perfect."

"I don't see why—" he began. There was no reason he could find for why Valerie should care that much about the details of his wedding.

Molly stared and swatted his arm. "Because she loves you. You're her only family aside from Malcolm, and you know how she feels about him."

It was Henry's turn to laugh. "I know." His sister had never said the words, only shown him. He hadn't known what familial love was until meeting his sister and seeing her stand up for him. "She doesn't need to express it by managing our wedding."

"I think it's also because she wants me to make an impression as leader of the Rebel Cause," Molly said, sounding resigned about the situation.

In Henry's view, Molly made an impression on everyone. She didn't need an extravagant wedding to do it.

The night of her and Gav's escape, Henry had packed some of his things, intending to flee to the guard's barracks for a while to train and vent his feelings. Then seeing Molly's face and wide eyes staring at him from the Gate's other side, he'd known he couldn't survive without seeing her again. She'd left an imprint on his heart on a day long before that, and the prospect of losing her forever had made him complete his most selfish act. "It doesn't matter what you wear, or what the decorations are," he said. "People already have an opinion about you."

Her shoulders sagged and her head dipped down. "Because of my dad," she said. "Great."

Henry enveloped her in his arms and stroked her hair. "Because of what you've done. Everyone saw our videos, and a lot of Colonists were present at the tower. They know your name and your face because of your dad, but your actions shaped their opinion."

"You sound like Marisa," she muttered. "She said I've earned a hero's reputation."

"And you don't believe it," Henry said, knowing the idea of it would make her uncomfortable. It was something they shared: a childhood spent blending into the background of society and expecting little.

"I'm not a hero," she said with a shake of her head. "I'm just trying to stop other people from losing everything like I did."

Henry dropped his arms from her and stepped away. The old urge to run returned, and he forced himself to stay in the room. "You don't have to settle for me, Molly."

Her eyebrows moved together, and she frowned. "Henry—"

He didn't let her finish as he fled from the room. Once in the hall, he slid his body down the wall until he hit the floor, his knees bent. He propped his elbows on his knees and covered his face with his hands. He'd been foolish to believe Molly when she'd said she loved him. He was her attempt to reclaim something as her own. She still wanted Gavriel; it explained why she was determined to help him.

Henry's eyes watered, and tears started to run down his face. He'd cried often after the Newsomes had brought him home when they'd placed more restrictions and rules on him than the Foster Centre had. He'd taught himself how to hold back his tears in front of them when they called him weak. He didn't care now. He got up, wiped away the wetness under his eyes and went to his sister; she deserved to know what was happening.

Valerie was sitting on the couch and looked at him with eyes wide. "What happened?"

"I can't do this," Henry said, as he sat beside Valerie. "I can't marry someone who's settling for me because the person she loves isn't here."

Valerie grasped his shoulders and gave him a firm shake. "Molly loves you. Anyone can see that."

"No. She said she lost everything." If he'd meant anything to Molly, she wouldn't have said that.

The door creaked open. Molly stepped through the gap and eased the door shut behind her. She'd followed him. "Henry," she said, her voice strangled, and her eyes bright and glistening. "Please. Can we talk about this?"

"I'll give you some privacy," Valerie said. She dropped her hands from Henry's shoulders and exited the room, shooting Molly a small smile as she passed.

Great, Henry thought. *My sister doesn't believe me.*

Chapter 19

I regretted my words as they left my mouth. They were true, but I hadn't thought of how Henry might interpret them. When he fled from the room, I paused, needing time to gather my thoughts. I heard him enter the room Valerie was staying in and forced myself to follow.

He didn't look my way when his sister left us alone, and my heart sank deeper every second. I crossed the room and knelt in front of him, trying to meet his eyes. "I meant what I said about losing everything, but not how you interpreted it."

"How should I have interpreted it?" he asked. He wouldn't look at me.

I exhaled and closed my eyes. "I'd give anything to have my mom back. When she died, my life fell apart. I lost my home, and the future with Gav I'd picked for myself. I don't want that to happen to anyone else."

Henry glanced my way then with tears flowing from his hurt-filled eyes. "You want to save him so you can be with him again. Why did you say you'd marry me?"

"Because I love you." My own tears fell. I yearned to reach out and wipe his, but I kept my hands down and clasped at my waist. He likely didn't want my touch. "And no. I don't want Gav back. You must know that, ."

"No one has ever loved me. Why should I believe you?"

Unable to stand the pain on his face another second, I wiped his tears with my thumbs. I cupped his face with my hands, and he didn't pull away. "I can't change your childhood or make the Newsomes better parents. I also can't alter my feelings for you. If it isn't obvious to you that I'm saying the truth, then I failed somewhere."

He stayed silent and averted his eyes, though he still didn't pull away.

With a gulp, I tried again. "I won't lie and say I didn't lose Gav. We both lost him, Henry; he was your best friend. But I don't want to marry him."

"If he was here," Henry said. "You'd be marrying him. Not me."

"No." I imagined Gav in the Colony, stripped of the comforts he'd enjoyed in the City. It wasn't how he'd pictured. He would've been homesick and miserable. "I wouldn't."

"He's still in love with you."

"I know." Gav's message to me in the video and the grief-stricken countenance on his face had made that clear. "But I don't love him. I'm not that person anymore. I just feel uncomfortable and sad when I think about him."

"You mean it," Henry said, meeting my eyes again. "You really don't want to marry him."

I shook my head and moved my hands from his face to cross my wrists behind his neck. He kept his eyes on me and let me pull him closer. "I want you, Henry. I wouldn't toy with your feelings if I still loved Gav."

Henry picked me up and placed me on his lap, my legs dangling over the couch. He kept his arms around my waist. "Sometimes it's easy for me to be jealous of Gavriel. He had it easier at the Foster Centre, and he's always known what he wants and how to get it. I faded into his shadow, and it's hard to believe you chose me over him."

"Gav is very charming," I said. "He made me feel needed, and I equated it to love when it wasn't. Kissing him never felt the way kissing you does."

"I'm sorry I didn't trust you," Henry said with a shy smile, his blonde hair luminous in the morning sun.

"I forgive you."

Before Henry could say anything, the door opened, and Valerie stuck her head in. "Have you two made up?"

"Yes," Henry said. "We have."

Valerie entered the room, leaving the door open behind her. "Good. Then get out so I can sleep."

Henry repositioned his arms to my knees and stoop up, scooping me up in the process. I gasped as my weight settled in his arms and he carried me out of the room. He toted me down the hall to our room. Its door was open from when I'd gone inside earlier searching for Henry. I hadn't bothered to close it.

Henry set me on the bed and closed the door. "Are you tired?"

"A bit," I said as pulled my boots off. "Wedding planning is exhausting."

Henry grabbed the hem of his shirt and pulled it over his head. My lips parted as I drank in the sight of his sculpted muscles. He was like a chiseled, golden statue. His cheeks coloured a faint pink. "It's so warm here. You don't mind, do you?"

"Definitely not," I said, my eyes glued to his chest. He'd never slept shirtless the first time we were in the Colony, but we'd been learning about our feelings then. This time was different; we were soon to be married.

I settled my nerves by pulling down the blankets as he took his boots off and came to me, barefoot and bare-chested. As he reached the bed, I scrambled to the other side and yanked the covers over my overdressed body. I rolled onto my side and watched as he lowered himself onto the mattress and turned to face me. How had I gone so long without noticing how attractive he was?

He brushed a lock of my hair over my shoulder and his fingers lingered on my face. Heat rushed to my skin and disappeared when he withdrew his hand. "You're beautiful," he said, pulling the blankets over himself.

"As are you," I said, tracing lines over his taut chest with my finger. I needed to feel him to know he was real. He might have had the appearance of a stature, but he wasn't one. His body reacted to my touch. And his skin was warm, like a blanket that warded off a chill. It was all I could manage to lower my hand and roll onto my back.

Henry stayed on his side and reached for my hand with his left. We fell asleep with our hands clasped. When I woke up hours later, the sun had set, and I was curled against Henry's body. I had shifted positions in my sleep, seeking his warmth. He stirred as I contemplated whether to wake him.

He sat up and stretched his arms above his head. His body was less statuesque in the moonlight, though he didn't appear as disheveled as I was certain I was. It made me jealous that he could be put together with such little effort.

"I need a hairbrush," I said as I climbed off the bed. "I'm going to check for one at the Market." I tugged my fingers through my locks and was glad there was no mirror as I didn't want to see the disaster on my head.

"Valerie shouldn't complain too much about that detour."

"She better not," I muttered. "Not if she wants me to look decent at my wedding."

Having untangled most of my hair, I dug through my bag and for a clean outfit. When I finished changing clothes, I turned to Henry. "Are you hungry? I'm going to cook."

"Yeah, a bit," Henry said as he retrieved his own bag and pulled out a fresh set of clothes.

When we were both ready, we headed to the kitchen for a breakfast of berries and porridge. Valerie, with her hair mussed, walked in as we washed and dried our empty bowls. She pulled a loaf of bread from the cupboard and eyed me. "You two seem ready to go."

"I need a hairbrush, so we're going early."

"That's right," she said as she grabbed a knife and cut a slice of bread. "We never picked one up in the City."

"You don't mind?" I asked, reaching for and clasping Henry's hand.

She shrugged as she placed her slice of bread in the toaster. "Nope."

"Great," I said. "Let's go, Henry."

...

I had just procured a hairbrush when someone called my name. I spun around, trying to locate the voice. It sounded familiar, but I couldn't locate the person.

"Molly!" the voice yelled, louder this time.

Someone tapped me on the shoulder, and I whipped around, ready to fend them off with my hairbrush raised. It was Katie, smiling wide. I lowered my arm.

"I found a sewer for your dress. Say hello to Alberto." She swept her hand in the direction of a man, in his thirties, wearing a business-like suit.

"Hello, Alberto," I said.

He walked a circle around me, his eyes raking over my body. I craned my neck to watch him, uncomfortable with him doing this in a public place. It felt he was scrutinizing me, and I wasn't sure whether I met his expectations.

"Yes, I can make you something exquisite," he proclaimed when he'd concluded his inspection. "Come when you're done here, and we can work up a design. Katie will show you where to go."

"Uh, thank you," I said, still feeling uneasy.

He waved over his shoulder as he departed the Market.

"I know he's a little forward," Katie said, giving me a cheeky smile. "Mama recommended him. He helped her with a few of her last projects. He's nice, I swear."

"I believe you," I said, having no reason to second guess her judgment. "But we have to go find Henry and wait for his sister. It's going to be a long night."

Katie didn't protest as I led her to the agreed upon meeting place. Valerie had claimed the benches near the storage shed, and Henry sat on one, waiting for me. He smiled as I approached with Katie. We had just sat when Valerie walked up scowling. Fearing something had gone wrong, I didn't dare ask what was going on. Henry, not sharing my trepidation, did.

"Kaydon is here," she groaned. "He hasn't spoken to me, but I'm worried he'll try."

I doubted he would while we were near and told her as much.

She deflated and plopped down on a bench. "Let's hope you're right and that we can get this wedding planned."

With the words barely out of Valerie's mouth, Katie piped in with her news about Alberto. The night felt endless, as I now had to choose fabric for

Katie and help design two dresses after the other tasks were complete.

To my joy, we worked out the location, decorations and food in rapid succession as there weren't many choices, or a lot of people Valerie trusted to execute my vision, though more than a few had volunteered once Marisa blabbed the news. To Valerie's credit, she deferred to my and Henry's opinions, if they weren't too casual.

Music was trickier to arrange as none of us knew if any of the Colony musicians were any good. We decided to hold an audition, and if none were decent, we'd forgo having any. With the major elements out of the way, our discussion turned to the ceremony. Valerie proposed a few candidates to conduct it, though none had names I recognized.

"We should meet each of them," Henry suggested. "Then we can choose who we like."

"I like that idea." It wasn't something I wanted to have a random person do. How would I feel comfortable trusting a stranger with that much responsibility?

"Alright," Valerie said. "I'll set it up."

Chapter 20

Juna ran over as Katie was about to speak. She stopped next to Valerie, doubled over and panting.

"What happened?" Valerie asked.

"Kaydon is looking for you," Juna said between gulps of air. "I thought you'd want to know so you can avoid him."

Valerie grimaced; her hands clenched into fists. "Where is he?"

"I'm right here," Kaydon said, stepping away from the storage shed. "It wasn't difficult to locate you when Juna led the way."

Valerie bristled and turned on her seat to face him. "What do you want?"

"To ask if we can talk." His voice was too casual. It didn't match his eerie face. "Privately."

Valerie drifted her eyes across me, Henry and Katie.

"Go ahead," I said when no one else spoke up. "Katie and I have things to do anyway."

Valerie sucked her lip and stood up. "Fine. Let's get it over with."

Kaydon led her away, and I tracked their path, making a mental note of where they turned.

"Are you sure this is a good idea?" Henry asked.

"Yes," I said as I rose, having lost sight of them. "I'm going to follow them. Meet me at Marisa's in half an hour, Katie." I ran in the direction Valerie had gone, not waiting for Katie's answer. I trusted her to know where to go and show up.

It wasn't difficult to find Kaydon and Valerie. They'd walked along the Market's entrance to the gap between the stalls and kept going, out of earshot of the vendors. I trailed at a safe distance as Kaydon led Valerie through the alley between houses. The challenge was to find somewhere in the open space where I could hide and still be able to listen.

"This is far enough, Kaydon," Valerie said, with a subtle glance back to the alley. I thought I saw her gaze in my direction, but it was so fleeting I could've imagined it. "If you want to talk, do it here."

"You're impossible," he growled. "Everything has to be your way, all the time. Now it's my turn." He stepped toward her, and she stayed put, her hands balled into fists at her sides.

I crouched, making my body as small as possible. From my vantage point, I could see her back and part of Kaydon, though her body blocked most of him from my view. I assumed she'd done that on purpose.

"Kaydon—"

"No!" he yelled. "This is your last chance, Valerie. Come with me."

"You know I can't. And I won't."

Kaydon's lips twisted into an angry snarl, and his nostrils flared. "I warned you. You're going to regret this."

"Leave my sister alone!"

I flung my hand over my mouth to muffle my gasp. As focused as I was, I hadn't heard Henry follow or pass me. He'd been trained as a guard; he knew how to manoeuvre silent and unseen.

He stood on the street, illuminated by the moon, anger flashing in his eyes and his own hands curled into fists. Valerie spun around; her face twisted by fear. I guessed it was for Henry, not herself. She always put him first.

Kaydon cackled. "Like you can stop me from getting what I want. I've known Valerie years longer than you have."

"She isn't your property," Henry said, forcing the words out through gritted teeth. "She said she won't go with you. Leave her alone."

Kaydon laughed again and addressed his words to Valerie. Henry meant nothing to him, evident in the way Kaydon swiveled his attention off him. "I'll go for now. Stay with your charity case look-a-like. You *will* regret this. Find me when you change your mind." He stalked off without receiving an answer.

As I lurked in the alley, Valerie ran at Henry and wrapped her arms around his torso, her body shaking. The impact made him stumble backward, but he was quick to hug her in return and regain his balance.

"That was a stupid thing to do," she said, tears choking her voice. "I love you for it anyway."

"Heh," Henry chuckled. "You've never said that before."

"I'm sorry," she said as moved one hand to her face to wipe her tears. "You deserve better."

I debated whether I should make my presence known before things got more awkward or slink back to Marisa's house without revealing myself. The second option became more appealing as I thought it kinder to let them have privacy. Settling on my choice, I turned, being as quiet as I could, and prepared to flee.

"Molly," Valerie called. "Come here."

I stood and stepped out of the dark alley, holding my hands up. "Sorry. I didn't mean to intrude."

Valerie and her brother stood side by side, no longer hugging. They both grinned, and Valerie laughed. "There's nothing to apologize for."

"Okay," I hedged. This was a weird reaction for her to have.

"I mean it," Valerie said. "I dallied on the way, hoping someone would follow. Being alone with him makes me uncomfortable."

"You shouldn't be alone with him," Henry said. "I don't trust him."

"Yeah," I agreed. "He's totally obsessed with you, in a creepy way." I couldn't forget his twisted face and wild eyes. He was more obsessed with Valerie than in love with her. People didn't make hostile demands out of love.

Valerie ducked her head. "I know. But enough about him. You have an errand to run and shouldn't keep Katie waiting."

I rolled my eyes and waved as I jogged back down the alley. *Typical Valerie. Right back to business.*

...

I found Katie waiting outside Marisa's house. She wrapped me in a hug as I told her about Kaydon's confrontation with Valerie, and we headed inside. Marisa wore another multicoloured dress and had her brown curls tied up. She beamed as we closed the door behind us.

"Come in, come in," she squealed. "I've been expecting you."

This time she had an array of fabrics laid out on the table. Katie and I sat side by side with Marisa across. "The final selection will be yours, Molly, as the bride," Marisa explained. "You can get your attendant's opinion if you'd like. And be careful not to choose something that will clash."

Feeling more at ease than when I'd chosen my dress material, I spotted a bright purple piece and knew it was the one. I grasped it and held it aloft.

"What do you think, Katie?"

"It needs something to contrast it, or it'll be too simple."

"Hmm." I scanned the displayed pieces until I spotted an iridescent silver swatch. "This will be perfect," I said as I pried it from the pile. "And this," I said as I noticed a darker, sheer, purple piece.

"You have chosen well," Marisa said. "Perhaps you would make an excellent apprentice. The fabric speaks to you."

"Thank you, I think," I said. "Though that isn't in my plan right now."

"Of course not child," Marisa cooed. "You're The Liberator."

I hadn't expected that title to reach the Colonists. Someone must've seen our latest video, or perhaps a Rebel Cause supporter had passed it on. I wasn't sure I wanted the weight of that title thrust on my shoulders on top of the expectation that came with being related to my dad. At least I had friends to help bear it. "I have a sewer to go see," I said, changing the subject and rising from my seat. "Ready to go, Katie?"

Katie nodded, and I bundled my selections in my arms and hurried from the house, glad for the sound of her feet behind me. Marisa chuckled as we exited, and I was relieved that she wasn't upset about my hasty exit.

I slowed my pace as I stepped on the street. Alberto's house was a mystery to me, and I hadn't a clue where to go. Thankfully, Katie did and pointed out the house, which was visible from Marisa's. We reached it within a minute, and Alberto threw open the door before we could knock. I imagined he'd been watching out the window for us as he bounced on his feet, giddy from excitement like a kid presented with a mountain of presents on their birthday.

"You're here!" he cried. "I have my sketching paper and supplies ready."

Katie and I shared a giggle as we walked into his main room. Where Marisa's had been chaotic, Alberto's was organized and immaculate. His table had a neat spread of sketching tools, paper and measuring tapes on top.

"First, the bride," he said with a flourished bow in my direction. "Stand over here."

I stood where directed and tried to keep my body still as he measured. The experience was a bit uncomfortable, though necessary for a custom dress, so I tried to ignore my nerves. He measured Katie after he'd written down my measurements.

I glanced around and spotted the fabric for my dress folded into a pile on the far side of the table. He'd laid Katie's dress material beside it when we'd come in.

"Now, Molly," he said. "You must tell me what you want. I have an idea of what would flatter your figure, but nothing matters except your wishes."

Since I had to wear a dress, I was thankful I got input in its design, even if I had no knowledge of clothing creation. "I want straps and a long, flowy skirt that I can move in. Otherwise, I'm not picky."

Alberto cupped his chin with his hand and pondered. "Ah," he mused as he darted toward his sketch paper and scribbled.

Whoever had smuggled it out of the City must've taken a large risk as it appeared thick and expensive. Similar paper had a hefty price tag in the stationary store Jax and I had visited in the City. When Alberto held a piece up to show me his drawing, I realized why it probably left the City; its edge was torn as if someone had ripped it off a larger piece or out of a book. No rich City person would've wanted it.

"I based this on the silhouette you want and your fabric pieces," Alberto beamed. "What do you think?"

My mouth dropped open as I studied the sketch. I couldn't have described anything more perfect. "It's beautiful. You can really make this?"

"Absolutely," he answered, drawing himself up to his full height. "It will be an exciting project. I'll need a week for it and the attendants' dresses. Valerie is dropping hers off tomorrow."

"What about Henry's outfit?" I asked.

"I assume Valerie will discuss that tomorrow," Alberto said as he picked up a new piece of paper. "She hasn't mentioned it."

He drew up a complimentary dress for Katie and showed it to us. She smiled, and I imagined both dresses would be the prettiest clothes either of us had ever worn. There'd been few occasions to wear fancy clothes in the City, unless you were rich, and there were none in the Colony aside from weddings. If Valerie was to be believed, most couples that wed in the Colony didn't wear anything extravagant.

"Thank you, Alberto," I said.

"You're most welcome," he glowed and gave me a bow. "It's an honor to design your wedding dress after what you've done."

I blushed. Marisa was right about me having my own reputation. It was another thing I'd have to get used to.

"I will get to work immediately." Alberto said. "You must come back in three days for a fitting."

"We can do that," I answered. "Right, Katie?"

"I don't have other plans."

"Fantastic," Alberto said as he escorted us outside. "I shall see you both then."

Chapter 21

Henry

Henry watched Molly jog back through the alley. Part of him wanted to follow, to be with her during every waking hour. But it was only an errand, and she could take care of herself. He'd believed that when he'd told Jack she didn't need protection. It was different now that they were getting married. He wanted to ensure nothing happened to her.

As he watched the spot where he'd caught one last glimpse of Molly, his sister grabbed his hand. She was grinning. "I love you."

It was different from when Molly said she loved him. This was a familial love that he was growing accustomed to. "I love you too."

"I'm sorry I was rotten when you first came here," she said. "I felt remorse every time I saw you. It was even worse when I realized you didn't recognize me. It meant I failed."

Henry encased Valerie's hands in his. "I'm not angry. You can stop blaming yourself for something I've already forgiven you for."

"You should put yourself first more often. I deserve to have you angry at me."

"There are enough selfish people," he said, thinking of Ben in particular. "I don't need to be one."

"You should for tonight at least," she said, a gleam in her eye. "We need to pick out your wedding suit."

That hadn't occurred to him, though it should have. How did his sister know so much about wedding planning? He groaned and released Valerie's hands. "You don't think Molly should have a say?"

Valerie waved his concern away. "She has enough to deal with. I think she trusts you enough to come up with something nice."

Henry didn't have any experience with wearing formal clothes. The Newsomes hadn't thought he was worthy enough to bring to their work dinners. And when he'd had his Courtship with Ben, he planned to wear a dress uniform commissioned from the Guard Corps, as was customary. He shuffled on his feet. "You'll help me, won't you, Val?" If her answer was no, he wouldn't be responsible for whatever creation he ended up wearing.

"Duh. As if I'd leave you alone to do something this important."

"Thanks. To Marisa's then?"

Valerie nodded. "If we take our time, Molly and Katie should be gone when we get there."

Henry strolled down the street after Valerie. He didn't know where Marisa's house was, but they were in no hurry, and he let his sister lead. She'd been right; Molly and Katie were no longer there.

Marisa was much bubblier than he'd expected. She bobbed up and down when he and Valerie walked in. "My goodness. The rumour is true."

"What rumour?" Valerie asked.

Henry supposed his sister knew the fabric vendor somewhat well, having lived in the Colony for years. He assumed Valerie knew all the residents, though he hadn't inquired as to whether it was true.

"That your brother is your double in image," Marisa said, like this was obvious. She turned to Henry and beamed. "You are Henry, aren't you?"

"Yes," he said, unsure how to feel about Marisa and her overly excited demeanor.

Marisa grabbed his wrist and pulled him farther into the room with surprising force. "Stand here," she said as she released him in the middle of the room. "I'll bring appropriate choices over, and you can decide."

Henry watched Marisa scurry around the room piling bolts of fabric onto her arm.

Valerie came to stand with him, her own eyes trailing Marisa. "Your suit has to coordinate with Molly's dress. She let Molly pick everything from scratch."

Marisa returned, arms weighted down with a massive heap of fabrics, as Henry was about to reply to his sister. His eyes bugged open, though he managed to keep his mouth closed.

Marisa set the heap on the table and separated it into smaller piles. Her organization made the selection a measure less daunting to him, and he was grateful for it. She gestured at the piles. "Go on. Choose the one that speaks to you."

Henry wasn't sure how fabric could speak to him. He examined the piles and picked his favourite: the one with a smooth, soft, charcoal grey piece on top of some white ones.

"Excellent choice," Marisa declared as she scooped up the pile and thrust it at Henry. "Give it to Alberto. He'll know what to do."

Henry adjusted his grip on the pieces of cloth. "Alberto?" He hadn't heard that name before.

"He must be the sewer Katie found," Valerie said.

"Yes," Marisa said. "He told me that he's been commissioned for the wedding. He's expecting you tomorrow."

"I need to pick my dress materials then," Valerie said, not sounding too enthused.

Henry didn't picture his sister as a girl that wore many dresses. He imagined the occasions for doing so were seldom in the Colony, and dresses seemed impractical.

Marisa whisked Valerie across the room to choose coordinating fabrics, and Henry stayed put. There wasn't much input he could offer, having as little experience as he did with fashion.

His sister walked over, arms loaded with cloth, after a few minutes. She hugged her bundle against her chest, like she wanted to hide it from him or was terrified of dropping it. Possibly both.

"Why can't we drop this off tonight?" Henry asked as they left Marisa's place.

"Molly and Katie might still be there," Valerie said. "And maybe Alberto wants to get a head start on theirs before designing ours."

"Okay," Henry said. "Let's go home."

...

Valerie had been correct; only Jax and Max were in the house when they returned. Henry saw his sister blush as Max noticed the fabric she carried and arched his eyebrow. He hadn't thought about Max when they'd been at Marisa's. Now he couldn't help imagining his sister's thoughts were on what Max might think of her dress.

He tried to stay out of Valerie's love life, knowing it was none of his business. He pushed past them to hide his fabric pile in the bedroom closet before Molly came home. When that was done, he entered the kitchen and poured himself a glass of water. He'd just sat and swallowed a gulp of it when Jax came in and claimed one of the other seats.

"You look worn out."

"Wedding planning is a lot of work," Henry said. *No wonder Molly was stressed.*

"Juna came by," Jax added. "She said Kaydon confronted Valerie again."

Henry set his glass down with a thud. "Yeah, he did." This was one area of Valerie's life in which he'd interfere. She deserved better than the way Kaydon treated her. "He wants her to fall in love with him."

Jax snickered. "He's been trying that since before I came to the Colony."

"Seems even worse now," Henry said, running his thumb along the rim of his glass.

"Because of Max," Jax said. "He's the first guy who might have interest in her that Kaydon hasn't been able to scare away."

"Valerie has the right to like whoever she does," Henry said. "Kaydon can't decide for her."

Jax lifted his shoulders in a shrug. "I know."

Henry rose from the table, grabbed bread and fruit to munch on and left the kitchen. He found Molly in the bedroom, lying on her back with her arms stretched out and her hair fanned around her head. He hadn't heard her come home.

She pushed herself upright and beckoned him closer, a smile on her face. Henry sat beside her and offered her some of his foraged snack. He'd gotten used to eating during the night on their last stay in the Colony. After a stay in the City, it was an adjustment again. And cooking an actual meal required energy he didn't have.

Molly picked up some bread and fruit and popped it into her mouth. "You know I can cook. I don't mind."

"I'm not that hungry," he said.

"Tomorrow then. We both need to eat something substantial."

Henry met her eyes. They were bright and a different shade of green than his own and Valerie's. They were the colour of fresh grass on the yards in the rich Quarters, vibrant and full of life. "Sure. You can cook."

She kissed him then, her lips soft and responsive. He cupped her face and deepened the contact and backward on the bed, Molly propped up on her elbows above him. Her hair, free of tangles, spilled over her shoulders like a curtain and framed her face.

Every nerve in his body screamed to close the gap between their bodies. He reached up with his arms, wrapped them around her torso and pulled her body down. Her lips parted, forming a small circle, but she didn't resist his tugging. She left a trail of kisses on his neck down to his collarbone and traced the path with a finger, igniting sparks along it.

He clutched her hair, brought his face to hers and nibbled on her bottom lip. She moaned. Her hands braced on the bed kept her weight off him. Henry slid his hands up her back, under the hem of her shirt. Her skin was smooth and warm.

Molly pushed his shirt up with one hand and planted it on his stomach. "I love you," she said into his ear.

Henry removed his hands from her back, pulled his shirt off and dropped it on the floor. "I love you too."

She slid her hand up and down his torso, over the contours of his abs. He'd never thought of himself as particularly buff, though guard training had given his muscles definition, and she might find that attractive. One of the kindnesses the Newsomes had given him was a steady supply of food, which had helped him be less skeletal than many City boys.

Molly rolled off him and curled into his side, pulled the sheets up over their bodies and rested her hand on his stomach again.

"You're tired?" he asked.

She bobbed her head. "The sun's coming up. And we have more wedding planning tomorrow."

"Alright," he said, as he slid his arm under her. "We can sleep."

Molly smiled and closed her eyes. She must've been exhausted as within minutes she fell asleep, her breathing even and deep. Henry watched her, wanting to brush her hair off her cheek. He refrained, not wishing to disturb her.

He fell asleep sometime later and dreamed of her standing in the sunshine, her brunette locks flowing in the wind. When he woke, the sky was orange from sunset, and Molly slumbered at his side. Henry grinned, his dream fresh in his mind, and waited for her to wake.

Chapter 22

When I opened my eyes the next evening, Henry was gazing at me. With a yawn, I propped myself up and crawled off the bed. His eyes followed my movements. "I'll make breakfast," I said, as I grabbed a change of clothes from my bag. Seeing his chiseled features the day before had heightened my insecurities. I felt ordinary and plain in comparison and needed a distraction.

"Sounds good," Henry said as he sat up and stretched his arms over his head.

I threw on a change of clothes and darted into the bathroom to brush my teeth before going into the kitchen. Scanning the contents of the pantry, I settled on toast and jam. As I waited for the toaster, the door swung open behind me.

I turned, expecting Henry. Instead, it was Valerie and Max, making eyes at each other. They froze as they saw me. "You two seem happy," I said to cut the tension. "Want some breakfast?"

"Sure," Max said as he sat at the table.

Valerie sat across from him and leaned forward. "I'll have some too," she said, never taking her eyes of Max's face.

The toaster popping brought my attention back to breakfast and I plated it. Henry, wearing fresh clothes, and Jax filed in the room. We ate our breakfast, and Max washed the dishes. Henry and Valerie headed to Alberto's, and I was alone at the table with Jax.

"We need a strategy," Jax blurted. "I know you, Henry and Val are busy with wedding planning, but we can't sit on our evidence and do nothing while there's an arrest warrant out for us."

"Evidence?" Max asked from the sink. "You found something useful in the books?"

"Yup," I said as I dove into a recap of what we'd uncovered.

"There's no point," Max said. "In releasing it while you're here. You'd come across like a coward, leaving citizens to fight for you."

Max's words made sense, and I couldn't disagree. Yet I didn't see a way to return to the City without being arrested, and he'd tried hard to convince me to come here. "You're right. But I can't solve that problem right now."

"It's not a problem you should solve alone," Max said. "We all share it. I fear my name will be added to the arrest list if I stay here much longer."

"You're not leaving, are you?" I asked, spinning around to stare at him.

"I cannot," he said. "It would equate to breaking my promise to your father."

That was an answer I should've expected. It was always about his vow to my dad where Max was concerned. Part of me also hoped that Valerie was part of the reason he wanted to stay. They each deserved happiness, and I thought they could find it in each other.

I held my tongue on that subject and turned my attention back to wedding planning. I pored over the already decided upon details and checked my lists. There was one major piece missing. "Jax?" I called.

He'd left his seat only long enough to get his hacker's tool and raised his head at the sound of his name.

"Do you know what Colonists can play music?" I asked.

He nodded. "I know a few. You want me to introduce you?"

"Actually," I said. "Can you arrange for an audition tomorrow? Henry and I want to choose that way, and I have enough other things to deal with tonight."

"I'll try," he said as he set down his multitool and rose from his perch.

Once Jax was gone, I groaned and refocused on ensuring everything was planned, or at least thought about. It was much more work that I'd expected, and I missed having my mom to help. I didn't leave the kitchen table until Henry, Jax and Valerie came home, and I remembered I'd said I would cook. After the meal, Henry and I went to bed and fell asleep without another make-out session, as exhausted as we both were.

The next night I woke refreshed and planted a kiss on Henry's lips. My good mood surprised even me. "Are you ready to hear some, hopefully good, music?"

"Definitely," Henry said.

...

Jax had rounded up a larger selection of musicians than I'd expected. Henry and I listened to them all and decided on a violinist and his singing partner after a quick deliberation. Happy tears had formed in my eyes during their audition, making the choice easy.

With music decided on, all the was left to decide was an officiant. This turned out to be a more difficult decision as none of Valerie's candidates resonated with me or Henry, and we agreed to decided closer to the date.

The rest of the arrangements fell into place. Katie and I went for our dress fittings, and I loved the dresses more than I had when they were only drawings. It amazed me how much I felt like a beautiful bride when I saw my reflection in the mirror, even with clips and pins marking where alterations were needed. It did a lot to soothe my insecurities. Afterwards, we went to the Market in search of shoes, both of us only having our everyday boots. As I selected a pair of sandals, a bejeweled hair clip caught my eye, and I had to have it.

Henry and I had talked about rings and given up on the idea. Jewelry was rare in the Colony, and the pieces that did trickle in were never more than costume jewelry. The prospect of not exchanging rings, as a City couple would, saddened me. We could always do it for an anniversary when we could afford to buy some, and I tried to accept that.

"Is that everything?" Katie asked, holding her own pair of strappy sandals.

"Not quite," I said as my eye settled on a smaller, almost matching, hairclip. "I'll take this too," I told the vendor as I picked it up.

When the transaction was done, I passed it to Katie. "For your hair, so we can coordinate."

"Valerie will be impressed," Katie smirked with humour in her eyes.

"She should. Sometimes she acts like she's the one getting married."

"It's a big deal for her," Katie said. "Her brother is getting married, and she's only recently united with him."

"I know," I said. "She's very protective of Henry."

"That's what older siblings do."

I rolled my eyes, doubting how she would know when she had no siblings, and we returned to our respective houses.

...

It was the next day, midafternoon, when an alarm blared. Henry and I bolted awake, the sun shining bright through the window. "What's going on?" I asked over the alarm.

"I don't know," Henry said as he sat up and pulled on a shirt and his boots. "We better go check."

It shocked me how fast he was ready to scope out the threat. The Guard Corps must have drilled that into him. I yanked my own boots on and tied the laces as he entered the hall to talk to Valerie. They were both exiting the front door by the time I was ready.

I jogged after them as they joined the crowd of people in the street, all shielding their eyes from the sun with their hands and wiping sweat from their faces. The air was scorching in the daylight. It felt like my skin was burning after mere moments in the sun. "Valerie! Why is an alarm going off?"

"Kaydon rang it when he saw a van approaching," Juna said from beside Valerie.

"Why?" I asked. "He didn't do it when we came back, and no one knew we were coming."

"Not sure," Juna said. She was much too calm about this and had likely expected it. She had been the one living with him the past few days. "I guess he wanted everyone to know someone's coming."

"Where's the van? And whoever was in it?"

"I have no clue," Juna said, with a shrug and a frown, like she was upset to be left out of that bit of information.

I pushed past her and ran to the north gate. Henry and Valerie shouted for me to wait, but I ignored them and pressed on. It was something I had to see.

The van was parked at the top of the incline, its doors open. That wasn't the interesting part, or what made me run faster.

"Dad!" I shouted as I sprinted to him and flung my arms around him. "What are you doing here? And why are you with Malcolm?"

Dad chuckled and hugged me back. "For a couple reasons. It's something your friends need to hear too. Where are they?"

"I left Henry and Valerie in the street," I said as I lowered my arms and stepped back.

"Obviously, they didn't stay there," Malcolm said.

I followed his gaze to where Henry and Valerie stood at the slope's bottom, their heads angled together as they discussed something. I should've expected they'd follow me.

"And Max?" Dad asked.

"He and Jax were in the house when I left. I don't know where they are."

"One thing at a time, Jack," Malcolm said. "My children are debating us."

Dad nodded, and we climbed down the slope. Henry and Valerie hadn't moved from their position, and both settled their eyes on Malcolm.

"Why are you here?" Valerie asked her father with the usual cold hostility she aimed at him.

He held his hands up in peace. "I only want to tell this once, Max and Jax need to hear it. And we need privacy. Can you send the others home?"

Valerie frowned and crossed her arms. I feared she'd object and demand an explanation.

Henry laid a hand on her arm. "Val, please."

"Fine," she huffed. "Tell them, Molly. They'll listen to you."

Together, Valerie and I stepped onto the street. The Colonists that had left their houses stood in the sunlight, still shielding their eyes.

"Everyone, go home!" Valerie called.

"There's nothing to worry about!" I added. "It was only a messenger delivering a wedding gift. They've left, and you can all go inside."

The crowd seemed appeased and trickled back into their houses. I concluded their sleepiness motivated them to believe my lie, at least in part. As the last straggler shut their door, I turned to Valerie. "Let's go fetch our dads."

...

I was relieved that they, and Henry, had stayed where we'd left them. Valerie and I led them home by skirting before the outer circle of houses. We darted inward only when we'd reached the gap leading to our destination. Jax and Max were still inside and waited by the front entrance.

"I thought it best to stay hidden," Max said as Henry, Valerie and I entered. Then my dad and Malcolm filed in, and Max's eyes widened.

Malcom nodded. "Smart decision. We come bearing news."

"Tell us already," Valerie said.

"Val, maybe we should go in the kitchen," Henry said, trying to control his sister's outburst.

She muttered something indecipherable under her breath and stomped her way down the hall. Jax rushed after her, never one for a confrontation.

Malcolm's eyes went somewhere far away. "We shouldn't keep her waiting." He stalked off, Max in tow, after Valerie.

Dad lingered by the door, and Henry hovered by my side. Dad's eyes went to my jewelry, and he smiled. "Malcolm bought those for your mother," he said to Henry. "I remember helping him decide what to buy."

"You helped him?" Henry asked, his eyes wide.

"Oh yes. Dina kept your mom busy while we went shopping. It was Malcolm's Courtship gift for her. He said he gave them to you, and I think I know what you did, considering Molly is wearing them."

"Henry and I are getting married, Dad," I said as we walked to the kitchen. "In three days."

Dad's arms wrapped around Henry and me. "Congratulations to both of you," he said as he released us. "We can discuss that later, after why we've come."

Inside the kitchen, I hopped on the counter, seeing as the chairs were all spoken for, and Henry climbed up beside me.

"I'll get right to it," Malcolm said. "Yesterday, Ben received a message saying all of you, save Max, were spotted in the Colony. I volunteered to investigate."

"A message from whom?" Henry asked.

Malcolm shrugged. "Someone named Kaydon."

"Kaydon?!" Valerie screeched, her hands balling into fists on the table.

"This must be what he meant when he said you'd regret not going with him," I said.

"He sent a previous message detailing your entry into the City," Malcolm said. "That's why the former Leader and the guards were waiting for you."

And why Ben, Gav and their dads were too, was the unspoken implication.

"Kaydon's a snitch," Henry said. "What do we do about it?"

"I have a few ideas," Valerie seethed.

"We banish him," Jax said.

"Banish?" That didn't sound very effective. Wouldn't he just come back?

"He means we drive him south and dump him," Valerie said, anger still radiating off her. "With only a flask of water and the clothes he's wearing."

That seemed like a viable solution. I had no qualms about it, seeing how Kaydon would likely betray us again if given the chance. "Let's do it."

Chapter 23

We agreed that banishing was the best solution for our Kaydon problem. Dad and Malcolm kept their opinions out of the discussion. I figured they both knew it was a necessary, albeit somewhat harsh, task.

Valerie consented to being bait. Henry, Jax and I trailed a safe distance behind her as the sun set and she walked to where Kaydon was staying. She knocked on the door, clasped her hands and hung her head, pretending at sheepishness, as it swung open. "Kaydon," she said, batting her eyelashes and gazing up. "I've changed my mind. Can we talk?"

He stood in the door frame and flashed a wicked grin. "I'm glad you've come to your senses," he said as he reached out and grabbed her arm. "You'll never leave my side again." He yanked, and she stumbled forward. She dug in her heels and pulled back, making him tug harder.

"We need to do something," Henry whispered from my side as we hid in the shadows between the house and the next.

He was right; Valerie had suffered enough. I nodded and stepped into the moonlight. "Think again, Kaydon. Valerie isn't staying with you."

He cackled like a madman. "Valerie is mine!"

I set my jaw and stared him down, my arms crossed against my chest. The Kaydon I'd known was easily swayed. Intimidation should've worked.

"My sister," Henry seethed as he ran to the door. "Is not a piece of property."

As Kaydon's attention flicked between Henry and me, Jax skirted along the side of the neighbouring house, lasso in hand, and sprang at Kaydon with more dexterity than he'd shown in the tower fight. In one smooth motion, he flung the rope over Kaydon and pulled it tight, pining Kaydon's arms to his side. The force freed Valerie's arm, and she spat.

Fury erupted in Kaydon's eyes. He opened his mouth, but Juna, standing behind him rubbing her bleary eyes, spoke. "What's going on?"

"Valerie's lackeys are trying to keep her from me!" Kaydon screamed as he struggled against the rope that Jax was knotting around his middle.

"I'll never go with you," Valerie said. Her repentant expression was gone, replaced by a fury almost scarier than Kaydon's.

Juna stopped rubbing her eyes as she noticed Jax. "Why are you tying him up?"

"He betrayed us to the Government," I said. "He told them where we are."

Juna's eyes widened. "The van," she breathed. "I'll help you." She wrapped her arms around Kaydon, stilling his thrashing body. Her strength outdid his by a fair measure, and she made fast work of subduing him.

Jax pulled more ropes from his pocket and wrapped them around various parts of Kaydon's body. Henry and I checked to see if the knots were secure. When Jax finished tying Kaydon up, I rolled a rag, stuffed it in his mouth and tied the ends around his head to stop the stream of angry words leaving his lips. I couldn't wait to be rid of him. He was nothing but trouble, and I had enough of that from other, more dangerous, sources.

Henry grabbed the rope encircling Kaydon's shoulders and dragged him. Juna flew out the door and grabbed hold of the rope. "Where are we taking him?"

I glanced at Valerie, and she dipped her head. "To the van we rode in on."

"Oh, a banishment," Juna said, sounding giddy and bobbing on her heels like this was an exciting event. She lived for the thrill of battle, and this fulfilled her desire for action.

Kaydon mumbled something unintelligible from behind his gag, and we all ignored him as Henry and Juna hauled his rigid body. Max had moved his truck from the street to the space behind Henry's and my old house, where Kaydon had stayed. It wasn't a long distance to drag him, but he resisted, and they went slow to increase his displeasure.

When we reached the van, I flung the rear doors open. Henry and Juna hefted his body and dropped him in the storage area. It was almost pitiful seeing him strewn on the floor. *Almost.* I slammed the doors closed, and Jax secured them with a padlock taken from his bag of tools. He handed me the key, which I pocketed it next to the flask I'd collected from the Market. "See you tomorrow," I said as Valerie and I walked around the sides of the van.

"Good luck," Jax said.

Valerie flashed him a small salute as she climbed on the driver's seat, Max's keys in hand.

Henry jogged over and hugged me. "Stay safe and come back."

I returned his embrace, glad to share one last embrace before this mission. "Like I could stay away from you. I'll be fine. Are you sure you can't come?" Having him along would've lessened my anxiety. What if he wasn't there when I returned?

Henry exhaled in a slow stream, a faint, embarrassed blush on his cheeks. "I wish I could, but I'd hate myself for giving up time with my dad."

"I know," I whispered. "I don't blame you, and Valerie and I can handle it."

He broke our hug and opened the passenger side door. I placed my hand on the inner door handle and hopped onto the seat. His fingers dropped from the exterior handle as I pulled the door closed and Valerie revved the engine. I shook thoughts of Henry from my mind. It was time to focus.

...

The sky grew dark as Valerie drove toward the south gate. I hopped out and opened it. It was obviously seldom used as the hinge screeched when I swung it wide using all my strength. Closing it after Valerie pulled the van through was no easier, even as I heard the latch click. I wasn't sure how we'd get back in without me hopping the fence since the latch only opened from the inside. That was a problem for later.

Valerie kept the wheels pointed straight; there was no road, so minimal changes in direction would help us on the return journey. I watched the barren landscape through the windshield, seeing nothing to break the scenery except trees in the distance.

"Are you sure this'll work? What if he sends Ben another message?"

Valerie didn't take her eyes off the land. "We'll search him before we untie him. If he has anything, we'll take it."

I reclined against my seat, doubts swirling through my mind. It sounded easy enough, drive south and drop Kaydon off. But there were no lengths Ben wouldn't go to in the name of revenge. That's what kept me on edge as we travelled south in moonlit darkness. "How far are we going?" The monotonous view made my eyes heavy. Sleep beckoned, though I'd only been awake since midafternoon.

"Until sunrise."

I groaned. After we searched Kaydon and untied him, we'd have to turn around and drive back. I was exhausted, and we weren't even halfway to our destination.

"You should sleep, so you can drive back."

I bolted upright on my seat. *Me drive?* "I don't know how."

"I'll show you. And you just have to go straight."

Aware that Valerie couldn't be expected to stay alert long enough to drive both ways, I gave in. Sleep didn't come easy with that in the back of my mind, nor did it last long. I had just dozed on when a loud clang jolted me awake. "What's that noise?"

Valerie had wrapped her fingers tight around the steering wheel. "Must be Kaydon. Go investigate."

I unclipped my seatbelt, twisted around and climbed into the backseat. Once I was there, I had a dilemma. The storage space was behind the seats, but the seats and the storage lid blocked it from view. The clanging was much louder with my head close in proximity. I forced myself to focus and tune out the racket.

I searched the area, knowing there must have been a way into the space where Kaydon was. Finally, my eyes landed on a lever at the top of the left seat. I pulled it up to a resounding click. The seat fell forward, folding onto the bottom half and leaving a dark hole into the storage space. With a deep breath, I crawled through.

...

Kaydon lay on the floor, rolling himself sideways into the doors. Each time he made impact, the doors clanged, and he grunted. I grabbed one of the ropes tied around his middle, braced my feet on the floor and yanked.

His lips curled as he bared his teeth and tried to hiss. I dragged him to the gap and shoved him headfirst onto the van's backseats. My chest heaved from the exertion as he resisted me the whole time. If he hadn't been tied, he would've overpowered me. I realized as he landed on the backseats that he'd held back during the fight at the Leader's tower. His terrible fighting had been intentional. With little strength left in my arms, I crawled after him, put the seat back into position and pressed the lever down.

"Did you get things under control?" Valerie asked, not moving her eyes from her straight-ahead view.

"I hope so," I said, eyeing Kaydon as he wriggled and struggled against the ropes.

"Knock him out."

Rage bubbled in Kaydon's eyes, and he snarled. I kept my distance from his face, sitting on the opposite end of the seats. This wasn't going to be easy. "Do we have anything heavy?"

"I doubt it," she said. "Just do it. Use the skills Henry taught you."

I exhaled in a slow, steady stream and fixed my eyes on Kaydon. With no tools to use, I balled my fist and struck him in the head. He twisted away just in time, and my fist connected with the seat. This was no time to be timid; I climbed on top of him, straddled his torso with my legs and punched him from close range. My hand smarted from the pain of the multiple blows needed. I hoped it would last long enough.

With him unconscious, I returned to the passenger seat and reclined it. I yanked my jacket hood over my face, wrapped my arms around my chest and tried to drift back to sleep to avoid thinking about him. It must've worked as, the next thing I knew, Valerie was shaking me awake. I moved my seat upright, pushed my hood off and shielded my eyes with my hand. The sunlight shining through the windshield was too bright.

"We're here," Valerie said as she lifted her hands from me. "Wherever here is."

I grabbed my flask and drank a long swig. My body ached from sleeping in the van, and I tried to shake out my stiffness. My stomach growled, and I realized a new problem. "Do we have any food?"

"Check the glove box," Valerie answered, titling her head to the small compartment in the dashboard before me.

I opened it and was ecstatic to find granola bars and apples. Max had stocked it well. I grabbed the food, handed half to Valerie and stuffed my share in my mouth in large bites. I'd never been happier to eat.

Valerie nibbled on her apple. "Might want to pace yourself. We have to go back."

"I'll eat when we get there. I'm starving."

She shrugged as she ate her apple and put the core in the van's centre cupholder. I added mine and wiped my mouth with the back of my hand. It was time to dispose of our cargo.

"Let's search him in the van," Valerie said, acting too calm about this. "There's no telling how hot it is this far south. I don't want to be outside longer than we have to."

We crawled onto the backseat and dug through Kaydon's pockets. His pants pockets were empty, as were his outer jacket pockets. But I felt something smooth and hard through the fabric. I squeezed my hand beneath his rope around his middle and under his jacket. In the lining, there was a small zipper, which of course was closed. With some blind maneuvering, I tugged it down and stuck my hand inside.

"Be careful. He's waking up."

I gritted my teeth and yanked the metallic object out. Once it was free of Kaydon's jacket, I stared at it. It was similar to the phone Malcolm had given Henry. Ben must've supplied it. As I puzzled what to do, its screen flashed and lit up with a message from Ben.

'Good to hear Malcolm has arrived. I anticipate his return with the fugitives. You will get your reward when they are in my possession. She won't object to your mercy if she has any sense.'

"Creepy," Valerie said with a shudder. "And he's wrong. I'd take the Government's punishment over being Kaydon's reward."

A heaviness settled in my stomach. "It won't happen," I said, picturing the pleasure Ben would get out of torturing me and Henry. The image fueled my resolve to finish what I started. There was no way I would let Ben win. "It can't."

She grabbed the phone from me. Mouth agape, I watched her tap out a message: **'Val is gone. I need a few days to find her.'**

She hit the send button and gave the phone back to me. I slid it in my jacket pocket, and my eyes landed on Kaydon's face, his own open and full of fury. He knew I had his phone. I wanted to smack him in the face with it. I might've done it if it wouldn't have damaged the phone.

"Let's get this over with." I removed the spare water flask from my pocket and threw my jacket on the front seat.

Valerie opened the van's side door and stepped out. I moved over Kaydon to join her. Sweat formed on my forehead and neck when the air hit my skin. The Colony was cool and refreshing compared to this sweltering heat, especially this early in the morning.

Valerie's grim face shone with sweat, and she grasped one of Kaydon's feet. I grabbed his other ankle and together we walked backward and pulled him out of the van. Halfway, I released his ankle, grasped the rope around his middle and pulled. When his head cleared the door, Valerie and I dropped him.

His body hitting the ground sent up a cloud of dust. The trees had no leaves, and the ground was arid. There were no signs of plant life. No wonder people didn't live here. It wasn't survivable.

I wiped sweat from my forehead and new sweat replaced it. I retrieved the water flask from the van's floor where it had fallen and threw it beside Kaydon's body. He scowled at us as he writhed on the ground.

Valerie rounded the van to the passenger door and dug through the glove box until she found a small folding knife. She dragged the blade along the ropes biding Kaydon. "Good luck," she said as she stood and sneered at him and refolded the knife. "You'll need it."

He pushed himself off the ground and got to his feet on shaky legs. "You can't leave me here!"

"We can," I said as I retreated with Valerie toward the van. "And we are."

I beelined to the driver's door, got on the seat, closed the door and grabbed the wheel, not knowing how to operate the controls. Valerie reached across me and pushed a button that locked the doors.

"Press your right foot on the left pedal and move the gear shift to D." I did as she instructed and glanced at her, the car not moving. "Move your foot to the right pedal and turn the wheel until we spin around. Try to line up with the tire tracks."

I stomped on the right pedal and the van shot forward. "Ease up!" Valerie yelled as she grabbed the wheel and cranked it to the right. I lifted my foot, my heart pounding in my chest, and the van slowed as we spun. She stopped the wheel when we faced our earlier tire tracks. "Now go straight until we reach the fence," she said as she reclined on the passenger seat, her jacket over her head to block out the sun. "Wake me if you get in trouble."

I caught a glimpse of Kaydon in the rear-view mirror, holding the water flask and glaring in our direction. With a sigh, I locked my eyes on the tire tracks and settled my nerves for the long trek home.

Chapter 24

Henry

Henry was conflicted as he watched Valerie and Molly drive away. They were both capable of anything that needed doing, but he didn't like being parted from Molly or his sister.

"I know you want time with your dad," Jax said, breaking Henry's train of thought. "I'll stay with Juna."

Henry nodded, and they left. He walked back to the house and went inside. Max was in his room while Molly's dad and Malcolm were still in the kitchen. Henry heard their muffled voices and opened the door. They quieted when he stepped through. He was nervous and gulped, though there was no reason for him to fear the men.

"They've gone?" Malcolm asked, arching a blonde eyebrow. It was the same shade as Valerie's and Henry's. It made him wonder what his mother had looked like.

"Yeah," Henry said as he clasped his hands to keep from wringing them.

"Have a seat," Molly's dad said.

Henry sat on the chair farthest away from the two older men. He wanted a relationship with his dad, and with Molly's, but being in a room alone with them made him feel like a specimen under study, and he wanted to bolt.

"You look scared," Malcolm said. "I'm guessing it's not all for Molly."

Henry hung his head. "No. I'm sorry. I just never had a good parental figure around."

Malcolm studied Henry. "I intend to fix that."

"I'll go talk to Max," Molly's dad said as he rose from his chair. "And give you two some privacy."

…

Henry's nerves grew once he was alone with Malcolm. The couple times he'd seen his father before, it hadn't been by himself or for very long. Either Molly or Valerie, or both, had been with him. A relationship with his dad was what he wanted, and it wouldn't happen if he was scared to be alone with the man. Pushing aside his nerves, he met his dad's eyes. "I proposed to Molly. That's why we came here. To get married."

To Henry's dismay, Malcolm beamed. "I hoped you'd do something like that with your mom's jewelry."

"You aren't going to tell me I made a mistake?" Henry wasn't used to having a supportive parent. The Newsomes had scoffed and chastised him whenever he'd tried to make his own decisions. And they'd berated him when he and Molly had confronted them. They had never been happy about anything Henry did except agree to a Courtship with Ben. Even that hadn't made them smile.

"No. I'm not," Malcolm said, his huge smile still on his face and a twinkle in his eye. "It doesn't matter what I, or anyone else, think, if you're happy and believe it's the right decision. You can't spend your life trying to please everyone else."

Henry, having gotten this measure of support, poured out the contents of his soul. He told Malcolm about his time in the Foster Centre, where his only bright spot had been Gavriel's friendship. And of how living with the Newsomes was as terrible, in a different form. He spoke of the day he'd met Molly, and how Gavriel sweeping in and charming her into a relationship had crushed him. Then he relayed Ben's offer of an escape from the Newsomes and a distraction from Molly being with his best friend, and he'd seized it, thinking there was love between them. He finished his tale with the events of his previous trip to the Colony, and their brief return to the City.

"I was scared she'd turn down my proposal," Henry said.

"She loves you," Malcolm said. "If she's anything like her parents, she won't hurt you."

"Sometimes it's hard to believe she didn't agree out of pity," Henry said with his head hung as he wrung his hands in his lap. "She would've married Gavriel if not for Ben's meddling. It's my fault their Courtship got denied."

Malcolm got up, walked over and sat on the chair closest to Henry. He placed his hand on Henry's shoulder and gave a gentle squeeze. "Don't blame yourself for anything Ben Henson did. His sole mission in life is to gain as much power as possible. He doesn't care whom he impacts. Besides, Molly told Jack she doesn't love Gavriel."

"She said that?"

"Yes," Malcolm said, his hand still resting on Henry's shoulder. "You need believe in yourself. There are people who love you."

"It feels strange." As a child, being loved was all Henry had wanted. He hadn't known what it felt like until he and Molly had been alone in that small wooden house and his love for her had consumed him. He'd spent most moments thinking about her and how he could make her happy. With anyone else, he would've been jealous of their bravery and crowd appeal. He was never jealous of Molly.

Malcolm hugged Henry. He was surprised with how comfortable the embrace was. Malcolm's arms felt safe. The Newsomes had never hugged him, not even when he'd had nightmares that woke him screaming and crying.

"I wish you'd had a better childhood," Malcolm said as he let go. "But you've found your place in the world. I'm proud of you, and your mom would be too."

"What was she like?" Henry knew nothing about his mother, besides the fact that she'd been a Rebel Cause supporter.

Malcolm's eyes misted over. This seemed like a painful topic for him. "She was never afraid to take a stand for something she believed in. She was also charming. That's how she kept out of trouble; she knew what to say to deflect negative attention."

She sounded like his sister, and like Molly. "I wish I'd known her." Henry didn't miss her, as he couldn't remember her. Yet there was a hole in his life where her presence should've been. He'd have to fill it with stories and information.

"She loved you," Malcolm said. "She named you after her grandfather."

His mother had loved him. Henry tucked that information in his heart. With it came a question he assumed he knew the answer to. Regardless, he hesitated before asking. What if he was wrong? "Do you?"

Malcolm's eyes focused and cleared as they landed on Henry. "Yes, Son. I love you."

No parental figure had ever said those words to Henry, not in his memory. This time, he initiated the hug. He launched himself at his father and wrapped his arms around Malcolm's torso. Malcolm, on his part, returned the hug and stroked Henry's back.

Henry acted on a leap of faith and admitted what he knew in his core was true. "I love you too, Dad." He'd first said those words to Molly, after she'd said them. Next had come Valerie. With this exchange with his father, he'd told everyone that mattered. After a few moments, Henry and his dad ended their embrace. Henry felt whole, though he'd spent his life not knowing there were gaps in it. He was grinning and powerless to do anything about it.

"When's the wedding?" Malcolm asked, bringing Henry's focus back to his immediate future.

"In three nights," Henry answered. It felt both too soon and not soon enough. "We didn't want to waste time, and Valerie's pushing Molly into putting on a show for the Colonists as leader of the Rebel Cause."

"I imagine she's earned herself a reputation here."

Henry nodded. She had one that she didn't want. Molly was much like Jack in that way. "When are you and Jack leaving?" he asked with an answer he hoped for and a different one he expected.

"That's to be decided," Malcolm said. "I volunteered to come for two reasons. First to make a show of loyalty to Carl Wessin and the Government. He thinks I'm here to bring the four of you back."

"And the second reason?" Henry knew his dad was a member of the Leader's Inner Circle, but he trusted him enough to think he wasn't really on Carl Wessin's side. Hopefully that trust wasn't misplaced.

"To see you and your sister, if she can stand being in the same room as me. And Jack came to see Molly. He was going to anyway, after he got Max's message."

This reassured Henry. His dad had come, at least in part, for him. He'd do his best to convince Valerie to be civil. It was the least he could do for his family. "You'll stay for the wedding?"

"I doubt I could convince Jack to leave before it," Malcolm said with a smirk.

"No, you definitely couldn't." Henry barely knew the man, but it was clear Jack wouldn't go anywhere before Molly's wedding.

"You must have details to work out," Malcolm said. "I can help, if you'd like."

This was a better idea than waiting for his sister and dealing with her over-management. "I would."

...

Henry half expected the suit fitting to be like clothes shopping with Eleanor had been. She'd always criticized how clothes hung on his frame and insisted on getting the cheapest and lowest quality items. Henry had thought that was why few things fit him well, though he'd kept that opinion to himself. Wearing his guard uniform and Ben's selected, better-quality clothes had almost been a relief.

When he got to Alberto's and tried on his suit, he kept his expectations low when he emerged from the back room. Alberto and Malcolm were in the main room, both of their sets of eyes on Henry. He bit his bottom lip as he stopped in front of them.

Alberto approached with a supply of pins and circled him. "Some minor alterations and you'll almost outshine the bride."

"He's right, Son," Malcolm said. "Molly won't be able to keep her eyes off you."

Henry tried not to move as Alberto stuck him with pins, but he couldn't help blushing. He craned his neck to see his charcoal grey suit, white shirt and purple tie. The purple tie, Alberto had told him, was to coordinate with Molly's dress. That was all Henry knew of her dress, that it was part purple. "It's not too much?"

"No, I think it's missing something." Malcolm stuck his hand in his jacket pocket, fished around and brought out something held between his thumb and forefinger. He walked to Henry and pinned the small object to Henry's suit lapel.

Henry grabbed his lapel and held it out to get a view of the object. It was round with an intricately carved edge and a stylized, swirly C engraved in the middle. The entire piece was gold coloured, and he assumed it was made of the precious metal.

"My father gave me this on my wedding day," Malcolm said. "The C stands for our family name. You should have it."

"Thank you. Do you want it back after?" Henry wasn't eager to relinquish a family heirloom, though if his father had said yes, he would've done it.

Malcolm shook his head. "I haven't been worthy of wearing it in a long time. I'd like it to get some use."

"Never turn down expensive gifts," Alberto said as he placed the last pin. "Especially ones without attached conditions."

"Really, Henry," Malcolm said. "It's yours."

Henry ran his thumb over the pin's face. It was smoother than he'd expected. He'd never imagined there'd be a Connor family heirloom for him to receive, but then he'd spent his life with only one link to his family: his last name. "Thanks, Dad," he said with a genuine smile. "I'll keep it safe."

"I'm sure you will," Malcolm said, his eyes tearing up. Henry hoped they were happy tears, not disappointed ones.

Alberto reached over and unfastened the pin. He deposited it in Henry's hand and curled Henry's fingers around it. "Start by not leaving it here. I won't be accountable if it goes missing."

Henry clutched it tight as he went to change out of the suit and put it in his jacket pocket. Seldom did he go anywhere without wearing that, even in the Colony's heat. When he re-emerged, he and his dad walked back to the house. "I'm glad you came," Henry said. "I like spending time with you."

"I wish your sister shared your attitude. I doubt she'll ever forgive me."

"She has a hard time trusting anyone," Henry said, thinking of how hostile and distant she was when he'd met her. The bunker stay had been awkward. She'd glared his way when she thought he wouldn't notice, and he hadn't known why. "She wasn't nice to me at first."

"What changed?"

Henry dove into the tale of his running out of Valerie's tour and her tearful confession.

"That must've been difficult for both of you," Malcolm said as they reached their door. "I'm afraid it won't work in my case."

"I'll talk to her," Henry said. "When she gets back."

Malcolm gave Henry another hug and a pat on his back. Henry returned the embrace, growing to like his dad's affection. When they parted, he followed his dad inside with the idea of food in his mind. There were still many hours before Molly and Valerie would come home, so he contented himself with eating and rehearsing his vows. He was almost happy, which was a feeling he was still getting used to.

But he couldn't fully relax while Molly was away, as hard as he tried. In the end, sleep provided the best distraction. When he woke, panic and worry flooded his system as the bed's other half was empty. He rose, ran into the hallway and doubled over with relief at the sound of feminine voices coming from the kitchen. *She came back.*

Chapter 25

The drive back was stressful, though uneventful. Kaydon stopped running behind the van after a few minutes, and I tried to relax and keep my attention on the road. The fact that I got to drive in daylight while our previous track was visible helped. All I had to do was keep my foot on the pedal and the van lined up with the tire tracks. It seemed simple enough to execute.

It was late afternoon when I drove up to the southern gate. Thinking I knew what to do, I pressed the left pedal and shifted it to P. The van stopped moving, which I assumed meant it worked. I unfastened my seatbelt, leaned over and gave Valerie a gentle shake. "Valerie, wake up and open the gate. We're here."

She groaned as she opened her eyes and removed her jacket to uncover her face. She flung her hand up to block the sunlight, moving slower than she would've if she'd been fully alert.

"Valerie, please."

She sat up and shrugged her seatbelt off. "I'm going," she said as she opened the door and got out.

I watched through the windshield as she scaled over the fence and opened the gate. I shifted the van back to D and drove through. Valerie closed the gate and latched it as the van's rear end came inside. I pressed on the left pedal again, and she reclaimed her spot on the passenger seat. It was as simple as I'd hoped. "Where are we leaving the van?" I asked as I followed the tire prints back toward the colony.

"Go to our house. Max can move it later if he wants."

I tried to orient myself and steer in the right direction. When we hit the drop off, I shrieked in panic as the van picked up speed and we barreled down the slope. Halfway through, I moved my foot to the left pedal and stomped. The van stopped, and I slumped onto the steering wheel, breathing hard. What had been easy was now a challenge I wasn't sure I wanted to try again.

As I moved my body off the steering wheel, I caught a glimpse of Valerie's pale face. Her wide eyes were on me, and her hands were white knuckled as she clutched the seat and door handle. "Sorry," I mumbled. "I don't know how to drive down hills."

"Just get us home so we can give Max back his keys," she said through clenched teeth as she clung to the handle.

I did as she said, and minutes later we stumbled into the house. My limbs were stiff from sitting still for such an extended period, making it hard to walk. Max was asleep on the couch, and my dad and Malcolm were in the other bedroom. I inched open the door to mine and Henry's room and found him in bed. Jax was nowhere to be found. That was a problem for later.

"Let's sleep in the kitchen," Valerie whispered.

I nodded and followed her into the room. Before joining her on the floor, I spread peanut butter on some bread and ate it in large bites. I emptied my flask to wash it down. The wood floor was cold under my body as I curled up on it with my jacket serving as my pillow. It reminded me of the night we'd slept in Malcolm's old house. Neither was a comfortable experience.

Being as exhausted as I was, sleep came surprisingly easy without Henry nearby, though it didn't last long. I woke as the sun set and saw Valerie standing by the sink, a glass of water in hand. I got up and stretched the knots out of my body. My limbs were still as stiff and sore as when we'd exited the van.

"I'm taking one of the beds in your room," she said, her gaze still fixated on the small window. "Jax must be with Juna. He wouldn't want her to stay alone."

Valerie sleeping in the same room as Henry and me would eliminate every shred of privacy we had, but there was no helping it. "You're probably right." Jax likely was with Juna, though I imagined it was to escape wedding planning and family reunions. He'd had gone through his own when we'd been in the City and wasn't the sentimental type.

"Have you written your vows?" Valerie asked, changing the subject and choosing now to look at me.

Oh no. "My vows?" I'd forgotten about that aspect of wedding planning. "No… I guess I need to start."

Valerie stared at me with her fierce green eyes. She shared less resemblance with Henry in that moment. "You really do."

Before I could reply, footsteps sounded in the hall near the kitchen door. Valerie and I both turned our heads toward the noise as the door cracked open. I tensed, though there wasn't anyone hostile in the house.

Henry walked through the doorway, a small, sleepy smile on his face. I ran and flung my arms around his middle, pressing my face into his chest.

"You came back," Henry said, returning my embrace. "I missed you."

"I missed you too." With my face this close to him, his scent filled my nostrils, and I realized how weird the last day had been without him. It was only with having him back that I was aware of the gap in my life when he wasn't near.

He placed his hands on my shoulders and stepped back to see my face. "I told my dad about the wedding."

"How did that go?" Valerie asked, walking over to us.

"Better than I'd expected," Henry said, though I could tell from his face this was a modest assessment for Valerie's sake.

Valerie's face darkened and she crossed her arms over her chest. "When's he leaving?"

Henry shook his head. "After the wedding. He hasn't decided past that."

After the wedding. I pushed past Henry and ran down the hall, my feet skimming over the floorboards. I didn't stop until I reached the door where Dad and Malcolm were sleeping. I raised my fist to knock, but the sound of my name gave me pause.

"Wait," Henry called after me. "Your dad's probably still asleep."

I dropped my arm and spun to face him as he caught up to me. "I'll wake him up."

Henry nodded. "Alright."

I knocked on the door. "Dad? I need to talk to you." He didn't answer, so I rapped on the door a couple more times. "Dad?"

The door opened as I was about to knock again, revealing my dad on the other side. He stepped into the hall and shut the door behind him. "What's wrong?"

"Nothing," I said, keeping my hands clasped to avoid fidgeting. "I just wanted to talk to you." I glanced in Henry's direction, only to find empty space where he'd stood. With us being the only people in the hallway, it was as private as anywhere.

"Oh?" Dad asked, arching an eyebrow.

"Henry said you're staying for our wedding."

Dad smiled. "Yes, I'd like to."

I hugged him, happy to have what was left of my family around for my wedding.

Dad returned my hug, his arms making me feel safe and secure. "Are you happy?"

"Yes," I said. "I love Henry, and I want to be with him."

"Then I'm happy too."

"I wish Mom was here," I said as I rested my head on his shoulder. She was the one missing piece I couldn't replace. Yet her death had indirectly allowed me to realize my feelings for Henry.

"I know," Dad said as he rubbed my back. "I do too."

"I'm glad you came," I said. "It would be strange getting married without you."

"I'll always be around when you need me," Dad said as we both ended the hug. "How is wedding planning going?"

My good mood evaporated. There was a lot left to do and such little time to do it. "We need to find someone to conduct the ceremony."

"I might have a solution," Dad said. "If you're okay with your old man doing it."

"You?" The idea churned in my brain. I wanted Henry and I to be the focus of our wedding, but I loved my dad and wasn't opposed to his offer. And who else could we trust with the job?

"You'll have to ask Henry, of course," he said, sensing my trepidation.

"Can I ask you something first, Dad?" He was the perfect person to ask the question on my mind. I trusted his advice.

"Anything."

"How did you know what to say in your vows to Mom?"

Dad's eyes softened. I hoped my question hadn't worsened his grief.

"I thought about what she meant to me and what I wanted to do for her then put all that on paper."

That was both helpful and daunting. First, I set out to find Henry to discuss Dad's offer. I followed his muffled voice to the kitchen where it mixed with Valerie's. I hesitated, not wanting to barge in on their conversation or wishing to eavesdrop. Making my choice, I tapped on the door. "Henry?"

Their discussion ceased, and Valerie sighed. I bit my lip, not liking that I'd interrupted. Then Henry opened the door and beckoned me in. "I was trying to talk sense into Valerie," he said.

Before I could lose my nerve, I plunged into what I had to say. "My dad offered to conduct our wedding ceremony."

"And you don't want him to," Henry said. He knew me so well that he'd sensed my hesitation.

"I don't know," I said. "He's a hero around here. He'll get all the attention."

"Oh, don't be ridiculous," Valerie snapped. "People are coming to see you. No one even knows Jack is here. And you don't have a list of other options."

I had to admit her words had some truth behind them. This wasn't solely my decision though. "What do you think, Henry?"

He put one arm around me and held me close. "I'd marry you regardless of who led the ceremony. And I like your dad, hero's reputation and all."

What he hadn't said was easy to determine: I was lucky to have a hero for a dad instead of one I didn't meet until I was practically an adult or none at all. Henry wanted what I had, a relationship and bond with a parent. "That settles it. I'll go tell him, and you can get back to persuading Valerie." I planted a kiss on his cheek as I darted out of the room to deliver Dad the good news.

With that task finished, I snuck into my room, dug the paper out of my bag and tore a bare strip off one of the sheets. I'd need an excuse if someone noticed before the wedding, but none of us had paid the books much attention since we'd left the Moris' apartment.

Pen in hand, I tried to think. Having limited space, I didn't do much writing until I was certain what I wanted to say. I filled one side of the paper strip with a draft and refined it on the reverse side. They weren't perfect, yet I knew in my heart the words would escape my mouth as I intended them. Henry didn't need perfection; he'd appreciate a more heartfelt touch.

Pleased with my effort, and knowing my private time was running out, I tucked the strip of paper in my bag with my personal items and picked up my hairbrush. I ran it through my hair as Valerie barged through the door, her personal belongings in her arms.

Chapter 26

Valerie dropped her things on top of one of the dressers. The idea of her in Henry's and my space made me eager to leave the Colony. As that wasn't happening in the foreseeable future, I decided to make the best of it. "Which bed do you want?" I asked as I set my hairbrush down.

"The easiest one to move," she said as she placed her hands on the bedframe not against the wall and started to push it across the room.

I struggled not to roll my eyes. Something was clearly bothering her; I didn't pry and let her work out her frustrations.

When she'd moved her bed, she plopped onto it and huffed. "Henry wants me to forgive Dad."

I waited, knowing she would have more to say.

"Why is it this difficult?" she asked. "I should be happy to have him back, not bitter and angry like I am."

"You can be upset about what he did," I said, remembering how angry I'd been when my mom had confessed to asking my dad to smuggle medicine for her. "But you don't have to hold a grudge if you can recognize he's changed, or even that he wants to. It seems he's putting effort in. You could meet him halfway."

She was silent as she pondered my words, and then resolve settled on her face. "I'll try."

I allowed myself a small smile, knowing this would make Henry happy. "Good."

...

The night before our wedding flew by. Katie and I picked up our dresses, and Alberto shooed us out as fast as he could bundle them in our arms. It was bad luck, he said, for Henry to see my dress before the event. On that note, Valerie convinced Henry to stay the night with Juna and Jax in our former house. Neither of us liked it, but we parted with a kiss and a hug in the name of superstition and keeping Valerie happy.

I didn't sleep much in the day. The empty bed unsettled me, and my nerves and anticipation also contributed to my insomnia. At some point I did doze off, as it was nighttime when Valerie's footsteps woke me.

Our wedding was scheduled to begin at dawn, so Henry and I could dance at sunrise. The early morning hours in the Colony were tolerably warm and wouldn't burn us, though our guests were free to leave anytime after the ceremony. Just because it was hours away didn't mean I had time to kill. I rose from the bed, untangled my hair and snarfed down a bagel. I didn't bother changing my outfit.

Katie came when I'd finished my breakfast so we could get ready together. I wasn't good at styling my hair and was grateful she offered to help. She twisted my locks into an elaborate bun, leaving some pieces hanging loose in the front, and pinned everything with a fistful of bobby pins. "When you get dressed, I'll add your veil."

"Thank you, Katie." I wished I could've helped do her hair. Instead, I watched her pin it into a less elaborate updo.

Valerie had roped Jax, Juna and Max into helping the Colonists in charge of catering, decorating and music set up. This was meant to make my night less stressful. It didn't work; I was anxious about everything.

"Don't tell me you're having second thoughts," Katie said, reading my face as I chewed on my lip and paced across the bedroom floor. "You'd crush Henry if you backed out now."

I stopped midstride. "I'm not backing out." Changing my mind about marrying Henry was unfathomable. I would never hurt him like that. "I'm just worried about how setting up is going."

Katie placed her hands on my shoulders and guided me to the nearest bed. "Sit and take some deep breaths. Everything will be perfect. Valerie gave detailed instructions, and she'd be upset if she knew you were stressing."

I did as she instructed and filled my lungs with air. Exhaling the large quantities or air did help settle my nerves, but I was still a bundle of nervous energy.

Katie did her best to distract me. She fetched our sandals, slid mine on my feet and fastened the buckles. Wearing shoes that didn't encase my entire foot was odd. Growing up in the City I'd worn boots. They were the practical choice for most citizens that didn't own cars and needed to walk. Even in the warmer Colony air, sturdy, lace up boots were the footwear of choice. It would be strange to walk wearing these strappy sandals with their thin, flat soles. Could I dance in them?

"Wait here while I change," Katie said as she darted from the room, her dress folded over her arms.

I sighed and rehearsed my vows in my head. Thinking about my impending promises to Henry offered a small distraction, and I wanted to be prepared. I'd just finished my second mental recitation when Katie reappeared.

She walked in, the purple fabric of her ankle-length skirt swaying as she moved. The silver material I'd selected for the straps and belt complimented her skin tone, and the close but not clingy cut of the dress flattered her figure.

"Wow," I said. "Your dress is beautiful."

"Not as beautiful as yours," she said, her face glowing as she smiled. "Speaking of which, you should put it on. We still have to do makeup."

I rose from the bed. Before I could cross the room to fetch my dress, Katie had it and offered it to me. Careful not to crease it, she deposited it onto my waiting arms.

"Don't mess up your hair," she warned as I exited the room.

In the bathroom mirror, I got my first glimpse of my hair. I almost didn't recognize myself, even before putting on makeup. It required effort to peel my shirt off without ruining the bun. My dress opened in the back, so I at least could step into it. There was no way I could've pulled it over my head without ruining Katie's hairstyling. With it pulled up, I slid my arms through the shoulder straps and contorted them behind my back. Unfortunately, I could only pull the zipper partway up. With a sigh, I went back to the bedroom to get Katie's help.

She gasped before I could ask. "You're stunning. Everyone's eyes will be on you."

That might be true, but at least one set would be on Henry. I was certain once I saw him, he'd have my undivided attention. "Maybe you can zip me up first," I said, twisting my head around in a vain attempt to see the open back. "Or they'll get more of a view than I planned."

Katie laughed as she approached, veil in hand. She slid the zipper up, fastened the clasp and pinned my veil to my hair.

I'd thought it would be cumbersome to wear such a long dress, but there was something nice about wearing a garment custom made to my proportions. I wasn't the slightest bit uncomfortable, even in the sandals, which I'd gotten used to after my trip to the bathroom and back.

"Sit and relax while I do my makeup," Katie said. "Yours should be as fresh as possible."

She left for the bathroom, arms loaded with brushes and cosmetics, and I followed. It was boring sitting alone in the bedroom with only my thoughts for company. I'd go mad if I had to recite my vows another time.

Katie was bent over the mirror, makeup brush in hand, as I entered the bathroom. She straightened up and waggled the brush at me. "You didn't need to come in with me."

I lifted my shoulders in a shrug. "I was bored. And this saves time anyway. The only mirror is in here." I perched on the edge of the bathtub as she rubbed her brush on the makeup compact and swiped it over her cheeks until they were a subtle, peachy pink.

I'd seen girls at school wearing makeup, which was a luxury my mom hadn't splurged on. Our money had needed to go to many other, more essential things. For a time, I'd been envious of those girls, more of their extra spending money than anything else. Now that I had a chance to wear makeup, I let myself be excited.

It hadn't been easy to acquire the cosmetics. Valerie and I had tried to no avail to find some at the market, and when that failed, sent a message to Charlie. He'd called in a favour with one of his contacts and had rushed a delivery. It was fortunate that the colours somewhat complimented my, Katie's and Valerie's complexions. Whoever Charlie's contact was, they had sent a variety of shades.

Katie was efficient at applying the powers to her face, making me think she'd done it before. She'd told me nothing of her life in the City, so it was very possible she had. She spritzed her face with a small spray bottle and then turned to me. "Your turn," she said as she gathered a selection of items and walked over. She laid the palettes and compacts at my side on the tub's edge.

I angled my face toward her and closed and opened my mouth and eyes when she said to. The feel of powders being brushed on my face was soothing in an unexpected way. Not as soothing was the mascara. I tried my hardest not to blink while it dried, but that only made me want to blink more. Somehow Katie kept it from smudging on my cheeks. I closed my eyes one last time as Katie picked up the spray bottle and misted my face. With our makeup done, it was time to leave for the Market.

…

The centre of the Market had been transformed. The set-up crew had pushed the vendors' booths out of the way to form a perimeter around rows of chairs and an arch on the platform. I got a peek at it, decorated with woven strips of purple and silver fabrics, before Katie pulled me behind one of the vendor's booths.

"It's not time for your entrance. You need to wait for Max and Valerie."

I sighed. "I know."

"You're lucky Henry didn't see you," Katie said. "That would've been bad luck."

I was tired of superstitions but nodded to Katie anyway. I thought the wait would be excruciating but we weren't that early. Only a few minutes passed before Max appeared, wearing his guard's dress uniform Charlie had picked up with the makeup and suits for Malcolm and my dad. Max's uniform was all black, and in the dark, predawn light, it would pass as a suit. No one would get close enough to see the sturdy material or militaristic construction. Even if they did, I doubted anyone, besides Henry, would recognize it as a guard's dress uniform. Valerie came moments later, wearing her own purple and silver gown.

The music began just after her arrival. This meant that Henry was standing by the arch and my dad under it. Katie and Valerie left for their slow walk together down the aisle, and Max turned to me, his arm bent and raised in offering.

I placed my hand on his elbow and counted to twenty. That was enough time for Katie and Valerie to make it to the front. I didn't hear an announcement asking people to stand, but everyone did when Max and I stepped onto the aisle covered in a long, purple cloth. My eyes found Henry. He stood on the right side of the platform, his eyes on me and the corners of his mouth turned up. It was the charcoal suit he wore, tailored to his body, that made my heart speed up. I needed all my self control not to run at a full sprint. If I hadn't had Max to steady me, I wasn't sure I could've maintained the slower pace. But he was there, and I did.

Chapter 27

Henry

Henry spent a restless night at the house he'd once shared with Molly. He missed cuddling with her and seeing her face, and it hadn't even been a day.

In the hours leading up to the ceremony, Valerie fussed over Henry. It had taken little time for her to put on her dress and do her hair and makeup. When she finished, she focused her attention on Henry. He didn't see the need. He'd put on his suit and shoes and slipped his written vows into his jacket pocket, and she smoothed out invisible wrinkles, wiped a cloth over his shoes to make their shine more lustrous and ran a comb through his already neat hair.

"Val," he said, grabbing his sister's hands as she smoothed his jacket again. "That's enough. I can't possibly have wrinkled it when you haven't let me move."

She stepped back on the wooden floor. "Your wedding needs to be perfect. I want you to be happy."

"I am happy. And Molly won't care if my shoes aren't shiny or my jacket has a crease." Molly was the opposite of Ben, who would've noticed and criticized Henry for those things. Everything Ben cared about was related to improving his own image, and he'd always seen Henry as damaging to it.

"No, she won't," Valerie said.

"Just like you don't care what Max wears."

Valerie pulled her hands from his grip. "Why should I?"

Henry shrugged. "Because you like him." He thought it was obvious given the way her eyes trailed Max's every move.

Valerie gave him a playful swat on his shoulder as a pink blush coloured her cheeks. "I won't comment on that. Not on your wedding day."

Henry chuckled. His sister had been quick to shut down the topic, which supported his belief. He walked over to the sink and poured himself a glass of water. The cool, crisp liquid helped settle his nerves as it trickled down his throat. The sky visible through the kitchen window was lightening, though there was still plenty of time before dawn.

It did mean, though, that Malcolm would come shortly. Henry returned to the couch where he'd slept and sat. On the table lay his gold pin with the carved C. With nimble fingers, he picked it up and pinned it to his lapel. He wanted something of his heritage with him during the best event of his life so far. His father's pin and his mother's jewelry on Molly's arms were enough family heirlooms to satisfy his sentimental mood. They were more than he'd ever expected to receive from his parents.

Malcolm arrived as Henry pondered this. He clasped Henry on the shoulder as Henry stood. "You look ready, Son. How are you feeling?"

Henry exhaled a slow stream of air. "Excited and nervous. I want to see Molly."

"It's not like you to be impatient," Valerie said as she approached, her hard soled shoes tapping on the wood floor as she walked. She halted a short distance from Henry and Malcolm and sucked in a deep breath to gather her composure. "I'm glad you came, Dad. At all, I mean. Not just tonight."

"I'm trying to help however I can," Malcolm said. "It won't reverse what I've done in the past, but I plan on being better."

Valerie raised her hand to brush her hair back, seeming to forget she'd tied it up. She dropped her hand and clasped it with her other. "And I'll try to be less hostile."

"Great that you've finally come to your senses, Val." Henry said. "But we need to go."

…

Henry had to restrain himself from running to the Market. When he and his family arrived, he wanted to bolt to his place at the front and forced himself to settle. He usually wasn't so jumpy. The hours away from Molly were making him anxious and edgy. What if she didn't show up?

When Jack got into position, and Malcolm took his seat in the audience, Henry wasted no time in moving to his spot. The music started and Katie and Valerie strode down the aisle. Henry paid little attention to them. As lovely as Katie and his sister were, he was eager for Molly's entrance. He had to wait until they reached the front, climbed the dais, went to their positions and left a space for Molly. Seconds passed with growing anxiety for Henry until Molly appeared at the end of the aisle, her hand on Max's arm.

Henry felt lighter. The tension he'd held since they'd parted was gone from his shoulders. She'd come and was actually going to marry him. He couldn't be jealous of Max anymore, not when he was marrying Molly. She was exquisite in her long, flowing gown. Wide straps on her shoulders led to a v neckline that showed a modest amount of her chest. The gown skimmed her torso and flared from her hips, though it wasn't a poofy ball gown. A swatch of purple made up the bulk of her skirt with translucent ivory laid overtop and underneath, and opaque ivory formed her bodice and straps. She wore a veil, trailing down her back from atop her head. Her eyes were wide and luminous, her pupils dilated, as she walked down the aisle. *Maybe,* Henry thought, *she's as eager as I am.*

Molly reached the base of the dais, where Max departed. She climbed the two steps to the top, claimed her place across from Henry and flashed him a small smile. The music stopped when she ceased moving.

Jack started the spoken part of the ceremony, but Henry only followed along half-heartedly. He was too captivated by Molly and nervous to give Jack's words full attention. His ears registered Jack's opening remarks welcoming the crowd and presenting the purpose of the ceremony; their meaning didn't absorb into his brain.

Then came words that resonated with Henry as important. "Before the vows, I must ensure this marriage is consensual." Jack turned his face toward his daughter. "Molly, do you enter this union with consent and your own free will, absent of coercion or force?"

"Yes," she said, her voice carrying over the audience, but her eyes on Henry.

Jack turned to Henry. "Henry, do you enter this union with consent and your own free will, absent of coercion or force?"

"Yes," he said, projecting his voice to the best of his ability. It felt like he and Molly were alone with Jack, which gave Henry courage. It didn't matter that there was an audience. The Colonists had come to see their hero, not him.

"Now, the vows," Jack said, turning back to Molly.

Molly closed her eyes. When she opened them, they shone with a determined spark. She kept her hands clasped in front of her, no sign of paper in sight. "Henry, I might've been slower to realize my feelings, but I promise they're true. I love you, and I will stick by you, support you, and stand up for you no matter the cost or obstacle in our way. You made me happy and were my anchor when my world crashed, and I can't wait to be your wife." Her eyes sparkled with tears when she finished, though her determination didn't waver.

Jack pivoted to Henry. Henry's hand gravitated to his pocket where he'd stored his written vows and his eyes followed. He hesitated. Molly had seemingly memorized hers, and he didn't want to appear inferior.

Molly reached and placed her hand on his arm. "Go on," she whispered. "It's okay."

She was his constant and reliable source of encouragement and strength. He could do this without reading. The words had implanted themselves in his brain anyway. With a deep breath, the words poured from his mouth. "Molly, you inspire me to be brave, and you empower me when I doubt my abilities. You entered my life as a beacon of light and showed me kindness when I needed it most. Every day, I realize how lucky I am to have you. I promise to always support you, to help you fight for justice and to love you."

"Molly, do you take Henry in marriage?" Jack asked, his face angled toward his daughter.

"I do," she said, her eyes still lingering on Henry.

"Henry," Jack said, his head swiveled in the other direction. "Do you take Molly in marriage?"

"I do," Henry said. There was nothing of which he was more certain.

"Then I pronounce you husband and wife. You may kiss."

That was all the encouragement Henry needed. He wrapped Molly in his arms, dipped her backward and kissed her, her arms hooked behind his neck. They kept it brief, mindful of their cheering audience, and descended the dais, hands clasped.

Henry didn't want to let go of Molly for a long time. They walked to the outer part of the Market where the benches and tables were in rows and a larger table on the side laid with food. Henry tried to scope out their seats and noticed Malcolm and Jack walking in their direction.

Malcolm wrapped Molly in a hug. She pulled her hand from Henry's to return the gesture. While Malcolm congratulated Molly and welcomed her to his family, Jack extended his hand to Henry.

Henry shook it as Jack spoke. "You make my daughter happy when I thought it might not be possible after Dina died. I'm proud to call you, my son-in-law."

"Thank you," Henry managed to say.

"Molly," Jack said. "I have a gift for you and Henry." He pulled two silver-coloured rings from his jacket pocket and offered them in his upturned hand to Molly.

Her fingers traced over the smaller one before she picked it up. "These were Mom's."

"They belonged to her parents," Jack said. "It's only fair that you two have them."

Molly picked up both rings and deposited the smaller one on Henry's hand. "We should put them on each other. That's traditional, right?"

Henry had to smile while Molly was now the nervous one. "Give me your hand," he said. She raised her left hand and stuck her ring finger, the one with his mother's ruby ring, out. He placed the silver ring between his thumb and forefinger. With an up-close view, he saw it had a craved edge circling it, and a short inscription etched on the inside. He read it before he slid it on her waiting finger until it sat flushed with the gold ring. *I will love you always.* Though someone else had chosen the words, they were appropriate for his marriage.

Molly, her face composed, placed the matching larger ring in her left hand. "Your turn."

Henry grinned, not caring if it made him look giddy. Marrying Molly made him happy, and it didn't matter who saw. He raised his hand, and she slid the ring onto his finger. He clasped her hand, and they both thanked Jack.

Henry turned to leave with Molly, but Malcolm stopped them. "I thought you might want some pictures," he said.

Pictures? "We don't have a camera."

Malcolm laughed. "I'll use my phone and send them to yours. You kept it, didn't you?"

Henry dipped his head. He'd left his phone on the bedroom's windowsill to charge, though he hadn't needed it recently.

Molly brightened at the mention of pictures, pulled her hand from Henry's and ran off to round up Max, Valerie and Katie. Henry chuckled. He liked her enthusiasm.

While she was gone, Henry scanned the surroundings for a good background. He and Malcolm decided on a spot along the fence where some strips of ribbon hung and twined with the wood, with the first rays of sunrise appearing behind it. It was as free of distractions as any spot, and Henry hoped Molly wouldn't disapprove.

Molly returned with the others, and they took turns posing for pictures. First was Molly and Henry. They kissed, embraced each other and held hands while Malcolm snapped pictures.

Next was a group shot with Katie and Valerie. Henry was glad to have evidence of his sister in a fancy dress as it wasn't a scenario she was likely to repeat. He put his arm around her and held her close. He would treasure these pictures, and someday, when they didn't have arrest warrants and bitter exes to worry about, they could reminisce over them.

He got pictures with Valerie, while Molly had some with Katie and then Max. And of course, Molly wanted one with Jack. Sadness shone in her eyes as she gazed at her dad and leaned her head into his side, the early sunlight making her radiant. Henry knew she must've been thinking of her mom.

Molly sprung over to Malcolm when she parted from Jack and said something that caused him to hand her the phone after indicating a certain point on the screen. Henry didn't have time to ponder this, as Valerie grabbed his hand and pulled him into position with Malcolm. This was the first picture they'd had since Henry was three years old, and he loved Molly even more for suggesting it.

With pictures done, they joined their friends and the Colonists in grabbing food, which was still warm. They sat alone at a table, Molly's right hand in his left. Henry couldn't get enough contact with her and was awaiting being able to sleep in her bed again, even with his sister in the room. He thought nothing could ruin his mood, but he was wrong. Molly had just lifted her glass, when she set it down with a thump and her face darkened.

Henry followed her eyes to three slim figures lurking against a side post of the Market entrance. He recognized the middle one but couldn't recall her name. As it happened, he didn't need to.

"Sage Parker," Molly said. "What's she doing here?"

Chapter 28

The wedding had gone like a dream until I spotted Sage flanked by two strangers – a girl with long, dark hair and hazel eyes and a boy with short brown hair and violet eyes. I tried to stand, but Henry tightened his grip on my hand. *She must have a reason for being here. I need to find out why.*

"She crashed our wedding," Henry said. "Either we both go, or neither of us goes."

If he'd stood with me, we could've been questioning her already. I didn't voice that opinion. "Then come on." Together we fled from our own wedding.

Sage stood with her hands in the pockets of her jacket. She grinned as we came up to her. "You didn't need to rush over, Little Sapling," she said, like she had no cares or responsibilities. "We would've waited."

"What do you want, Sage? And who's your backup?" There was nothing about this girl that made me want to trust her. And the strangers on either side of her did nothing to lesson my unease. Were we that big of a threat that Sage needed to bring others?

Sage smirked. "This is Peter and Evelyn. We come with another message from The Devout. The new Leader has impacted our business, and you need to fix the mess you made."

"Why should I care about your business?" I had larger problems to worry about.

"Oh, we don't expect you to, Little Sapling. You might care about the arrests of citizens and the end of this Colony though. The Government has forbidden us from selling or supplying goods to anyone associated with the Rebel Cause. We stand to lose a lot of money and influence."

That included Charlie and explained how she found us. I hadn't thought to ask Charlie how he got supplies to bring here. What better way was there than to buy from an established group that had permission from the Government, who likely got a cut of the profits?

"Who's been arrested?" Henry asked.

Sage stared at him like she found the question tedious. "I'm sure no one you know personally. Some common people who thought they were helping you."

People were being arrested because of me. This felt like Ben's reaction to not getting what he wanted. I couldn't let this continue. But there was one thing I had to know. "When did this start?" No one had been in danger outside our immediate circle when we left the Moris.

"About four days ago," Peter said. Up close, his eyes unsettled me with their brightness. Evelyn bit her lip like she wanted to laugh and was trying hard not to.

Kaydon. It coincided with his betrayal too closely for him not to have been what set this in motion. "I'll stop this," I said, wanting Sage and her cronies to go away. "You can tell your group you've convinced me, and I don't need more messages."

Sage smirked. "Words are easy. Action isn't."

"I'm serious," I said. "I'll fix it."

"Not alone you won't," Henry said, tightening his grip on my hand like he never intended to let go.

There was only one way to end things and it required Henry as much as me. "No, I'll need your help," I told him before I turned back to Sage. "Tell your group it's being taken care of."

She shook her head and frowned. "They'll want more details than that."

"I can't give you more tonight." This girl was difficult to work with. She made demands and never gave anything in return. "I'll send word through Max. Will that satisfy you?"

"It could be sufficient," she said. *Apparently, neither of us trusts the other.* "We'll leave you to your morning. If I hear nothing within a week, I'll be back."

She slipped from the Market with Peter and Evelyn and disappeared into the shadows between some houses.

This time, I tugged on Henry's hand. "Let's eat. I'm starving."

He gaped like I'd lapsed into gibberish, but he went with me back to our table and, now lukewarm, food. I ate anyway. The caterers had put effort into cooking a fancy meal. Even at a colder temperature, it tasted better than anything I could've prepared.

When the food was gone, many of the Colonists gave us their congratulations and departed. A few lingered, and the music started up again. Henry and I swayed, holding each other close, under the early morning sun. Jax danced with Juna; Valerie, beaming with glee, danced with Max, and Katie twirled in time to the music. It felt peaceful, being held in Henry's arms and moving with the song. But this peace wasn't real, and the illusion couldn't last. No longer could I ignore what was necessary. "You know what we need to do, don't you?" I asked Henry, gazing into his emerald eyes. I tried to memorize them, along with all his other features, the warmth of his hand and how strong, resilient and kind he was.

He nodded, keeping one hand on my waist and the other holding mine. "I think so."

"Valerie won't like it," I said.

"My sister is strong," Henry said, his mouth close enough to me that his scent filled my nostrils. It was another thing I tried to commit to memory. How would I survive without reminders of him? "She'll realize it's for the best." His eyes had darkened, and the corners of his mouth pointed down.

I planted a peck on his lips, trying to ease his worry. This was still our wedding night. *We deserve to enjoy it.* As one song ended and another began, I moved my hand to his wrist. "Come home with me," I purred into his ear. "While it's empty."

"I don't know," he groaned, his eyes flitting over our dancing friends. "We need to prepare."

I dropped his wrist and cupped his cheek. My eyelashes fluttered as I made eye contact. "Don't you want time alone with me?" If that didn't break him down, nothing would. I wouldn't beg.

"Yes," he said. "But we have to—"

"It can wait," I interrupted, not giving him the chance to appeal to my responsible and logical side. "We've earned time alone as a married couple."

Resolve warred across his face with desire until desire won out. He smiled, his eyes sparkling like polished gemstones. "You're right. Let's go."

We snuck out of our own wedding celebration and left our friends and family dancing in the cleared-open part of the Market. The house was empty.

Under other circumstances, I might've tried to memorize its layout and little details. But that wasn't a high priority on my list as Henry and I rushed to our bedroom.

The bed, twin-sized since Valerie had claimed the spare, was cramped as we fell on it. He lay on his back, and I suspended myself atop him. We kissed, but I wanted more. Part of my brain screamed not to ruin my hair or makeup, yet the wedding was over, and my ensemble wouldn't last forever. As I adjusted my weight to balance on one hand, enabling me to touch his chest with my other, I noticed a small, round gold pin on his jacket lapel. It had escaped my focus earlier, and I stared at it now.

"My dad gave it to me," he said as he saw where my eyes were. "When you and Valerie were dealing with Kaydon. It used to be his. He wanted me to have it since he doesn't wear it anymore."

I sat up, and he did the same. His family, which I was glad he was getting to know, was rich. It made me feel inadequate, and my fingers moved to my bracelet. Even the rings my dad had gifted us were cheap in comparison. "I don't have expensive things to give you," I said, my eyes on the blanket and unable to meet his. "Are you sure you want to stay married to me?"

Henry chuckled. "Usually, I'm the one with doubts about being good enough. I don't care about how much money you have. I love you the way you are."

"Someday you might care," I said, gathering the courage to look at him.

Henry cupped my face. "You forget I didn't grow up rich. My dad's wealth is new to me too, and he hasn't really shared it with me. Just given me some old jewelry he didn't want anymore." The tone of his voice indicated this was no big deal, but I sensed the lie mixed in. He didn't do it to hide anything, only to comfort me, so I left it unchallenged.

I unpinned the veil in my hair and dropped it to the floor. It would only get ruined and tangled if I kept it on. Trying to recapture my previous joyous mood, I shimmied across the mattress, inching closer to him, his eyes tracking my advance. I stopped when my face was millimetres from his. A kiss on his lips eased the tension in his body. We had almost resumed where we left off when the door opened, and someone entered.

"I should've known this was why you two crept away," Valerie said.

Apparently, we hadn't been subtle. Not that it mattered now. I backed away from Henry and sat up. "We just wanted some alone time as a married couple."

"Love birds," Valerie grumbled with her arms crossed over her chest. She would've appeared frightening if she hadn't been wearing a fancy dress and makeup and had her hair up. As it was, she just seemed annoyed. "You couldn't have waited another hour?"

Henry sat up and shook his head. "You don't understand. Sage Parker showed up with another message."

Valerie frowned and wrinkled her eyebrows. "The girl from the fire escape?"

"Yup, with back up," I said and repeated Sage's warnings and what Henry and I knew we had to do.

"You two are seriously planning on going alone?!" she shrieked. "How is that a good idea?"

"We have to," Henry said, trying to diffuse his sister's emotions.

That strategy was doomed and required my intervention. "We need you to stay here to help Jax. And I'll leave Kaydon's phone with you to send Ben off track and contact Henry."

"I don't like this," she said. "But I know I can't talk either of you out of it. Have you told anyone else?"

"No," Henry and I said in unison. This was something we had to remedy. Our plan involved the help of some other people, but we'd agreed on it without even discussing it amongst ourselves. I wasn't sure what this ability to wordlessly be on the same page meant for our relationship, though it seemed like a good thing.

Valerie swept her arm toward the door. "Might as well tell everyone now."

"She's right," Henry said, sounding none too pleased about admitting it. "There's no time to delay with the deadline Sage gave us."

I forced myself to my feet and trudged out of the room. Henry and I followed Valerie back to the Market. We hadn't been gone long enough for our absence to draw much notice and none of our other guests batted an eye as we returned.

Not eager to resume dancing, Henry and I surveyed the remaining food, and I piled pieces of dessert onto a small plate. At least I could enjoy it while it was available. After I'd devoured the pastries and cake, it was time to share our plan. The music still played, though fewer people were actively dancing. Summoning my courage, I found my dad with Malcolm and Max. This was as good a group as any to tell first. Henry remained by my side the entire time.

Our dads' eyes, and Max's, settled on us when we came near and told them about Sage and her message. Max tensed when hearing her name. There was history of some kind between them that I lacked time to delve into.

It didn't shock me as I outlined the plan that Henry nodded along in agreement. This had been the only clear solution; it was a relief he realized that too.

"We'll leave tonight," Malcolm said, his eyes heavy as they focused on Henry. "Send Ben a text from Kaydon's phone." This last remark was for me, though he kept his gaze on his son.

"Valerie will handle it," I said, mentally reminding myself to give her the phone. It would be of little use to me in the foreseeable future, if I'd even be able to keep it.

"You're ready for this?" Dad asked. "Once you start, there won't be an out until it's over, in one form or another."

"I know." There wasn't a better option. The other possible course of action was to ignore what Sage alleged was going on in the City. That was cowardly and selfish, and I didn't want that reputation. "I'm ready."

Chapter 29

Henry and I returned home with the others once we'd filled Jax and Juna in on the plan. Jax had his part to play, and I handed over the books and pages of notes with slight hesitation. He'd safeguard and make good use of them, but it was difficult to hand them over.

"No one else can do this," he said, seeing the worry on my face. "And you can't bring them."

"True," I said. "Just don't damage them, or Max will blame me."

"They'll be in the same condition," Jax said. "Don't worry."

I gave him a nod, and he put his arms through the backpack straps. With my imminent departure, Jax and Juna were moving back into the house to stay with Valerie. She refused to go where they were staying, and we all gave up on trying to change her mind.

Having gotten the books, Jax went to his room. Henry and I had discussed trying to sleep, but it was impossible for me with my nerves on high alert. I'd taken off my wedding dress and retrieved my veil from the floor, then given them to Katie with my sandals for safekeeping. Henry had done the same with his suit and shoes. Katie's mama, being a sewer and garment lover, would ensure no harm or stains came to them.

With the makeup washed off my face and my hair unpinned, I

commenced my preparations. I'd gotten the book handover done with first when I still had the nerve. But there was another task that needed completing.

I fetched Kaydon's phone from my bag's pocket and went to find Valerie. She sat at the kitchen table with Henry and Malcolm. They all stopped talking as I walked in and placed the phone in front of her. "You're in charge of this. And you need to send Ben a message."

She swiped it off the tabletop. "Has he sent anything since we dealt with Kaydon?"

I shook my head. "No."

She opened the conversation with Ben and tapped out a message. She turned the screen to show me, a question on her face, before she sent it.

'Malcolm is bringing Molly and Henry back. Jax fled south, and Malcolm decided he wasn't worth finding since you and Gav have no personal interest in him. He will likely perish. I found Val and have her with me.'

I tapped the send button. "Good enough."

Malcolm plucked the phone from Valerie's hand. He tapped the screen a few times and then passed it back. "Now you can message Henry and me. I updated the contact list," he explained.

I was apprehensive about leaving the communication to Henry and his family, but there was no way to avoid it. If Kaydon's phone was trackable, it had to seem like he was still in the Colony. "We're set then," I said as sat beside Henry.

"It would be a good idea," Malcolm said. "To leave your jewelry behind. It will draw suspicion, and you can't announce your marriage."

Malcolm was right. When we left the Colony, Henry and I would have to act like the wedding hadn't happened. No one in the City would recognize it as legal.

Henry gripped my hand with his hand that wore my grandfather's ring. His eyes migrated to my wrist where his mother's ruby bracelet lay. Since he'd proposed, I'd only removed it and the ring in the Moris' apartment.

"We'll leave all of it with my dad," I said, more to Henry than the entire room. "He'll safeguard it in his house."

"That's likely the best solution, unless you leave it here," Malcolm said.

"No offence, Val," Henry said. "I agree with Molly. Everything will be safer with Jack."

"Doesn't bother me," she said. "His house is more secluded. Less nosey people poking around."

With that settled, Henry and I ate one last meal before saying goodbye to everyone except Malcolm. The stew's taste barely registered on my tongue as my mind ran through the plan on repeat, though its conclusion wasn't clear. The only reassurance I possessed was the knowledge that the path I'd stepped on when I first left the City would come to an end, for good or bad.

When we finished eating, Henry hugged his sister. I slipped from the room as they said their goodbyes, not wanting to intrude on a personal family moment. Dad and Max were in the main room preparing for their own journey back to the Outskirts in Max's van. I entered, not bothering to knock. They were sitting on the couch, their bags on the floor at their feet. "Dad?" I called. "Can you keep our rings safe, and my bracelet and Henry's pin? We can't bring them."

"There's nowhere safer than with me," Dad said.

"Are you sure you want to go through with this?" Max asked, his intense eyes boring into me. His disapproval was made evident by his frown.

"I have to."

"It isn't safe," he said, ever my protector.

The time for hiding behind his protection was over. "It's necessary. You can't change my mind."

"Molly's right," Dad said. "If there was a safer way, she and Henry would take it."

They were both worried about me, which would serve as my motivation and fuel. The upcoming days would be a challenge I hoped I could overcome. I hugged my dad and ran to Henry so we could store our jewelry and deliver it to Dad.

Henry still had the box his mom's jewelry had been in. We placed the ruby ring and bracelet back in it and nestled our silver rings and his pin on top. With everything in the box, I handed it to Dad. His frown and sad eyes made it difficult to walk away. A small section of my brain screamed not to leave this comfortable and safe place for a den of people that wanted me arrested and punished. With effort, I silenced it and maintained my bravery.

After a quick goodbye to Valerie, Henry and I trailed Malcolm to his van. Malcolm carried his own bag, while we walked with only the clothes on our backs. It felt weird, lugging no backpack around. I followed Henry onto the van's backseat and curled against him. We had a few precious hours until we'd need to put on an act.

"Try and rest," Malcolm instructed as he drove to the northern gate. "You'll need your wits when we arrive."

...

Sleep came easier than I expected, and I didn't wake until we were in the

Outskirts. The van kept moving as Henry roused beside me. He reached for and grabbed my hand. That little bit of contact was a lifeline for me. I wished I could hold it forever but settled for until we reached our destination.

Malcolm drove into the City, the sun now up and the pass on the van's windshield automatically opening the Car Gate. "There are water flasks and some food in my bag, Henry," Malcolm said as he made eye contact with his son in the rear-view mirror. "I'll pass it to you." Without moving the steering wheel, he reached with one hand, lifted his bag off the passenger seat and held it back to Henry.

Henry grabbed it with his free hand and set it next to him on the seat. One-handed, he unzipped it and unpacked the flasks, apples and bread. I accepted my share and let the sustenance calm my growling stomach and soothe my dry throat. The food had come from the kitchen and were things Valerie was willing to part with. I was grateful, not knowing what, or when, my next meal would be.

I lost what remained of my appetite as we passed a street covered in glass shards. There was a crowd near a Government office with smashed windows in Apartment District 12. They mobbed the building, limbs flailing in all directions, while others fled from it, and a group of guards holding shields formed a line to restrain them. On the far side of the scene, two guards dragged a struggling woman to a black van with tinted windows and open back doors. They threw her inside and slammed the doors behind before they turned back to the mob. *Another arrest. This must be what Sage was referring to.*

The people were too far away for me to hear their shouts, and I squeezed my eyes shut and buried my face in Henry's shoulder. The incident added to my list of things I needed to fix. This couldn't go on. I imagined the van was full of arrested people that would suffer because of me.

Henry stroked my hair with one hand and held me with his other arm. We sat in silence as we travelled, and I dared not peak at other districts. The odds were high that similar events were occurring throughout the Apartment Districts, and I didn't need more images to haunt me.

My nerves grew as we passed through the rich Quarters. I clung to my resolve, reopened my eyes and drew comfort from the fire in Henry's. He'd execute his part without fail. He was braver than he gave himself credit for.

"Put your phone in my bag, Son," Malcolm instructed as we moved onto the tree-lined road. "I'll get it back to you later. And remember, we all have a part to play. Try to forget what I say and do around the others."

"I know," Henry said as he dropped his phone in Malcom's bag. His calmness helped to settle my nerves. Malcolm's act would be worse for Henry than me.

When our van cleared the trees, six guards in uniform stood ahead of us, shoulder-to-shoulder and blocking our advance. Between them and us were Ben and Gav. Malcolm exited the van and opened the back door. I slid from the seat, letting my hand fall from Henry's as he climbed out after me.

Malcolm put a hand to each of our backs and nudged us onward. We kept our heads down. Acting defeated didn't come to me easily, but I played my role. It only needed to last until I was alone.

"I doubted you would show up," Ben said. "I'll admit I'm pleased. Aren't you, Gavriel?"

"Yes," Gav deadpanned. I could feel the weight of his eyes on me, though I didn't look at him.

Ben continued as if he didn't register Gav's tone. "You can leave Molly with Gavriel. I'll deal with Henry," he said to Malcolm. "I'm assuming you don't want to discipline him yourself."

"He means nothing to me." Malcolm's said. "I have no claim to him, so he's all yours."

Henry didn't as much as flinch as his father spoke and pushed him in Ben's direction. I didn't have time to react or see whether Henry stumbled as Gav gripped my arm and yanked me around the row of guards.

Gav led me halfway to the stone walkway and he halted. He faced me and kept my arm in his grip. "What are you doing here?" His voice sounded the way it used to.

I titled my face to meet his. "I'm giving up. Henry and I are turning ourselves in."

"I don't believe you. You'll tell me the truth eventually."

I should've known he'd distrust me, but I needed him to believe me. "I told you the truth. Do you really think we'd come here alone and try something?"

He rolled his eyes and huffed. "Fine, keep up that act." Without another word, he walked, and I let him drag me. We crossed the walkway and entered the tower after Gav typed in the passcode. I tried to watch over his shoulder, but he'd positioned his body to block my view.

He led the way to the door by the elevator. There were blood stains still visible on the floor of the great room, which was empty and quiet except for the sound of our footsteps. It was almost easy to forget fighting in it. Gav didn't give me much time to reminisce as he shouldered open the door to the right of the elevator and pulled me through into a small room, like an entry of a house or lobby of a building. Familiar metal rivetted plates covered these walls. Someone had gone to lengths to fortify this place.

"Stop gawking," Gav said, cutting of my inspection. "We need to be out of here before Ben comes with Henry."

"Why? Are you scared I'll say something to Henry?"

Gav fixed his eyes on the ceiling and his lips moved as he silently counted to ten. When he finished, he lowered his face. "Will you just trust me? You don't want to see it."

Trust him? He couldn't expect me to agree to that, not with how we left things. I wouldn't get anywhere by arguing though, so I went with him through a small door and up a narrow set of stairs. This staircase crossed the rear of the building, while the one I'd traversed with Jax went up the side.

I counted four flights before Gav steered me to the exit. My arm was still in his hand, like he'd forgotten he held it. It was possible he knew and just wanted to touch me. That didn't help matters. We walked down the hall, which belonged to a different part of the tower than the offices Jax and I had found. This felt colder, not as much in temperature as in the overall aura of the place. Dark tiles covered the floor, and dim lights ran the length of the ceiling at even intervals. Gav stopped at a nondescript metal door with no number or other marking. He pulled a key from his pocket, inserted it into the knob and swung the door open.

Chapter 30

Henry

Henry didn't lower his head when he was face-to-face with Ben. Where once Ben's face and colouring had been attractive, it was now twisted with fury and hate. Henry wasn't scared; Molly had faced far worse, and he could survive this. "This is what you wanted, isn't it, Ben?" How he managed to keep his tone neutral was a mystery to him.

"It's a start," Ben snarled. He turned his head over his shoulder to command the guards. "Search him."

Henry stood still, realizing now why Malcolm had taken back the phone. Maybe it would've been safer with Molly, but he wanted to keep something from his father. It was his lifeline to his sister too, and he'd preserve that to the extent of his abilities.

Three guards from the row broke ranks and circled him. Even with Henry's training, outrunning and escaping them wasn't possible. Knowing Ben, he'd probably ordered them to shoot if Henry tried. Henry extended his arms out to his sides as the guards reached him. They patted him down and turned his pockets inside out. He half expected them to order him to strip. That never came.

Ben, who watched with a critical eye, called them off. This had been meant to humiliate Henry, and if the guards had found anything, Ben would've considered it a bonus. The guards went back into line and Ben moved behind Henry. He gave Henry's back a hard shove. "Start walking, and don't try anything."

"I see you haven't gotten any nicer," Henry said, his feet moving him forward to the tower where Molly and Gavriel had already gone.

Ben cackled. "You don't deserve me being nice. Not after what you did. You made this harder when you didn't let your parents turn you in. I might've taken pity on you. But I won't now."

The Newsomes. He didn't regret taking Molly to their apartment. He'd rid himself of years of judgement and expectations by doing that. And he didn't need Ben's pity. "They aren't my parents."

Ben snorted. "And you were never their son, or the one Molly is in love with."

Henry ignored Ben's baiting. He regretted being blind to Ben's nature for so long. Possibly part of him had always known and ignored it. He'd agreed to Ben's Courtship offer because of the attraction he'd felt and because he'd been trying to put Molly out of his mind.

Molly. No matter what Ben said, Henry knew she loved him. Her face flashed through his mind, and pain spread through his body as he realized he had no idea how long it would be until he saw her again. The best course of action was to focus on one thing at a time, and the first item on his list was finding out where Ben was taking him. "Your anger has made you worse," This earned Henry another shove on his back. He kept his footing; guard training had been useful for drilling balance into him if nothing else.

The guards had broken into two groups, and one had gone into the tower before Ben and Henry, leaving the door open. The other half trailed them. Apparently, they all thought Henry was a flight risk.

Henry couldn't see Malcolm, but he didn't try too hard as he couldn't make it obvious that he was searching for his father. He gave up entirely as Ben led him to a narrow staircase, the guards having left them in the small entry room.

Henry climbed the stairs, mindful of Ben's fist making constant contact with his back. They ascended eight flights before Ben ordered him to exit. The hallway was narrow, with a row of dim lightbulbs dotting the ceiling, metal panels on the walls and dark tiles on the floor. Ben pushed his back again, a gesture Henry was growing tired of.

"Walk," Ben commanded.

Henry did it to avoid fighting Ben in the hallway. It wasn't that he didn't want to punch Ben as much as this wasn't the right time or place. He needed information and an idea of where Molly was before he could do anything too brazen.

"Stop here," Ben said when they reached an unadorned metal door, the tenth from the stairs, if Henry had counted correctly.

Ben unlocked it with a key from his pocket. When the door was wide, Ben shoved Henry inside and slammed it behind him. Henry heard the click of the lock, as he'd expected. There'd been no chance of Ben giving him freedom to wander or leave.

Left alone in the room, he surveyed it. The space was small, though not cramped as it contained few pieces of furniture. A metal bed frame bolted to the floor and wall was the biggest. There was a metal chair, also bolted down, by itself on the opposite wall next to an open door leading to a tiny bathroom.

In that was only a toilet and sink. Henry tested the faucet, and clear water flowed from it. At least he wouldn't perish from dehydration if Ben planned to leave him locked in without food.

The bed had a thin mattress on it, akin to the one he'd slept on at the Foster Centre. He sat on it and sighed. There had to be a way out of this room, so he could help Molly. Henry knew Gavriel, at least the former version of Gavriel, enough to be certain he'd treat Molly better than this.

Henry stretched out on his back on the hard mattress. The ceiling had four lightbulbs suspended from it: one in each corner. There was no switch to turn them off. The room's small window also let in light. It had no curtains, shade or blind and displayed nothing except endless water and sky. With nothing to do, he tried to sleep. He'd just closed his eyes when he heard the turn of a key and bolted to his feet. Whatever threat was coming, he wanted to meet it head on.

It was Gavriel. He stepped in the room and scanned it. His eyes landed on Henry last. "So, this is where Ben's keeping you."

"Why are you here?" Henry asked, wary of his former best friend after how they'd left off. There was no trust between them anymore.

Gavriel smirked. "You've gotten touchy. Did Molly rub off on you?"

Henry ignored this, sensing Gavriel was trying to trigger him. "I know things aren't great between us, Gavriel. Can't you at least answer my question?"

Gavriel gave a slow and exaggerated shrug and leaned against the door jamb. "I want to talk. Molly won't tell me the real reason you two came here. All she'll say is she's giving up. Unless you've broken her, it's an obvious lie. I thought you might tell me the truth."

"I don't know what made you think I'd contradict Molly." The idea was ridiculous. She'd been smart to tell Gavriel what she had, and Henry wasn't about to tell him anything different.

Understanding lit in Gavriel's eyes and a sly grin formed on his mouth. "Ah. You've always been her guardian, haven't you? Perhaps I came too soon. Ben hasn't worn you down yet."

Henry had lived with Ben and survived it. This wouldn't be worse unless Ben really did mean to starve him. "Why do you care? I thought you'd be happy to have Molly back. Isn't that what you want?"

Gavriel's browed creased and he frowned. It wasn't the reaction Henry had expected. "She isn't my Molly anymore. She's changed, and I can't undo it."

"Sounds like you're feeling sorry for yourself."

Gavriel pursed his lips, and his hands twitched at his sides. "You're the one who changed her. You couldn't have left well enough alone. No. You had to swoop in to rescue her the minute I was gone."

Henry wished he'd had to power to change someone as easily as Gavriel thought he could. It would've been a handy way to deal with Ben. In truth, Molly was the one who'd changed him. Getting this through to Gavriel when his current image of Henry was of a backstabbing criminal would be difficult. "I didn't rescue Molly. She's never been a damsel in distress. Nor is she as weak as you think."

"If you were ever my friend, you wouldn't have stolen her from me."

Stolen her? Molly wasn't a book or a piece of furniture. Henry shook his head. "I was a better friend than you realized. It's not my fault you were blind to everyone's feelings except your own."

"What are you saying?" Gavriel asked, most of the malice gone from his expression and voice. If Henry didn't know differently, he would've thought Gavriel was hurt.

"You only met her because of me." This confession was like lifting years of piled up weight off his shoulders. It felt good to deliver this piece of truth, and he couldn't stop until he said it all. "I didn't have words at the time for what I felt when I saw her. I felt jealous when you helped her, and she smiled at you. All I could do was stand frozen. Later, I realized I had a crush, but you'd already made your move. I couldn't take your chance at a relationship away."

"You could've told me," Gavriel said, sounding almost like the boy who'd been Henry's friend. He was much easier to defuse than Ben.

Henry ran a hand through his hair and exhaled. "And what? You wouldn't have broken up with Molly if I had."

"That's why you got together with Ben," Gavriel said, as if he'd just gotten clued in on a secret.

"He offered me an escape from the Newsomes. Besides, he isn't bad looking, and I thought I could do worse."

"What about now? Do you still have a crush on Molly, or is it something more?"

Henry didn't trust Gavriel enough to give a completely honest answer. Plus, he didn't want to add to the crimes on his arrest warrant. "It's more than a crush."

Gavriel hung his head and shook it side to side. He then lifted it and met Henry in the eye, his own dark eyes turned cold again. "I'll have to wait for Ben to break you enough that it overpowers your loyalty to Molly. If she breaks first, I won't need you. You'll tell me why you're here if you have any desire for self preservation."

There was a warning, or possibly a threat, in Gavriel's words. Maybe it was both. Henry didn't get to ask what he meant, as his former best friend exited the room and locked the door.

Henry returned to reclining on the bed. With no way to communicate with Molly, or leave his small room, it was best to keep his mouth shut. If Gavriel or Ben came to ask more questions that was.

No one came for a long time. Henry tracked the sun's motion as his only passage of time. He didn't starve, at least not to the extent Ben had probably hoped. Sometime after Gavriel left, but definitely still the same day, footsteps came, stopped at his door and someone slid a food tray through an almost invisible flap blended seamlessly into the bottom of his door. Once the tray was in his room, whoever had made the delivery walked back the way from which they'd come.

Henry rose and went to collect his meal. On the small, rectangular, steel tray were some apple slices and a peanut butter and jam sandwich. Beside the food was his phone with a message on its screen:

'This isn't much, but you'll need your strength. Hide your phone in the wall behind the bed frame, and the tray wherever you can until you hear five knocks on your door.'

Henry grinned as he picked up the phone. Malcolm had given him a lifeline, though it did nothing to connect him to Molly. It did give him a way to contact Valerie and that would keep him sane. He clung to that as the time passed, knowing he could at least do something.

Chapter 31

Gav left as soon as I was inside the room. I heard the lock click and let my shoulders droop. The room wasn't fancy, nor was it a dungeon. It had beige – not white, walls, a news screen, a tiled floor and thin, cream curtains. A large, round light in the middle of the ceiling lit up the entire space, minus the small, connected bathroom.

A twin sized bed made with a grey and white plaid comforter, nightstand and upholstered armchair were the only pieces of furniture. There was a mirror in the bathroom, so I could at least see my hair to detangle it. The bathroom also had a shower stall with a bar of soap. I guessed the accommodations had been Gav's doing. Ben would never have put me somewhere this decent, which made me worry where Henry was.

I sat on the surprisingly plush bed. This room wouldn't be terrible as a prison and at least wasn't monochrome white. Yet sitting in here would accomplish nothing. There had to be a way out, and my only hope lay with Gav. My mind spun all night, trying to think of a way to convince him. The Gav I'd known had to still exist. I just needed to help him find himself.

Gav came back the next day. He opened the door and walked in carrying a tray of food. I still didn't trust him, but I needed him on my side. My eyes followed the food, my stomach rumbling, as he walked to the bed, kicking the door closed behind him. He set the tray next to me. His brown eyes lacked their usual warmth, though his voice was the same as it had always been. "I thought you'd be hungry."

"Thank you for the food," I said, keeping my eyes away from him as I picked up the pear.

"Henry told me he has feelings for you."

I lowered my arm, the pear halfway to my mouth. Why was he bringing this up? "And you're jealous?"

"I'm angry," Gavriel said as he sat on the other side of the tray. His eyes bored into me; their weight made me want to squirm.

"Why? Henry can't help how he feels anymore than I can."

"I'm not angry with Henry," Gav snapped. "I'm angry at myself for being naïve and for what I have to do now."

What he had to do? He was acting like the one with problems when Henry and I were the prisoners here. "What is that?"

"The Leader says someone has to pay for sparking riots. Ben wants to sacrifice you to hurt Henry. I'm trying to sway him. You need to help me, if not for my sake, then for yours."

"Sacrifice?"

He closed his eyes and winced. "Pin all the blame on you."

Of course, Ben knew punishing me would hurt Henry as much as me. It would wound both Gav and Henry, which would be even better in Ben's mind. Neither scenario was agreeable to me. I couldn't hurt Henry by offering myself up, nor could I save myself at his expense. Maybe there was a third choice. "Gav, listen to me. You can't want what Ben does. Even if he agrees to spare me, you'd hurt Henry. He was your best friend. I know he meant a lot to you once."

"It's too late to spare you both. You two betrayed me. Maybe I should just let Ben have his way."

"That's not what you want," I said, forcing my eyes to find his. This was a mistake, though it also gave me some hope. If I hadn't known him for years, I wouldn't have spotted the regret in his eyes or the slight frown on his mouth. "The Gavriel Kingsley I was going to marry wouldn't turn away from those he cared about."

"It's not that simple," he said, shaking his head. "If it was only going against Ben I might, but it would mean going against the Leader and I can't."

Carl Wessin. I'd realized it would be difficult to convince Gav to disobey his foster dad; I hadn't realized how deep his loyalty ran. "What is your loyalty gaining you? By going along with it, you'll punish me or Henry, and we'll both despise you."

"It's kept me alive."

My temper turned to embers in my veins, not quite lit but awake and waiting for a spark. "You're not the one locked in a room with an arrest warrant out for you. When did you become such a selfish coward?"

"A coward?! You'd rather have me dead?"

His words struck the match and lit my temper aflame. "I'd rather you do what we both know is right! You can't live as someone's puppet. It'll tear you apart, or I will."

"Eat," Gav said, ignoring what I said and nudging the tray toward me. "I was summoned to fetch you, and you need energy."

With a huff, I grabbed the pear and bit into it. When I finished, I dropped the core on the tray and wiped the juice from my mouth with the back of my hand. Gav pushed the plate of crackers and peanut butter my way, and I downed them in as few bites as possible. When there were only crumbs left, I turned to him, my anger still burning inside me. Was the Gav I knew really gone and replaced by this Government puppet? "Happy now?"

"I'm glad you ate," he said. "But no. I'm not happy. That isn't possible with how things have to be."

I tried again to appeal to his conscience. He at least had one, unlike Ben. "You don't have to do this. Our relationship not working out is no reason to punish Henry. You're better than that."

"I can't do what I want," Gav growled in a rare show of anger. At least he was showing emotion. "Only what I have to. Are you saying you want me to punish Henry over you?"

I tossed my head, my anger fading. "I'm saying don't choose between us."

"You don't understand. Someone is going to choose between you. The Government is adamant that one of you must pay"

It was obvious Gav thought he was helping, but there had to be a way to sway him. "Who summoned me?"

"The Government," he said. "We need to go. Can I trust you not to run away?"

"There's nowhere to run." This was true, whether Gav believed me or not.

"Just in case, give me your hand." He stood and extended his hand, waiting for me to take it.

I got to my feet and clasped it. The once familiar contact felt wrong now, and my body yearned for Henry in his place. As hard as I tried, the off feeling of Gav's touch was unshakable.

He led the way back into the narrow hallway and to the staircase. We descended to the small lobby and into the great room with the elevator. Gav pressed the call button, and we waited. "The back rooms aren't used much," he said as the elevator descended to us. "No one connected them to the elevator system as they're prison cells."

"I thought prisoners were sent to the Outskirts." That was where the prison was.

"The cells here are for people who committed treason and are waiting for sentencing."

If anything counted as treason, it was what I'd done. Henry and the others had supported me, but the former Leader was dead because of my direct actions. "I'm surprised you're talking to such a criminal as me."

"I understand why you think what you did was necessary," Gav said, with a tone that said the opposite. "I still love you," he confessed and held up a hand to prevent me from speaking. "Before you say anything, I know regaining what we had is impossible."

His feelings were why he was determined to spare me. I could work with that. "Hurting Henry won't persuade me to start our relationship again."

The elevator door chimed and opened; neither of us moved to enter it. I tugged my hand from Gav's, hugged my arms tight around my torso and forced myself not to flee as he gazed at me, his eyes warm and his pupils dilated. He placed his hands around my waist, pulled me close and pressed his lips on mine. I froze at the unexpected and unwanted gesture. Wrong. It was all wrong. I wiggled my hands free, put them on his shoulders and shoved.

He was already backing away, his eyes wide and sad and his mouth frowning. "I'm sorry," he said. "I had to know if that felt the same."

I wiped my mouth with my hand. It took every part of my willpower not to scream or lash out. "Did it?"

"No," he said. "You've changed."

"I've changed?! You're the one that went and became a loyal Government lieutenant."

Gav backed up a step, his brows wrinkled. He gulped and pressed the elevator call button to reopen its doors. "We have to go."

I didn't want to appear in front of a hostile group of people that wished to punish me. However, I had no choice. There was nowhere to run. Even if I got outside, a guard would likely shoot me. I expected Government-loyal guards were stationed near the tower.

Against my every instinct and my judgement, I got in the elevator with Gav and rode it upwards. We stopped at the tenth floor, and Gav moved to grab my arm. *Not again.* I sidestepped him and beat him out the doors. His time of pulling me around was over.

Gav was a mere step behind me and pointed at the door at the hallway's end. "That's where we're headed."

I walked with a weight on my shoulders I couldn't shake. There was little hope both Henry and I would get out of this unscathed, and it was difficult to come to terms with that. I would do all I could to prevent it.

My mind was clear enough to notice the differences on this hallway. The walls were familiar with their metal panels, and the tiles on the floor were the same. But there were no offices or doors aside from the one we headed to, which was perpendicular to the walls. Evenly spaced sconces ran down the ceiling, providing the only light since there were no windows. A carpet runner went down the middle of the floor, like the ones used at fancy events for the rich that I'd seen in magazines.

My legs grew heavy as I forced them onward. This had to be done; there was no choice. Knowing that did nothing to calm my nerves. Beads of sweat accumulated at my hairline, and I wiped them away. Going into battle hadn't made me as nervous or anxious as facing a room of hostile enemies who wanted my downfall. I'd had a plan before; now I was going in blind with no time to prepare.

Gav stopped short of the door and reached for my arm. He didn't grab it this time, rather rested his hand on me as if to comfort me. There was sadness in his eyes. "Don't show fear. I'm going to protect you as best I can."

He still saw me as the naïve girl who knew little of the world outside her district. I backed away, sliding out from under his hand. Swallowing around the lump in my throat, I forced my eyes to land on him and my voice to stay even. "I don't want your protection."

Gav closed his eyes, inhaled and let his breath out in a slow stream. He reopened his eyes, now focused and determined. "You're getting it whether you like it or not." Without another word, he walked to the huge, metal double doors, pushed the left one open and waved me forward.

It was time to face my fate for the second time. The first time I'd been spared, but there was no one to bail me out me now. I didn't need a hero. I was the leader of the Rebel Cause, and I could save myself and Henry. With this small resolve growing inside me, I raised my chin, brushed past Gav without giving him a second glance and marched into the room.

Chapter 32

The doors opened to a large chamber set up like a courtroom sometimes displayed on the news. In the judge's position across from the door sat Carl Wessin wearing the Leader's full regalia. I hadn't told Gav that I knew the Leader's identity. That secret seemed safer kept. On left and right sides of the room, perpendicular to the Leader, were two long desks with three people sitting behind each. On the left were three women, none of whom I recognized. Three men, all familiar to me, were on the right.

Though I had met all the men before, only one was a comfort. Malcolm had the middle seat, sandwiched between Bob Henson and Humphrey Walston. My former escort appeared contented in his role and gave me a smirk; he'd never support me over the Government.

As I walked into the room, Gav on my heels, I shifted my attention to the women. The dark haired one on the end closest to Carl Wessin and opposite Bob Henson shared Ben's features, making me assume she was Annette Henson from Malcom's note. The woman in the middle seemed to be in competition for most glamourous with the one on the end closest to the door. They both had their hair done and wore heavy makeup on their faces. Their V-neck garments each showed enough cleavage that it bordered on being unprofessional.

"Sit at the table," Carl Wessin commanded in the robot voice of the Leader, bringing me back to my one-on-one combat with his predecessor.

While I was scoping out the Inner Circle, I hadn't noticed the small metal table across from Carl Wessin's bench with two chairs behind it. With a gulp, Gav and I moved to it and sat. We faced a room of mostly hostile people. There were few good endings that could come out of this, and I still doubted whether Gav would help me spare Henry or not.

"Do you know why you were summoned before the Government?" Carl Wessin's robotic voice hadn't changed from the previous Leader's, which left me uneasy. Visions of a falling figure cloaked in black, with sharp tipped gloves swam through my mind. It made concentrating on the current proceedings difficult.

"Gav- Gavriel didn't tell me," I said. My previous brow wiping had been futile. New beads replaced the old ones, and my palms dampened.

"You were summoned," Carl Wessin said. "So, we can decide on your punishment."

I squirmed. What I did was illegal under the Government's laws, obviously, but it had been necessary. That didn't mean there would be no consequences, especially since I'd come here of my free will. It had seemed the only solution when Sage delivered her ultimatum. Now, faced with a room full of most of my enemies, I second guessed.

"Who of the Inner Circle has a piece to speak?"

Bob Henson stood. His cold features lacked Ben's hatred, but they still put fear in my veins. "What happened was a young girl throwing a tantrum out of disappointment over her Courtship rejection with the backing of some outcasts that blame us for their misfortune and poor choices. We should make an example of her to stop others from pulling similar stunts."

"Really, Bob?" the woman on the left end asked. She rose to her feet, her fingers twirling her straight, black hair. Her brown eyes shone against her dark skin. "You think this was a stunt?"

"What is your theory, Carli?" Bob Henson asked.

Carli smirked, her bright-red painted lips not making her welcoming or friendly. It was more akin to a murderess taunting her next victim. "This was a deliberate act. She broke into our City and, our tower with the intention of a coup and assassination. Any one of us could've been her victim."

"I have personal experience with Miss Birch," Humphrey Walston said, taking his turn to stand, while Carli and Bob sat. "She is not capable of malicious, preplanned acts. Though our entire acquaintance she did nothing except mope over the rejection of her relationship. I see no motive for that changing. She simply blamed our Leader for her heartbreak."

"Miss Birch," Carl Wessin said. "Why have you come?"

I couldn't admit my true intention to this room. Nor did I have a plan to lead me to my goal or save me. My mind spun, trying to grasp a single, useful idea for anything I could use in the immediate time to help myself and Henry. Helping the Rebel Cause could come later, when I was assured I could help it.

"Stand and speak!" Carl Wessin ordered.

I got up on shaky and unsteady legs. All I could manage was standing with my fingers gripping the edge of the cold, metal table. "I came because I realized it was over. Too many people are suffering because of me." What I said was true. How they interpreted it would hopefully lead them astray.

Carl Wessin cackled. It was not a human laugh, and it sent shivers throughout my body. "There was no immediate threat to you, and you've come here. You must place little value on your own existence."

The ash blonde woman sitting next to Carli stood. She had to be Scarlet Everbee from Malcolm's list. "Since she seems eager and willing to fix the mess she created, I propose we take her up on it."

"How do you suggest we accomplish that, Scarlet?" Malcolm asked, not rising from his seat.

Scarlet brushed her hand over her blonde bun and smiled at Malcolm. It was full of charm, and she batted her eyelashes to add to it. "We put her in front of a camera to denounce her acts and the Rebel Cause on a live stream and then we execute her."

Executed. It had come to this. I froze. My mind was unable to process Scarlet's words, and my body was unwilling to move.

"That is an appealing solution," Annette Henson said. "It would remove the threat of her inciting and rallying the masses."

The voices of the Inner Circle members turned to a senseless hum in my ears as they debated my fate. I was desperate for a way out of this, for my own sake and Henry's. My eyes clouded over, and I collapsed onto the chair. My brain needed all my energy to try to fix this latest mess. Then, one voice, well known to my ears, cut through the din.

"She cannot be executed!" Gav shouted. He was on his feet and had curled his hands into fists, though the likelihood of him landing a winning punch was non-existent.

"I'm aware that you have history with Miss Birch, Gavriel," Carl Wessin said, the words carrying no emotion or comfort. "And I'll remind you that you'd fare better by sitting down and staying out of matters that don't concern you. I expected you to be grateful for the privilege of watching this process."

"This does concern me!" Gav shouted. "You gave me control over Molly. As long as I have it, I won't stand her for being executed."

This had to be one of the rare, if not the only, times Gav stood up to his foster dad. His eyes blazed with fury, and I wasn't grateful. It did nothing to help me protect Henry.

"Perhaps," Malcolm said, his words measured and detached, though I spotted a glimmer of intense sadness in his eyes when he glanced my way. "It would be more beneficial to deal with the boy instead. Killing Miss Birch may set off further outcry amongst the people. They have no allegiance to Henry."

I believed Malcolm suggested executing his son to show his loyalty to the Inner Circle members. I had to. Otherwise, the man who'd given his late wife's jewelry to Henry was a cruel fraud and a better actor than I'd imagined, which didn't fit with the picture I had of Malcolm Connor. He'd helped us before when he had no reason to. He wouldn't turn on Henry now.

"The boy is weak," Carl Wessin said. "With Miss Birch removed, he can be brought into line. Perhaps in time, if he proves his loyalty, you can take charge of him, Malcolm. That's something you must want."

"Time will tell if he's worthy," Malcolm said, shooting me a brief glance that I didn't have time to decipher.

"It is settled then," Carl Wessin said. "Miss Birch will denounce the Rebel Cause and be executed. As for you, Gavriel, if this doesn't suit you, I can assign someone else to watch her."

And so, it came. The Inner Circle had decided my fate.

Gav's eyes darkened. "That won't be necessary."

"Then you are dismissed and can take Miss Birch back to her cell."

Gav grasped my arm and led me from the chamber. I didn't resist, my head still spinning its wheels, trying to find a way out. This couldn't be my end.

"Mol," he said as the doors closed behind us. "I won't let this happen to you."

I pulled my arm away, making him drop his to his side. My arms wrapped around my torso, and I hung my head and shook it. "Don't, Gav. I don't want to be saved at Henry's expense."

"You love him."

I walked toward the elevator. Now was not the time to restart this conversation. If Gav couldn't handle me having feelings for someone else, I didn't want to deal with it.

He caught up to me, though he kept his hands to himself. "We'll find a way out of this. I swear it."

"We?" I asked as I kept walking, almost at the elevator now.

Gav sped up and got ahead of me. He blocked my path and moved as I tried to sidestep him. "When I arrived here, I thought you'd come for me. When you didn't, I was devastated and angry. I didn't want to believe you and Henry had real feelings for each other, but I can see it on your face. You love him."

"I can't let him die in my place," I said, choking on the words as my eyes filled with tears.

"I know," Gav said, the words serious and quiet. "I shouldn't have—"

The chamber door opened, cutting Gav off. He sprung away from me and jabbed the elevator call button. The doors didn't slide open before footsteps neared and stopped just shy of where we stood. With a gulp, I spun around.

Malcolm was there, alone, his eyes glistening and fixated on me. He had his hands in his pants pockets, the stance casual. "Molly, is there anything you'd like me to tell Henry? I've gotten permission to visit him."

"Tell him it's over," I said, thinking it best Henry heard from me, through his father, instead of finding out through a different source.

Malcolm frowned. "It needn't be," he said, flicking his eyes on to Gav and back to me. "Perhaps, we can find a more private location to discuss this further."

"Whatever you have to say to Molly," Gav said. "You'll say in front of me."

Malcolm kept his attention on me. "Do you trust him?"

Once, that question would've been easy to answer. In the days when things were simpler, I would have answered yes without hesitation. Now, I wasn't sure. There were few people to trust in this place. "Enough."

"Very well. We should still find a more discreet place to talk."

The elevator doors opened, making me jump. "Tomorrow. And you must go to Henry first," I said as we stepped through the doors and Gav pushed the lobby button. If Malcolm dallied near me, someone would get suspicious. I was sure they had ways to monitor his, and probably everyone else's, activity and whereabouts. "Tell him it's time. He'll know what that means."

Chapter 33

Henry

It was the next afternoon when five knocks sounded on Henry's cell door. He sat up and watched as the door opened. The ceiling lights illuminated a head of blonde hair, the same shade of his own. *Malcolm.*

His father stepped into the room and closed the door behind. "I have a message for you, from Molly."

Henry perked up at her name. His dad had seen her. "What is it?" He itched to leave the room and find her, which wasn't possible.

"It's time," Malcolm said. "She said you'd know what it meant."

Henry puzzled over the words. They could only mean one thing. "I do. I'll take care of it."

Malcolm gave a slight nod. "There's more I should tell you, Son," he said as he leaned against the wall, his face grave. He recounted the events of Molly's hearing and the planned outcome.

Henry didn't flinch as his father told of suggesting his own execution. That act of Government-loyalty had given Malcolm this opportunity to visit Henry. "Gavriel won't side with the Leader over this." His former friend loved Molly too much to let her die. "Do you have contact with Max?"

"Not until he checks in."

"Let's hope he does that soon." They'd need the guard's help.

"I'll be in touch," Malcolm said. He approached Henry and sat beside him on the bed, his eyes on Henry's face. "Ben will come. Don't tell him anything about helping Molly or why you're here."

"I know." Henry didn't need this warning. The trust he'd once had for Ben had long ago vanished.

Malcolm squeezed Henry's shoulder, made his exit with the food tray, and Henry was alone.

...

Henry pulled the phone from where he'd hidden it under the loose plate of metal behind the bedpost. He tapped out a message to his sister, being hoping she'd answer sooner than later.

His frustration grew when her reply came: **'Jax and I will handle it. Give us a few days.'** *Days.* He slouched. His only hope, as he re-hid the phone, was that it would be fast enough.

Malcolm hadn't brought more food, so Henry went into the bathroom to drink from the faucet. After that, he collapsed on the bed and stared at the four, always turned on, light bulbs. With a groan, he rolled onto his stomach, pressed his eyes into the mattress and crossed his wrists under his head. There was no pillow, only a fitted sheet and a thin top sheet.

He didn't find sleep easily, but he did find it hours later after the sky had turned as black as Ben's hair. When his rumbling stomach woke him and he opened his eyes, the sun was back in the sky. Some foreign sense compelled him to check the phone. There was no message from Valerie.

Two sets of footsteps approached his door, and someone unlocked it. He could make out voices, though not the words they spoke. Henry just had time to jam the phone in his pocket and sit up when the door to his cell opened.

It was his father with a woman about Malcolm's age with ash blonde hair. She smirked at Henry with red painted lips and sashayed into his cell. Her dress was cut close to her figure and accentuated her hips as she walked. It also had a deep vee neckline. Henry tore his eyes away.

"He looks like you, Malcolm."

"He's my son, Scarlet," Malcolm said as he stepped into the room after the strange woman – Scarlet Everbee from the list of Inner Circle members. What was she doing here?

"Yes, and yet he could resemble Amelia. Small mercies he doesn't."

Amelia? Henry didn't know that name and felt his brows move together.

Scarlet laughed, her hand with painted nails the same colour as her lipstick covering her mouth. "Poor, unfortunate boy. Has no one told you your mother's name?"

His mother? "You knew her?" Inner Circle member or not, if Scarlet had information she was willing to divulge about his mother, he wanted to hear it.

"Oh yes. She got between your father and me. You see, my parents and I planned for me to wed Malcolm." Malcolm closed his eyes and winced at this retelling. It appeared to Henry his father hadn't liked this plan or wanted to go along with it. "There was nothing I could do when he chose your mother instead. Not until she died."

"Scarlet, is this necessary?" Malcolm asked through clenched teeth.

"It is. If we keep him in the dark, we can never be certain where his allegiances lie as he cannot choose."

Malcolm sighed and tossed his head.

Scarlet brushed a stray piece of hair over her shoulder and continued her tale. "After Amelia's death, I let Malcolm have time to grieve. Then, when a Government position opened and he'd wasted his fortune, I offered him a choice. He could've stayed with you and your sister, and whatever reminders of Amelia he wanted, but he made the wise decision to leave that behind. He had nothing to gain from the memory of a Rebel supporter and her children," Scarlet spat as she said the word 'Rebel'. "Now you've gotten involved with a Rebel and traitor. It's time to decide whether you'll go down with her or see reason."

Molly. Henry didn't believe for one second that Malcolm would've abandoned his wife had she lived. Why should Henry? And his father hadn't abandoned him and Valerie out of carelessness. Malcolm had sacrificed for what he thought was right. "What difference does it make when I'm locked in here?"

"If you want out, you'll choose the right side," Scarlet said as she turned on her heel and sauntered out of the room.

Malcolm lingered with pain and regret in his eyes. "I'm sorry, Henry. She insisted."

Henry fixed his eyes on his father. "Why didn't you tell me my mom's name?"

Malcom's face crumbled and his shoulders sagged. "It was too painful."

If the Government succeeded in executing Molly, maybe Henry would feel the same. He didn't want to. Molly deserved to be remembered, as his mother did. "You might've lessened the pain by sharing it with Valerie and me."

Malcolm hung his head and stuck his hand in his pants pocket. He dug around and produced a wallet sized piece of paper. It was face down on his hand when he slid it to Henry; it felt glossy and cold on his palm.

Henry went to turn it over, but his father covered it with his hand. "Keeping this was a giant risk, and it needs to stay secret. Hide it well."

Henry let Malcolm leave then. He sat on the bed and flipped the paper over. The last time his father had showed him something this size, it had been Macolm's ID card as proof of their relation. He expected another document this time, something of his mom's with her name on it maybe.

It was an old and faded photograph. He could still make out the people in it. There was Valerie as a toddler, dressed in a red dress and grinning wide with mischief in her eyes. Valerie had never been that happy and carefree since they reunited. She was sitting on a woman's lap, and the woman was holding her and a baby swaddled in a white and grey polka-dot blanket with tufts of blonde hair peeking out from a blue, cotton cap. Henry had never seen a baby picture of himself before, and it was strange.

But it was the woman holding him that made his eyes water. She had purple bags under her hazel eyes and her brown hair tied up in a messy bun. Her skin had the pale, grey hue of someone ill, yet she was smiling and gazing with adoration at Henry and his sister. *His mother Amelia.* Henry ran his thumb over her face in the picture. He retrieved his phone, removed the back and tucked the picture in. This way it would stay with him.

…

Days passed with the occasional tray of food slid under Henry's door. When it was a week since he and Molly had arrived, Valerie woke him with another message: **'Streaming in five.'**

He'd barely had time to process the message and get off the bed when fast, heavy footsteps pounded down the hallway. Henry stuffed the phone in his pocket as his cell door banged open.

Ben stood in the opening radiating more fury than he had during the battle, which Henry hadn't imagined was possible. "You're lucky the Leader thinks you'll be useful," he growled.

"Why?" Henry kept his voice calm and uninterested. He had nothing to lose and might as well make things difficult for Ben.

"If you can manage to be anything other than a dolt, now is the time."

Another insult. Henry would've believed it before Molly and his family entered his life. He gave an exaggerated shrug. "Why are you angry now?"

Ben stomped into the room, each step a loud smack on the tiles. "The girl who claims to be your sister just hijacked the stream with that boy you brought last time you were here. Care to explain why?"

"I have no idea," Henry lied. "I didn't see it. There's no screen in here."

Ben pursed his lips and stepped closer to Henry, their faces almost touching. The last time Ben's lips had been this close to Henry's was one of the rare times they'd kissed. That train of thought sent Henry's mind to Molly. Ben's lips had always been demanding, never yielding to Henry's. He tried desperately to focus on the present.

"You've developed an attitude," Ben said. "After what you've done, you'll be lucky if I let you rot in here instead of beating you to a pulp."

Henry smirked. The idea of Ben beating anyone up was ludicrous. And Ben had been the one to force Henry into the Guard Corps. His deluded belief that he could overpower, let alone land a punch on, Henry made Henry want to laugh. "If the Leader finds me useful, I doubt you'll get away with either."

Ben cackled. "Go ahead and place your hopes on that. It requires you being obedient. I imagine once the girl is taken care of, you'll join our side."

Henry had never wanted to strangle Ben more than he did hearing those words. "You're wrong. Losing Molly won't make me cooperative."

"I'm glad," Ben spat as the anger in his eyes grew. "Your lack of self preservation means I can watch you suffer. Try not to lose your wits in here. There's no telling when I'll be back, with the execution being tomorrow."

Ben turned to walk away, and something in Henry snapped. He couldn't stew in this cell as Molly faced an untimely demise. He'd never be able to live with himself. As Ben reached the halfway point to the door, Henry lunged. He tackled Ben who flung his arms up to protect his head as he fell. When his body hit the floor and Henry landed atop him, Ben snarled and tried to strike.

But Henry was the one with combat training. He dodged Ben's slow swipe and pinned his arms down while he dug through Ben's jacket pockets until he found a keyring. With it in his grasp, Henry jumped to his feet and bolted from the room. Ben yelled and cursed and was slower to stand. Henry beat him to the door and slammed it closed.

Grinning, he inserted the key and engaged the lock. Ben pounded on the door's inside. Henry ignored it. Whoever was in earshot could think he was going crazy and begging for an escape.

Henry sent Malcolm a message saying he'd gotten out of his cell and not to come by. He didn't wait for an answer as he jogged down the hall, retracing the route Ben had led him on. The most important thing was getting to Molly. There had to be a way he could help her.

…

The staircase was quiet, which presented a problem of its own. Molly's location and that of her execution weren't known to Henry. He sat of a step and pulled out his phone. The only thing to do was send Malcolm another message.

Before he could, an answer came to his prior message. **'Max is coming to get you. Stay put.'**

Max. He had shown up. Henry pocketed his phone and waited. The guard didn't come immediately, and Henry grew impatient. The longer he lingered on the stairs, the higher the risk became of someone discovering him. The logical part of his brain told him to stay, but the irrational part wanted him to flee. He was about to give in and leave when he heard footsteps coming from below. Facing an incoming threat sitting down was a bad idea, so he sprung to his feet and readied his battle stance.

"Relax," Max said, his features coming into focus as he neared. "We need each other's help, but I'll fight you if that's what you want."

Henry dropped his fists. "I don't. It would be counterproductive."

Max flashed him a grin. "I can see why Molly likes you. You've got sense."

Henry hoped she liked him for more than that, but he accepted it as a compliment anyway. "Where is she? Have you seen her?"

"Not yet. Gavriel's with her downstairs."

"Gavriel?" Henry tensed. He'd known Gavriel since they were both little kids, but his former best friend was a different person now. Could Henry trust him?

"Yes," Max said, arching an eyebrow at Henry's tone. "He's the one with a key to her cell. Turns out he's not on board with her dying."

Obviously Gavriel had selfish reasons for helping Molly. This also told Henry that his own life meant little to his former friend. His heart hurt at this realization, yet now wasn't the time to dwell on it. He had a goal that needed his focus. "I expected that."

"Good. File it as a mutual interest. You don't have to trust him as long as what you both want aligns."

Henry sighed. "Can we leave this staircase now?"

Max's laugh lit up his face. Henry saw in it what drew his sister to him. "Yes." Max descended the stairs and didn't check if Henry followed, so Henry rushed after him.

There was a similarity their gaits shared, probably from guard training. In Henry's short stint as a guard, he'd never met Max. If they'd been in the same place, he hadn't known it. Max was his sister's age and likely had years of service in and long ago been promoted from Gate duty. "How'd you get involved in the Rebel Cause?" Henry asked as they passed the seventh-floor door.

"That's a boring story," Max said, not sparing a glance to Henry. "You sure you want to hear it?"

"That's why I asked."

Max wiped a hand over his face and upped his speed. "Becoming a guard made my life marginally better. But it isn't about helping the public as I thought. It's about repressing them. And it didn't help my family. I'm sure you know that already."

"My foster parents and Ben were the ones who forced me into the Guard Corps. None of them care about the public." They hadn't even cared about him.

"You do."

Max didn't phrase this as a sentence, so Henry didn't reply. It was true on one level, but it was also difficult for him to care about a vast number of strangers. Molly and Valerie were the ones with a strong desire to help people and the bravery to act. Henry was no leader.

He mulled this over as he and Max walked down to the fourth-floor landing. Max held a hand up to stop Henry from following him out the door. Once he was gone, Henry cracked the door open and watched Max stride down the hallway until he got out of sight.

Henry felt useless hiding in the stairwell, but he couldn't wander the halls when he was supposed to be locked in a cell. It still frustrated him, having Molly so close yet out of his reach.

"Did you see Molly?" Henry asked as Max when Max returned.

The guard tossed his head, a slight frown on his mouth. "No. Only Gavriel. He told me to bring you."

"Fine," Henry said. He could tolerate Gavriel if that's he needed to do to see Molly.

"Let's go," Max said held the hallway door open for Henry.

They walked the dimly lit hallway to a plain, metal door Gavriel leaned against. He didn't make an intimidating sentry, but he was an obstacle to anyone trying to entre the room, plus, as Max had said, he had the key.

Gavriel's eyes landed on Henry as he and Max neared. Henry thought there was guilt in his expression, though it might've only been what he wanted to see. "Ben must be furious," Gavriel said, keeping his eyes on Henry and his tone level.

Henry crossed his arms and planted his feet. Why did Gavriel feel now was the time to discuss Ben? It was annoying being toyed with while Molly was on the other side of the door Gavriel propped himself up against. "Probably," Henry said in as rational a tone as he could.

"Perhaps this can wait," Max said to Henry's relief. "There is more important business to intend to." He slanted his head toward the door separating them from Molly.

"You really want to help her?" Gavriel said, twirling the key in his hand and his focus now on Max. He sounded like he didn't believe it was possible that one of the guards would help a criminal slated for execution.

Henry himself wouldn't have believed it if he was still a guard. He'd never been approached by ones like Max with Rebel Cause sympathies, probably because of his relationship to Ben.

"I promised Jack I would, and I intend to keep my word," Max said, his voice and stance exerting his authority.

"Alright," Gavriel turned and unlocked the door.

Henry followed Gavriel and Max inside. Across the room, standing and gazing out the window, was Molly. All he wanted to do was take her from this place they'd mutually agreed to come to, but he forced himself to stay put. "Molly," he said. He wasn't sure she heard him; he hadn't spoken loudly. She must've as she turned from the window, her eyes damp, and sprinted to him.

"This isn't a dream, is it?" she asked.

"No," he said, wrapping his arms around her for what he hoped wasn't the final time. "It's not a dream."

Chapter 34

Gav and I left Malcolm when we exited the staircase and returned to my cell. Malcolm kept climbing, heading to Henry. Being alone with Gav was the last thing I wanted.

"I'm sorry, Mol," he said when we reached my door and he unlocked it. "I'm going to fix this."

I hung my head and delayed entering the room. "Gav, I told you—"

"I'll protect Henry too. You shouldn't have to suffer losing him like I lost you."

This was a change in attitude I hadn't expected. Yet, deep inside, I had always known it was possible to get through to him. Gav had been hurt, had felt betrayed and had heard lies, which made him go against us. Now, though I remained unsure how much I could trust him, I was glad he was becoming more like his old self.

"I'm holding you to that," I said as I stepped inside my cell. There was no point in dallying in the hallway. I had nowhere to run or escape to. I shut the door before Gav could reply. Solace was what my mind craved since I couldn't have Henry.

...

The next day, in the late afternoon, there was a knock on my door and the sound of a key unlocking it. I assumed it was Gav, but Malcolm opened the door and stepped inside, carrying a tray of food.

"I gave Henry your message with the other news."

"Thank you," I said as I accepted the tray. It meant a lot to have someone I could trust without fear. "You'll take care of Henry afterwards, won't you?"

Malcolm sighed. "He's my son, and I'll help him however I can. As I intend to help you to prevent the worst."

"I want to be prepared," I said as I picked the peanut butter sandwich off the tray and ate a bite. More than anything, I wanted to survive and feared the worst. It didn't help that I couldn't see a clear way out of what was coming

"There are people who will help you, so don't worry too much. You don't want to show fear," Malcolm said.

"I'll try," I said as I ate another bite and guzzled the small cup of orange juice.

"Good," Malcolm said, taking the tray and empty cup. "I'll leave you to your preparations. Try and rest."

He left me alone. I didn't sleep, just lay in bed running through the coming events my mind. In the morning, I stretched my muscles and sat on the bed. There was an indefinite amount of time to kill before someone fetched me. No one had told me when my execution was. As sleepless as my night had been, I wasn't tired. Knowing their demise was imminent would do that to anyone.

...

It was Ben who came when the sun reached its peak in the sky. I'd expected Gav walk into the room when the door unlocked, and Ben's ink black hair caught me off guard.

I stood as he shut the door and leaned against it. "What are you doing here, Ben?" Why wasn't he somewhere scheming or watching Henry?

He smirked. "So distrustful. I come to offer help, and you can't even be polite."

Help? He couldn't be serious. I crossed my arms. "What are you talking about? You'd never help me."

He laughed, and it almost sounded natural. "You're not the person who wronged me. I have no animosity toward you."

That was true in its own way. All his rage was directed at Henry. Still. What help could Ben give that I'd want? "You think because I'm locked in here, I'll join your side?"

"I know you had a motive for coming here. You and I are alike. There's no way you'd give up when you had relative freedom. And I know you can't really support the Rebel Cause. You're a sacrificial figurehead to them. Surely you see that."

"You think I'm like you?" There was no worse comparison. It warranted more attention than him calling me a figurehead.

"Yes," he said with an eye roll and impatient tone that implied I was missing the obvious. "We both had things taken from us and are willing to do whatever is necessary to achieve our goals. This time, I believe our goals can align."

"What are you proposing?" My curiosity made me want to hear what he was offering.

"The Leader thinks Henry is useful. And he might be, to the Government. Not to me."

I shoved down my anger. It was no secret that Ben hated Henry. "What does that have to do with me?"

He stared at me like I was foolish for not understanding. "You want the Leader dead, and I want their job."

Ben as Leader would be worse for the City than Carl Wessin. Voicing that opinion would not go well. "Why not just get out of my way then?"

Ben laughed again, like I'd made the funniest joke in the world. "You'll be executed, and the Government will give the Leader's job to someone else. I'm not on the list. With your help, I can seize it. The people will follow me if their beloved Liberator is my wife. It would be a marriage for show. I won't expect anything intimate."

Hearing those words from Ben's mouth made me feel sick. How could he think I would ever agree to that? "No deal. I'd rather die than marry you."

Ben stood straight and lifted his shoulders in a casual shrug. "You've always been reasonable. And we've already helped each other."

"What are you talking about?" I had never done anything for Ben. There hadn't been reason to.

"I know you don't love Gavriel. I got you out of marrying him, and you gave me an excuse to end my Courtship with Henry. This can be mutually beneficial too."

There was nothing I wanted to do less than marry Ben. It would last as long as he benefitted from me, and there would be no stopping him from killing me after. The marriage itself would be torture, even if just an act. And I'd already assumed he was behind mine and Gav's Courtship denial, though I didn't view that as helpful. "I didn't help you on purpose before, and I definitely won't now."

He turned the doorknob and opened the door, giving me a smirk. "You value your life more than that. My offer stands. Tell Gavriel to fetch me when you change your mind." He stepped out and locked me in before getting an answer.

I spent the next three days hardening my resolve that I didn't need Ben's deal. What kind of life would I have without Henry? If Ben didn't kill me, my own shame and grief would. Even if Ben spared Henry's life, to be stuck with Ben would be agony.

When a week since Henry's and my return to the tower had passed, the wall screen flicked on. I hadn't expected it to work and, at first, it didn't draw my attention. Most times the screen turned on for a news cast or Government propaganda. Neither of those things held my interest. Then, a familiar voice played through the speaker.

"People of the City," Valerie said. "You've been lied to."

She and Jax sat side by side on a couch I recognized from my dad's house. The stream only showed their torsos, not the pile of books that had to be nearby. It also didn't display the surrounding room.

"We have proof of atrocious acts carried out and ordered by the Government," Jax said. He bent forward and ducked his head. When he straightened back up, he held an open book to the screen and recited its contents.

I already knew them as I'd poured through the books in detail. Still, it was harrowing hearing the information read aloud. Jax and Valerie alternated in delivering the bits of information, one reciting while the other picked up the next source.

Gav, if he was watching, must've been devasted when Jax announced the sale of children from the Foster Centre to their new families. Jax had opened with that piece of evidence, being the one who hadn't lived within its walls. It would've been too personal and painful for Valerie.

She delivered the next bit of evidence. This one she'd found when we'd gone through the books in the Moris' apartment. "I'm sure many of you know someone who went to the End Camp. What you weren't told is that residents are fed meals laced with poison."

"The Government also executes prisoners, usually, but not always, those with long sentences," Jax said, holding up the next book. "Some are poisoned, others shot, and some beaten to death."

"Murdering citizens isn't the solution to crowding and overpopulation," Valerie said. "The Government should, and can, do better."

"The Government cares about nothing except their own power, wealth and control," Jax said. He and Valerie both had circles under their eyes from exhaustion, though there was a spark of fury in both of their gazes. This was a challenge for them, streaming when they usually would sleep. I was grateful for them and their show of support despite the physical distance between us.

"To help, you can—"

The stream cut out halfway through Valerie's sentence, and the screen turned off. The Government had heard enough, and I imagined they were furious.

I sighed and got to my feet. After pacing the length of the floor, drinking from the sink and trying to smooth my hair, I went to the window. The ocean hit the tower's side in crashing waves, fueled by a strong wind I heard once I jimmied open the window. No one had bothered to install bars on it or lock it. The jump to the ocean would kill anyone that tried that escape route.

I had doubts about it being opened in recent times though as my arms were sore by the time I slid it open wide enough to fit my hand through. The air was cool on my fingers, so I thrust my other hand in the gap. It didn't take long for the windowsill digging into my wrists to hurt. I removed my hands, closed the window and drank in the view. There was something soothing about watching the waves, even with my memories of the previous Leader plunging into the depths.

The sound of the lock disengaging shook me from the tranquil place the water had brought me too. *Ben is back already.* I didn't want to deal with him now, not when I'd found a measure of peace. What made me turn around was the sound of my name spoken by a voice I'd yearned to hear, though we'd parted just a week prior.

Henry. "This isn't a dream, is it?"

"No, it's not a dream." He smiled as he wrapped me in his arms and held my body against his.

I never wanted to leave his embrace. "What are you doing here?"

"Your ex told me to bring him," Max said. I hadn't noticed him in the room as distracted as I was over Henry. And Gav was there too; he'd been the one to unlock the door.

I disentangled myself from Henry's arms and turned to Gav. He and Henry had been at odds last time I spoke to Gav. What had changed? "Why?"

Gav was leaning against the wall by the door, his arms crossed over his chest. "Because I have something to say, and you both should hear it."

"Then say it," Henry said.

Gav closed his eyes and ducked his head. His shoulders moved up and down as he sucked in a deep breath and exhaled. He opened his eyes and rested them on Henry. "I'm sorry. I should've trusted that you two didn't hook up to spite me."

Henry tensed. "Yes, you should've."

I'd never seen Henry act that cold toward Gav, but I understood why he did. I wasn't sure either how much I could trust him. Yet, we had little choice. "Great. Now that you've come to that realization, what next?"

Gav sighed. "I'll help however I can. I won't let you die, Mol. Or Henry."

"You'll help by staying here," Max said. "You need to escort Molly to the execution tomorrow."

Tomorrow. The Government had set a date. Ben must've given up on me accepting his deal. *Good.*

Gav frowned. "That's not—"

"Running away isn't the answer." It hadn't been successful the first time. "It would only end with both of our executions."

"You have to," Henry said. "The Leader needs to think you're still following orders."

Gav groaned. "Fine."

Max nodded at Gav and then swiveled his head to Henry. "You're coming with me, and we need to leave now."

Henry gave my hand a quick squeeze and followed Max to the door. That's when I remembered they couldn't leave yet. "Wait!" I called. "Max, you have to get a message to Sage."

Max froze near the door and spun on his heel.

"The deadline she gave me is today," I said. "She'll go to the Colony if you don't. Please. Just tell her everything will be over tomorrow. I've taken care of it."

"I'll find her," Max said as he ushered Henry out.

...

Gav left with the promise of procuring food. If I'd believed I was going to face my demise, I would've refused it. But that was a fate I didn't intend to meet. When he returned, we ate the sandwiches and apples, sitting side by side on the bed. It was almost like the old days at school when we shared a cafeteria table. Except everything had changed since then.

"Are you scared, Mol?" Gav asked once he'd swallowed the last bite of his meal.

"Yes." How could I not be? This was the biggest threat I'd ever faced, and it could mean never seeing Henry or my dad again.

"What about the last time you were here? Were you scared then?"

Leave it to Gav to fixate on this line of questions. His motives didn't matter; I would appease him. "Not as much."

"You need to be brave." He adjusted his position to face me, and he clasped my hands. I could almost remember the feeling of letting myself be comforted by him. I wasn't that girl anymore though, and Gav's touch no longer stirred anything in me. Maybe it never had.

"And you need to act," I said. "Are you up to it?"

"I've had practice," he said with a pause. "There's something you should know. The reason why it's hard for me to go against the Leader."

"He's your foster dad," I said, saving him the admission. His eyes widened, and his lips formed a circle. "I already know."

"Max told you?" Gav asked, his brows wrinkled together.

"No. Valerie did."

"Henry's sister? How?"

"Someone from the Rebel Cause told her." I couldn't put Malcolm in danger by naming him, especially without his consent or being certain I could trust Gav.

Gav sighed. "So, you understand why this is difficult? He's the only family I remember having."

"He also had you kidnapped."

"Your mom would've done the same if she'd had the means."

I bristled. Bringing my mom into this was low. "That's not fair."

"I just mean he did what he thought was best as my father."

"This is the man who insulted you in front of me and your best friend, and who put out arrest warrants on us. Beyond that, he's in charge of the City, and the current reason why things are as bad as they are." If that didn't motivate him to go against a man he wasn't related to, who bought him from the Foster Centre, nothing would.

Gav shook his head. "I know. But if this ends badly, I won't have a home."

Gav had become selfish. He'd been here, in the Leader's tower, being fed propaganda and brainwashed while Henry and I had trained, fought, and survived. "Join the club. Just know, this was never about you."

Chapter 35

Gav put his support behind me. To him it was all about saving me, and Henry by extension. He didn't care about the public. Why should he when he'd grown up rich and privileged? Gav had never made it to the Colony and couldn't relate to the hardships and suffering that had driven people to desperation and propelled them to flee their homes. I let him ease his conscience by deciding to help me. It aided my plan if he didn't back out. It would also help him move on from being a Government puppet.

The next morning, when my door opened, I rose from the bed expecting Gav and frowned at the sight of Ben stepping inside. His skin was marked with bruises where Henry had tackled him to the floor. His blue eyes were like ice when they landed on me. "Last chance to accept my offer. There's still time to stop your execution."

"My answer is still no." Being executed was still more appealing than being Ben's wife. At least it would be a shorter torture and had a clear ending.

He scowled, his icy eyes darkening with his fury. I didn't flinch. There was nothing he could do to me that would be worse than what was coming.

"I'd say you'll regret that decision, but you won't live that long." He exited my cell and slammed the door. I heard his angry footsteps as he stomped away.

...

It was another hour before Gav fetched me. I followed him, not sad to leave my cell. One week had been long enough. It was past time to end things. We traversed down to the large room where the battle had taken place. Through the door, the blood stains on the tile floor were still visible, a large filming camera on a tripod was set up near the exit, and uniformed guards lined the walls.

As I stepped into the room, Malcolm swooped in on me, placed a hand on my arm and steered me to the side. "Say what the people need to hear. And when it's time, give the signal."

"What signal?" I didn't understand. Was I supposed to cue my own death? Why would I do that?

"Brush your fingers across your forehead. They'll see it."

"Who will?" I asked, but he'd already taken his hand from my arm and walked away.

"What did Malcolm want?" Gav asked, approaching me from behind.

"He told me to tell the people what they need to hear." I still didn't understand what Malcolm's message meant.

"Gavriel," Carl Wessin said in his robotic voice. "I see you've brought Miss Birch on time." He was walking out of the elevator now, followed by the Inner Circle members, minus Malcolm of course.

"As promised," Gav said. He'd spent the hours after our meal playing at being a loyal Government follower. They didn't suspect otherwise.

"Malcolm," Carl Wessin said, switching his attention away from Gav and me. "Are the guards prepared?"

"Yes," Malcolm said, shooting me a brief glance I couldn't decipher. "I told them what to do."

"Excellent," Carl Wessin said. "Gavriel, get Miss Birch into position."

"This way," Gav said, his voice low and in my ear. He gripped my arm and directed me forward.

As I approached the camera, the set up came became clearer. There was a metal backdrop, which only reached my chest in height, across from the camera with a red cloth draped over it that extended along the floor to the front. There was a sole, square, red cushion atop the cloth on the floor.

"Kneel on it," Gav said, pointing to the pillow.

I lowered my knees onto the cushion. Though it would've been worse without the cushion, this was meant to humiliate me. I would be a disgraced criminal in the eyes of the public. And everyone would watch. That's what happened when the City's screens turned on.

The camera's red light blinked on; its lens focused on me. A spotlight shone above my head, casting the surroundings into shadow. The playback screen showed a glimpse of me, small and dejected. This wasn't the girl who led the Rebel Cause. What had happened to her? Why was my face, on that screen, dejected and defeated?

I lifted my chin and set my jaw. This wasn't the time to give up. Gavriel had backed away when the camera turned on, and I didn't allow search for him. My eyes zeroed in on the small, red light. There was nothing else.

"Miss Birch," Carl Wessin's robotic voice boomed over the room. I couldn't pinpoint its direction. On the playback screen, his words appeared in written form. *Leave it to the Government to conceal their identity even now.* "Let us begin with a pressing question. Henry Connor disappeared yesterday. Where did he go?"

I clung to the hope that Henry was somewhere far from here and safe. As to his whereabouts? I hadn't a clue. "I don't know."

"Perhaps some pressure will bring out the truth." This time I heard Humphrey Walston's voice, though again the words appeared as text on the screen.

The playback screen showed a uniformed guard approaching me from the right. He was holding a thick baton that would hurt to be hit with. Then he pressed a button, and the baton crackled with electricity and a blue spark. My body tensed, and I squeezed my eyes shut as the baton touched my arm and current surged through my body. I yelped and toppled forward, landing on my hands on the cloth.

"I guarded her cell the entire time," Gav said, his voice projecting authority he usually didn't possess as he stepped between me and the guard. "She never saw him." If Gav's lie wasn't a sign he was on my side, nothing was.

The guard carrying the electric baton withdrew, called off by a signal I couldn't see. With strength returning to me, and the pain in my arm abating, I adjusted my position to kneel on the cushion again.

"A more pertinent question then," Bob Henson said, the words still appearing on the screen as text. "Who orchestrated the attack on our City's Government?"

For a split second the playback screen showed my terrified face. Hopefully, my lapse in self-control was brief enough that no one guessed at the secret I kept. They likely thought I feared the stun baton. "I did," I lied. They wouldn't get the truth from me, not that Valerie and my dad had been more instrumental in planning the attack. Some people were worth protecting more than myself.

"That's difficult to believe," Annette scoffed. "How did you convince a group of runways to follow you?"

It was time for a hint of the truth. Too many lies and they would get suspicious. "The Rebel Cause was alive before I heard about it. I just provided the final piece."

"Only a joke of a movement has a sixteen-year-old child as leader. No wonder it failed, and you've given up," Carli said.

"Yet Rebel Cause supporters are running amok and destroying our City," Scarlet said. "Surely Miss Birch's demise will stop them."

"They won't stop unless Molly calls them off," Malcolm said.

The Inner Circle members quieted, and I squirmed under the weight of countless sets of eyes. Beads of sweat accumulating at my hairline went unwiped. Malcolm hadn't explained what the signal would indicate, or to who. I wasn't going to use it now. Not when it could summon my end.

"Miss Birch," Carl Wessin's voice bellowed, the effect lost on the public reading his words. But it made me flinch, which was a result the Government would accept. "You have lost. In defeat, you must call off the rioters."

Tell the people what they need to hear.

"Citizens, thank you for your support. The time for riots is over. Please, put down your weapons and go home. No one else should get in trouble because of me." My image on the screen wasn't of a defeated girl. Even on my knees, there was determination across my face. "This is my battle, not yours." If these people had ever listened to me, they had better not stop now. Rioting in the streets and damaging property had never been the answer.

"Listen to Miss Birch," Carl Wessin said. "If the riots continue, each participant will be arrested on the spot."

Please let this work. No one else can be harmed in my name.

"Now, Miss Birch," Carl Wessin said. "Do you have any final words?"

This was it. What I dreaded most had arrived, and there was no one and nothing that could save me. Had everything been worth it? Nothing substantial had changed for the better; the general population was as suppressed as ever, if not more so. Yet, if I could've gone back and done it over, I would have done the same. That had to mean it was worthwhile. If my actions motivated someone else to make lasting change, I could be satisfied.

"Henry," I said to the camera, my voice clear and strong despite the tears threatening to flow from my eyes. "If you're hearing this, forgive me. I love you, and I hope you can be happy." Wherever he was, he had to be safe. I needed to believe that in my last moments.

"A very sweet sentiment," Carl Wessin said in what was meant to be a sarcastic tone. Through the voice box, it was thunderous and creepy. "And now it's time to finish things."

I gulped down the lump in my throat. This wasn't the time to show fear. If I could achieve nothing else, I could face this with courage. Getting to my feet was an appealing prospect; no one wanted to die on their knees, but the camera was framed to fit my kneeling form. If I stood, my upper half wouldn't be in the picture.

"People of the City," Carl Wessin said. "Molly Birch is guilty of treason, attempted overthrow of our Government, breaking and entering a Government building and instigating a rebellion. The punishment for these crimes is execution by gunshot, which will be carried out forthwith."

If there had ever been a time for the signal Malcolm provided me, this was it. With no knowledge of what it signified, I wiped my fingers across my forehead. Nothing happened. As I knelt, refusing to hang my head, a lone guard stalked toward me with a slow and measured pace. *My executioner.*

He dallied, drawing this out to increase my torture. In his right hand, he held a gun: the weapon he'd aim at me when he got close enough to kill. I put my eyes on him and tried to read his name badge. It was too small and far away, not that it mattered. The guards who'd sworn loyalty to me were all unnamed to me, except for Max, and he was somewhere else with Henry.

Whoever the guard stalking toward me was must've been loyal to the Government. I scanned his uniform, searching for weak points as Henry had taught me. If he came close enough, it might be possible to land a strike. Then I wouldn't go without a fight. The last image the public saw of me wouldn't be a kneeling girl dying without resisting.

The guard anticipated my intentions. He stopped metres away, past the edge of my reach. The most foolish thing possible would be to throw myself at him. I'd be dead well before I made contact. Fuming, I scowled as he planted his feet. With practiced ease, he raised his arm, straight as a line, and aimed the gun. He squeezed the trigger; I closed my eyes, and the gun went off.

Chapter 36

Henry

Max hurried down to the lobby leading to the tower's main section. Henry sped after him, his feet flying over the stairs. When they got to the bottom of the staircase, Max held up a hand for Henry to wait and stuck his head out the door to the battle room. He waved Henry forward. "We have to be quick, so no one sees us."

"Are you going to tell me where we're going?" Henry asked as he followed Max to the exit.

"To find Sage." They were in the entry now with only the large metal door separating them from outside. Max turned left, opened a door that blended seamlessly into the wall and ducked into the small closet on the other side. "Get in here."

Henry inhaled a deep breath and stepped in after Max. It was full of guards' gear. Just what he wanted to see again. Max thrust a uniform at Henry and pulled on his own. Henry stared at the uniform pieces. When he'd dumped his at Malcolm's abandoned house, he never thought he'd wear one again.

"Don't stand there gawking at it," Max said as he pulled on his gloves. "Put it on already."

Henry hesitated. This was a part of his past he didn't want to revisit.

"If we walk out of here with you dressed like that," Max said, sweeping a gloved hand over Henry. "You'll end up on the execution list too."

Henry caved and pulled the pieces on. It wasn't a bad fit considering this was a random set Max had thrown at him. The boots were on the small side, but he could deal with squished toes for the short term.

Max threw their shoes into the back of a wardrobe and slid his helmet over his head. Henry did the same. It was strange viewing the world through a one-way window again.

"Let's go," Max said. "If we run into someone hostile, I'll do the talking."

Henry nodded, his heavy helmet bobbing down and up. The eye screen had one benefit of lessening the sun's glare as they stepped outside and fetched Max's van. He was glad no one approached them, though it was eerie being the only two people in sight. And it had been the same on his first arrival to the tower, only him and his traveling companions exposed and treading across the grainy, shifting ground. Guard boots at least had good traction.

Maybe there were hidden guards with their eyes on Henry and Max. He didn't let his mind go down that path. And he didn't tear himself apart over how cowardly it was to flee while Molly was in danger.

Henry removed his helmet when Max drove the van down the forest road. It was always better to view the world with his own eyes, not filtered through a thick lens. "How do you know Sage?" he asked Max as they drove through the trees.

Max sighed, his grip tight on the steering wheel. "We grew up together. Our parents are friends and wanted us to get a Courtship."

Henry couldn't imagine Max and Sage married. They were wildly different, but there was a familiarity between them. "You didn't?"

"She joined the Devout, and I joined the Guard Corps and later the Rebel Cause. We have different goals and don't love each other. We never applied for the Courtship. Luckily she was still too young when we decided against it."

Henry wished he'd seen the truth about Ben before he'd agreed to their Courtship. At least he'd gotten out of it. Sensing Max didn't want to give more details, Henry asked a different question. "Where is she?"

"Hopefully in the same place as last time," Max said.

"Which is?" Henry was growing frustrated. The older guard insisted on ditching him with the girl he'd almost married and wouldn't even say where that was.

"The Devout headquarters, in Apartment District 1."

"Great." Max was dumping him in rich person territory.

"She better cooperate and agree to come," Max said.

Apparently, Max meant to drop off Henry and go back with Sage. Henry wasn't thrilled. There was nothing he could do though since they were on route to the Devout headquarters, and he wasn't about to throw a tantrum over being dumped there. He should've been grateful for the safety, yet he only felt annoyed that he couldn't help Molly and guilt-ridden because of it.

…

Apartment District 1 was opulent. The buildings shined like someone polished their exteriors on a regular basis. There wasn't a single piece of dirt or litter on the streets that had potted trees at even intervals along the sides. He'd missed all this in the dark when he'd followed Valerie through the City. More pressing matters had occupied his mind then as well as during their retreat to the Moris'. And on the drive with Malcolm, he hadn't been interested in sightseeing.

Max stopped the van at the edge of a large lot and removed his helmet. The open space was mostly asphalt, like a parking lot with no lines, and had a concrete path running down the middle toward a wide, squat building that was out of place amidst the surrounding high-rises. He was halfway down the path before Henry stopped staring. Henry jogged to catch up, his too-small boots digging into his feet. He'd have blisters later, which wasn't a high priority currently.

Max veered to a door in the centre of the building's front. He pushed it and walked inside with practised ease. *He's been here before,* Henry thought as he rushed through before the door closed on his face.

"Max Alexander." A familiar young man, in his late teens, reclined on a grey couch set against the white wall opposite the door. His arm rested on the couch's back, and he had one knee bent to prop up his foot on the matching cushions. He wasn't the only person in the room. People lounged and stood, filling the vast space. "Why are you here?"

"And with a wanted criminal, no less," piped up the also-familiar girl sitting next to him.

"Peter, Evelyn" Max said, nodding his head to each of them in turn and avoiding answering Peter's question. "Where is Sage Parker? Molly Birch sent me with a message."

Peter sat leaned forward with his elbows on his knees. "The Little Sapling? Interesting. Sage said there was a guard tagging around. You can find her upstairs. *He,*" he said, pointing his thumb at Henry. "Stays here."

Max shot Henry a quick glance. "Stay put," he ordered before sprinting to the staircase at the left side of the room.

If Henry was going to be stuck here, he might as well move from the door. He felt like a specimen being studied as he walked forward on the black lacquer floor.

Peter eyed Henry, with one eyebrow arched and amusement written on his face. "You didn't want to go hunt down Sage with Max Alexander, did you? I thought I was doing you a favour."

"I only want to help my wife," Henry blurted before it hit him that he probably shouldn't announce his relationship to the room. There was no reversing it now.

Evelyn sat up straight and stared wide-eyed at Henry. "Your wife? It was your wedding we crashed, wasn't it?"

"Yup." Henry decided halfway to these two was enough and leaned against the nearest support column holding up the ceiling of the enormous space. He guessed the entire ground floor of the building was this one room. He didn't see any doors, only the staircase Max had run up. As Henry settled against the column, his phone vibrated in his pocket. He fished it out, which was a difficult task when the guard uniform blocked his own clothes, thinking it was Malcolm. It wasn't.

'We're coming.' Those two words were all his sister wrote. *Coming for what? To rescue him?* Knowing Valerie, she'd try. Ever since they'd reunited, she'd acted like his personal protector. It was strange, though it might've felt natural if they'd grown up together.

'Help Molly,' he sent back. **'I don't need it.'** He shoved the phone back in his pocket. His head wasn't in the right place to argue with his sister.

Max walked down the stairs with Sage behind him. Henry expected them to exit the building, but they turned deeper into the giant room.

Sage climbed atop a stool, cupped her hands around her mouth and shouted. "Listen up!"

All the lounging people quieted and focused on her. It was reminiscent of Molly's speeches in the Market, though Sage had more impatience and less charisma to her tone.

"Sitting here while the Little Sapling is in trouble because we told her to fix things makes us cowards."

"She caused this trouble and ruined our business," a man in the crowd said with a dismissive wave. "Let her clean it up."

How could he say such a thing? A rare spark of rage ignited in Henry. He moved away from the column to pounce at the man, but Max gripped his jacket and held him back. That didn't quash Henry's anger.

"She can't fix it alone," Sage said. "Nor should we expect her to! It's time we picked a side. I, for one, don't want to be at the Government's mercy."

An older woman stepped from the crowd and faced Sage. "You forget," she said, her voice wise with age though it lacked volume. "Without the Government, the Devout wouldn't exist. Before the Little Sapling's interference, they let us conduct business for a reasonable cut. We cannot choose the side that will bring our ruin."

"The Government is expediting our ruin!" Sage screeched. "They stopped our deal with the Colony. How much longer until they shut down all our operations? They'd rather have all the money than a cut of ours."

Henry could only see Sage from behind. Her entire slim frame shook with rage. This was a change from how she'd been when delivering her messages.

It made him wonder what Max had said.

"Sage is right," Peter said as he stood and walked over to her with Evelyn in his shadow. "It's time we tried to save ourselves, not rely on someone else to do it for us."

The room broke out into arguments then with everyone talking over each other. The din hurt Henry's ears. How was he supposed to survive staying here?

"Enough!" Max shouted. He dropped Henry's jacket and walked to the side of Sage's stool. "Argue later! I've delivered my message, and I'm leaving to recoup before tomorrow. If any of you," he paused to shoot Sage a look, "Want to help, come outside." With his short speech delivered, he walked back to Henry, regripped his jacket and ushered Henry out the door.

"Wait," Henry said as his feet synched with Max's pace. "You aren't leaving me here?"

Max laughed. "If only things were that easy."

Henry shoved Max's hand off his jacket. "What does that mean?"

"We need your help. I can't leave you here, even if it kept you safe and Molly happy. And before you ask," he said. "You had to come. Leaving you in the tower would've added your name to the execution list."

Sage came outside as Max spoke, followed by Peter and Evelyn. Henry also heard footsteps coming from the road, which made the hair on the back of his neck stand up. At least whoever it was, only two people based on the sound, didn't outnumber them.

"Great," Max said, his eyes on road. "Did you know they were here?"

Henry squinted and saw two familiar figures: Valerie and Jax. How did they find him? He jogged over to his sister. "Val, I told you to help Molly."

"We intend to," Jax said.

"Jax tracked your phone's location," Valerie explained before Henry could ask his next question.

Of course.

"Don't tell me you aren't going to help your wife," Valerie said, her eyes boring into him.

"I want to." More than anything else, he wanted Molly to be safe.

"Then let us come," Valerie said, her voice softening as she rested a hand on Henry's arm. "We'll be stronger together, you know that."

He couldn't send them away. And his sister had a point. So, he led them to Max and the others, and they all rode to Max's small, one-room apartment. When they got there, the sun was on its way down, and Henry was happy to gobble his portion of the meagre meal of rice and beans that Max threw together. He drained the cup of water he'd procured from the tap, stripped off his guard uniform and joined his sister and the others preparing to sleep on the floor.

With his head propped on his jacket, he turned his neck to gaze at his sister. "I don't know what to do without Molly." How could he live in a world without her? She was his strength and his model for courage and kindness.

"Don't talk like that," she said as she rested her hand on his arm. "Molly will survive. It's what she's always done. But, *if* she doesn't, you'll have me. Family is supposed to stick together."

Family. That reminded him of his mom's picture he'd hidden. He pulled out his phone and removed the back and the picture. He slipped his arm from under her hand as he sat up. With the picture face down on his palm, he slid it to Valerie.

She flipped it over, her eyes misting as she sat up and shielded the picture with her other hand. Even without a warning, she knew how dangerous the picture was. "Where did you get this?"

"Scarlet Everbee brought Dad to my cell and told me about Mom. He gave me the picture after she left."

Valerie closed her eyes and stroked the picture with her thumb. Henry wasn't used to seeing her on the verge of tears and could tell she was using every bit of her willpower not to weep. She turned the picture back over and passed it to Henry.

He re-hid it in the phone. There was too much risk in keeping it in the open.

"Henry?" Valerie asked and waited until he looked at her. "Thanks for showing me that. No matter what happens tomorrow, we'll stick together. That's what Mom would want."

"Of course, Val." Henry lay down and rolled over. He was grateful to have her, but she wasn't a substitute for Molly. In the morning, he swore to himself, he'd find a way to save her.

When the sun rose, Max threw apples and barely toasted bread at the group and herded them to the van. Once everyone was buckled in, he drove back to the tower. Henry had put the guard uniform on helmet on again at Max's insistence. Sleeping on the floor had formed knots in his muscles and donning the sturdy uniform did little to help. Molly had to have slept better than him, if she'd been able to at all.

When the van reached the coast, Sage, Peter and Evelyn vanished into the tree line with Valerie. Jax stuck near Max and Henry as they trod inside the tower. Once in the door, Max ushed Jax into the guard uniform closet.

When Jax re-emerged wearing a uniform, Malcolm came over. "Henry, I have something for you," he said, extending his hand to the group, there was no way to distinguish which person was Henry as the name tag on his borrowed uniform didn't identify him.

Henry lifted the gun from his father's grasp. He'd learned how to use one in training, but he'd never fired one since as he'd largely been on Gate duty as most new recruits were.

"I hope your aim is good, Son, and that you won't lose your nerve."

"If you're asking me to shoot Molly, I can't." He'd made a grave misjudgment of his father if it was true.

"No," Malcolm said with shake of his head. "The bullet isn't for her. You'll only get one shot, so make it count. She'll give the signal."

Henry nodded as his father described what he needed to do when Molly brushed her forehead. It was immense pressure, which was only fair after what Molly had gone through. He stood across from the backdrop at his father's instructions. Could he really kill someone? He thought so if it meant saving Molly.

Malcolm had stocked the room with guards who'd sworn loyalty to her. Henry was between Max and Jax, who was beside the door, lowering the chances of someone noticing he wasn't meant to be there.

He saw Molly enter and Malcolm talk to her. Her face displayed her determination when he'd expected fear. Anyone else would've been terrified, but she was brave, even more than any guard he'd known.

Henry watched as she endured and answered the Inner Circle's questions and the stun cane tap on her arm. He cringed as she toppled forward, and Gav swooped to her defense. His former best friend's lie and show of loyalty to

Molly came far too late for Henry's liking.

Henry shattered when she spoke her final words at Carl Wessin's command. "Henry," she said, unshed tears filling her eyes. "If you're hearing this, forgive me. I love you, and I hope you can be happy." He wanted to run to her then and forced himself to wait. It wasn't time, and acting early would ruin everything.

She gave the signal when Carl Wessin declared her death sentence. Henry summoned his courage and moved to her. He went slow, trying to suss out the best target. Another advantage of the guard helmet was that no one could tell he was surveying the room if he didn't turn his head. Directly behind Molly stood Carl Wessin. That was the easier shot and the best target. Yet, beside the Leader was Ben, whom someone had freed from Henry's cell, with hatred in his eyes and bruises covering his body. When Henry got to a couple metres from Molly, who scowled at him, he made his decision. He got in his shooting stance, pointed the gun and pulled the trigger.

Chapter 37

For the second time, my life was spared from a gun shot meant to kill me. This time I heard the bullet hit its target. A robotic voice grunted as it made contact, and a body thudded to the floor. *Something didn't go according to the Government's plan.* The last thing I wanted was to stay on my knees while the room dissolved into mayhem. As hard as I tried, I couldn't make myself move.

The guard holding the gun dove toward me, and I flung my arms up to fend him off. He dodged and pinned my arms down as a female Inner Circle member screamed. This couldn't be my end, pinned down and broken by a guard.

"Molly, you need to focus."

I raked my eyes over the guard, analyzing his crouching form. "Henry?" It couldn't be him. This had to be my mind playing a trick. Maybe the bullet had hit me, and I was hallucinating.

He nodded. "Max and I went to fetch help. You need to take charge; all the guards in here are loyal to you, and they need your orders."

With a nod, I let him pull me upright. Once I was on my feet, Henry vanished, and the scene hit me. Someone had tilted the camera up and zoomed it out to show more of the room, including Carl Wessin's dead body that lay in a pool of blood. It was one more stain added to the dried ones dotting the room.

"You!" Scarlet Everbee seethed. "This is your doing!" She tried to pounce on me, but one of the guards restrained her.

"Some things need doing personally," Ben said. He strode toward me, taking the direct path through the puddle of blood like he didn't have a care in the world or notice it splashing on his pants. He was holding a stun baton.

"Very true," I said, matching his nonchalant tone. "I'm sure Henry would love to deal with you personally."

Ben rolled his ice blue eyes. "He's always been weak and ungrateful. Maybe his execution will work the first time."

"We'll have a double execution," Bob Henson said, coming up behind me. "After you tell us where Henry is."

The other Inner Circle members, including Scarlet, who had broken free of the guard's grasp, circled me on all sides. Malcolm only hesitated a step behind the rest. Over Carli's shoulder I saw the camera swivel to capture the scene.

If they wanted a show, I would provide one. "I don't see why I'd do that, considering I'm not the one at a disadvantage."

"Nonsense," Annette said with a flick of her hand. "We should end her and be done with it."

"As appealing as that is," Humphrey Walston said. "How do you suggest we accomplish it? Are you willing to kill her with your bare hands?"

I tuned out the Inner Circle and Ben as they bickered. Malcolm kept silent, his focus on me. The intensity of his gaze was unsettling. Why was he staring at me? I closed my eyes. The bickering faded to the background as I focused.

"That's enough!" My shout ceased the arguing as the Inner Circle members stared in various states of shock. "You have no power anymore. Guards! If you meant what you pledged to me, arrest them!" The guards moved from the room's perimeter in unison at my request and closed in on the Inner Circle members. *I'll be crushed in the middle if things continue this way.*

Malcolm retreated into the wave of incoming guards, who let him through. His departure gave me an opening, and I ran for it. The remaining Inner Circle members and Ben inched closer together until they formed a tight knot. I'd just squeezed through the gap left by Malcom when they bumped into each other, a wall of guards surrounding them, stun batons and guns drawn. I tuned ignored their shouts as the guards formed a solid perimeter. None of the Inner Circle were strong enough to fight their way out.

Seeing Gav standing over Carl Wessin's body with a frown on his face, and his hands clenched into fists stopped me mid run. He angled his face in my direction. "I'm an orphan all over again," he said with a hollow voice. "He was the only family I can remember having. Did you order this?"

I shouldn't have been shocked that he'd blame me. What else was he to think? Still, I didn't want to take credit. Even now, hearing his flat and emotionless words, I yearned to help him. "Really, Gav? When do you think I had time or opportunity to do that?"

"Before you came here," he said. "I knew you had a reason."

There was no denial to that I could give. I had come with the goal of toppling the Government. Killing Carl Wessin hadn't been a direct order from me, yet it went toward accomplishing what I set out to do.

"He wasn't the best person," Gav said. "I know that. It's just, I thought I'd always be connected to someone, whether you or him. Now I have no one."

"I didn't order anyone to kill him. Nor will I pretend it doesn't help my plan." There was no reason to tell Gav that Henry had pulled the trigger.

"And what is your plan?" he asked. I expected his eyes to be filled with sadness or anger, yet they were lifeless.

"It's under construction." It wasn't easy to admit I hadn't planned this far ahead. I had believed I'd be dead, and the fight would be someone else's to finish.

"Tell me what you need," he said. "I said I'd help."

He really means that. I surveyed the room. The guards were maintaining a barrier around the Inner Circle and Ben. Malcolm was in conversation with one of the guards not circling my enemies, presumably Max, who nodded his head.

"This is an outrage!" Humphrey Walston cried. "Back away you traitors!"

"Yes," Bob Henson said in a calmer manner. "Each of you will be discharged and arrested for your part in this treason."

"Go tell whoever's manning the camera to move it over here," I instructed Gav and nudged him toward the camera as an idea came to me. "We need to unmask Carl."

I walked in the direction of the guards. "You'll arrest no one, Bob. The guards listen to me. I'm in charge now."

"You?!" Carli said. "Like anyone would listen to a child."

I flashed her a wide grin. If she wanted to continue underestimating me, it would hurt only her. "They already do. Guards! Take them somewhere secure until they can stand trial."

The guards moved as one mass, guiding the Inner Circle and Ben out the door. I didn't like them leaving my sight, yet I had more pressing things to worry about.

Gav returned with a guard carrying the camera and its tripod. A cord attached to the camera draped down, leading to the guard's pocket. There was something familiar about it.

"Your friend was way too eager to bring the camera over," Gav said.

"It was boring standing over there," the guard said in Jax's voice.

So that was the help Henry and Max had fetched. "Well, this'll give you some excitement," I said as I walked to Carl Wessin's body.

Jax tracked my movements with the camera, not needing my prompting. Mindful of the pool of blood, I found a bare spot to crouch by Carl Wessin's head. "People of the City," I said to the camera, my hand on the edge of his hood. "The Government deceived you. I killed the previous Leader, a woman, and I'm about to reveal the identity of this Leader." With one smooth motion, I tugged the hood off to reveal his white-blonde hair.

"The Government can't even be honest about a change in Leadership," I said. "Their regime ends today. The rest of the Government is in guard custody and will stand trial for the injustices they've committed. Change is coming, and it will be for the better."

"Molly," Gav whispered. "You need to show the people who killed him."

I bit my lip and avoided his gaze. How could I thrust Henry in the spotlight and flaunt his actions in front of Gav?

"It doesn't matter who it was," Gav said. "The people need to know who your saviour is. Besides, your face is betraying his identity, so go get him already."

Gav knew me too well, even after recent events that had torn us apart. Before I could lose my nerve, or Gav's impatience could grow, I sprung to my feet, searched the room for Malcolm and jogged to him.

…

Malcom leaned against a wall across the room, his legs crossed at the shin. He peered my way with an arched eyebrow as I approached.

"Where is Henry?" I asked as I caught my breath.

"In the uniform room shedding his borrowed one. He couldn't stand wearing it anymore."

He'd need to be convinced to don it one final time. Hopefully, it wasn't too late. My feet propelled me in the direction Malcolm indicated. And there was a cracked-open door. With a deep inhale, I barged in.

…

Henry spun around at the sound of the door opening. He held his helmet in one hand, and the rest of his uniform was still on his body. His face went from wide-eyed, to a large grin as he saw me. "Molly."

I ran to him, like one magnet drawn to another, cupped his face in my hands and pressed a kiss on his lips, my body coming alive from the touch of his skin against mine. Before he could react, my fingers twined with his gloved ones, and I steered him from the room. "Gav and I need you."

His gloved hand was bulky in mine and didn't fit as well as his bare skin. Still, this contact was better than none, so I held on. One-handed, I got the door to the battle room open and pulled Henry through.

"Need me for what?" he asked as he swerved around the door as it closed behind us.

"Gav said the people need to know who killed the Carl Wessin."

Henry stopped walking, the halt in motion yanking my arm back and throwing me off balance. "He's okay with that?"

"As much as he can be," I said. "He's right about the people needing to know." They needed to put a face to their latest hero, and Henry could bear the attention.

"Alright," Henry said.

I led him to Carl Wessin's body, and he slid his helmet on as we reached the camera.

"Your ex has been speech making," Jax said. "I'm glad you're finally back."

I'd been gone a couple minutes at most, so there couldn't have been much for Jax to complain about. And Gav had stopped talking as we arrived, preventing me from forming an opinion on his words.

He stepped out of frame and ducked behind the camera. "I'll introduce you and then you can take your helmet off and say what you need to."

"Gavriel, I'm—" Henry started.

Gav held up a hand. "Save it for later. We have business to take care of."

Gav stepped back in front of the camera, its lens broadcasting his entire frame, Carl Wessin's body and the pool of blood. "People of the City," Gav said, his voice projecting power though I knew he was still in shock and upset. "The Leader shot today was my foster father: Carl Wessin. He wasn't a good man, and he wanted to execute Molly Birch for trying to improve things for everyone. There was nothing I, or Molly, could do to stop it," he said, regret flashing in his eyes. "Someone else, who's much braver than I'll ever be, found a way. I present, the saviour of our City, and the vanquisher of the Government: Henry Connor."

Chapter 38

I nudged Henry when Gav conferred the title: The Vanquisher. It suited him. He'd been brave doing what was necessary to save me and the City. I'd be forever grateful.

He stepped into frame and stood to Gav's side. Once in position, he pulled his helmet off and focused on the camera. "All I did was save Molly's life. I couldn't lose her, so when an opportunity presented itself, I seized it," he said with a broken voice, lowering his shining eyes and flicking them to Gav. "Molly is the hero. Not me. Without her, the City would be in worse shape than it was before she joined the Rebel Cause."

I sprang into the picture, grabbing Henry's gloved hand as I stood on his other side. "A rebellion can never be effective with only one person. The Rebel Cause formed long before me. It's taken many people to accomplish its goals. We provided the final pieces, and now it's time to celebrate our victory."

In the periphery of my vision, I saw gazing Henry at me. "I know one way," he said, wearing a knowing smile like Gav wasn't standing beside him.

I matched his smile with my own, the stream and audience forgotten. What did we have to fear now? "Show me."

Henry pulled his gloves off dropped them on the floor. He wrapped his bare hands behind my back, cradling my body as he dipped me backward and kissed me. My arms twined behind his neck, and I'd just crossed my wrists to secure them when Gav cleared his throat. Henry helped me up, my cheeks warm with a blush.

"I'm sure everyone loved seeing that," Gav muttered.

Jax laughed. "I stopped the stream when they started eying each other."

"Heh. Good call," Gav said, gifting Jax a grateful smile.

"If the stream is over," I said. "We can get out of here, right? This place has too many bad memories."

"Yep, I agree, there's too much blood in here," Jax said. He unplugged his tools, abandoned the camera and headed to the exit.

"Are you going to let me take this uniform off now?" Henry asked.

I crouched and picked up his discarded gloves, a smirk on my lips. "I don't know. Maybe you should wear it all the time. It's kind of attractive."

"Get my shoes from the wardrobe Max stuffed them in and I might consider keeping the rest if you like it that much," Henry said with a sparkle in his eyes.

"Where is Max?" I asked. Henry and I were alone in the large room. Even Gav had left us.

"Probably with Sage," Henry said with a shrug. "Or at his van."

"Sage?" Nothing good came when she was around. What was she doing here?

"You sent us to give her a message, and Max convinced her to help."

Help from Sage? She had too many interests of her own that conflicted with my goals for that to work. "I don't see—"

"She's outside with Val. They kept an eye out for Government-loyal guards."

"Let's go. I know you want to see Valerie." Maybe Valerie had kept Sage in line.

Henry grabbed my hand and we sped out of the tower, after a brief detour to the uniform room where he stripped off his borrowed one and retrieved his shoes from a wardrobe. He didn't drop my hand again once we stepped out into the sunlight.

Off to the far right, the guards were herding the Inner Circle members and Ben into their vans, the windows all tinted black. It wasn't something I wanted to be involved with, so I tore my attention away and ignored their protests.

From the tree line, Valerie and Sage sprinted toward us, Peter and Evelyn a step behind. They all appeared rumpled, with messy hair and dirt on their clothes and faces. Valerie collided with my body, her arms wrapping tight around my torso. I froze in shock at the contact, having expected her to embrace Henry.

"I'm glad you're safe," she said into my ear.

"Henry saved me," I said.

"We know," Sage said from a metre away, a flat, rectangular metal device in her hand. "Jax gave us a portable screen to watch, which we did after fending off some rogue guards lurking around. You both did well. Even the staunchest Devout members will have to admit things will be better now."

I had never dreamed I'd hear anything near praise from Sage Parker. It was too much of a shock for my mind to form words.

"Even if they don't," Henry said. "That shouldn't be something we have to deal with."

"The Devout will get over it," Peter said as he swiped at the dirt on his shirt. "You did a good job, Molly, and it seems like you've sprouted."

"We can't call you Little Sapling anymore," Evelyn giggled, looking like a giddy toddler that had found a fun way to get covered in dirt.

I frowned. What were they doing here? It was bad enough that they'd crashed my wedding.

Evelyn laughed again on seeing my expression. "We came with Sage to help. I even got to punch a guard."

"It was better than sitting in headquarters while everyone argued," Peter said.

They'd agreed to help and actually fought? This was a change. "Thanks," I said, with a blink. "I think."

"Don't worry," Henry said, giving me a peck on the cheek. "They're not that bad."

My skin reddened where his lips had landed, and I grinned.

"You two are so cute," Evelyn squealed, bouncing on her heels. She was a constant source of bubbly energy. I didn't see how Sage was friends with her. They were very different.

"Adorable," Peter said with a roll of his eyes. He placed his hand on Evelyn's arm and turned her around. "Let's give them some space and go clean up. You coming, Sage?"

"Sure," Sage said. "See you later, Molly."

I watch her, Peter and Evelyn veer toward the road through the trees and disappear. I hoped they wouldn't return with another cryptic message. I'd had a lifetime's worth of those.

...

Max walked over after Sage left. The purple circles under his eyes betrayed his tiredness, though he tried to smile when he got near us.

Valerie lit up and ran to Max, her eyes on him and a wide grin on her face. She flung her arms around his neck, pulled his face down and planted a kiss on his lips. As Henry and I stared agape, Max cradled Valerie's torso and returned her kiss. They shared their intimate moment, each lost in the other, until they broke apart, and Max traced his fingers down Valerie's arm as she stepped away.

Max glanced her way, his eyes shining as he did, but he spoke to me. "I have orders to drive you two out of here when you're ready."

Max and his orders. He didn't act solely on what Malcolm and my dad told him to do. Part of him helped me because he wanted to on a personal level. If only he could've admitted to it, or to wanting to stay with Valerie. I was sure he did want that. His dilated pupils and the lopsided grin on his face gave that much away.

Henry and I shared a glance. "We're ready, but we don't have anywhere to go."

"I'll take you to Jack's house," Max said as if it was the obvious answer.

Dad. I wanted to see him. Did Henry mind? Or did he want to return to the Colony? That felt like hiding, and I was done doing that. I peered at him and chewed on my bottom lip. "Is that okay with you?"

Henry squeezed my hand. "It doesn't matter where we go or where we live as long as I'm with you."

I beamed at Henry and clutched his hand. "Take us home, Max."

...

Valerie said her goodbyes as Henry and I left. The look on her face told of her reluctance to let Max and us leave. Jax had sent Charlie a message to arrange a ride for him and Valerie: Jax to his parents' apartment to give them the news, and her to the Colony. That was the closest place she had to a home. Henry hugged his sister, both of them with misty eyes. "We'll keep in touch, I promise," she said.

"I know," Henry said. "I love you."

She smiled and hugged him tighter. "I love you too."

Tears pooled in the corners of Henry's eyes. "Come on, Molly. We should go."

"Yeah, best not to keep Dad waiting."

He laughed as we walked with Max. I hadn't felt this carefree in a long time. Max had lent his van to the guards carting the Government members away, as they wanted to put one member per van to avoid them plotting an escape. So, he had commissioned a small car to drive us.

Jax and Gav stood near it, talking to each other. They stopped and turned their heads as Henry and I approached, our feet shifting and crunching the grainy ground with every step. Henry tensed when he spotted Gav.

"Gav," I said, trying to dictate the mood before it got awkward. "Where are you headed?"

He sighed, his eyes on Henry though he answered me. "With Jax, for now. Being alone in a giant house that was never mine doesn't feel right, even if it was available to me."

"Your foster dad didn't leave it to you?" Henry asked.

"No." Gav inhaled a deep breath, like he was summoning his courage. "Henry, I'm sorry for being self-centred our entire friendship. You deserved a better friend."

Henry gave him a small grin. "It wasn't the entire time Gavriel, and our friendship doesn't have to be over. Just, I won't pretend I don't love my wife because you used to date her."

"Your wife?" Gavriel asked, speaking the words slowly as he blinked and glanced at me with glazed over eyes.

Jax chuckled, and Max rolled his eyes as he went to ready the car.

"Henry and I went to the Colony to get married," I said, trying to quell my panic. Kissing in front of Gav was one thing, but announcing our marriage was dangerous. However, Henry had declared it, so giving details couldn't make things worse. And Gav did deserve to know. It was time he realized what we'd had was irrecoverable. "It wasn't possible to do it here."

"It isn't legal then," Gav said, his voice still slow and distant

I shook my head. "It doesn't matter whether the Government or a random citizen thinks it's legal. Henry's my husband."

Gav nodded. "If you're both happy, then congratulations."

"Thank you," Henry said.

"Yes. Thank you, Gav." It was weird that I'd once planned to marry Gav. How different had things and even I been then? It was difficult to imagine that life now. I didn't crave it as I once thought I would.

"If you're done," Max said, the car doors unlocked and open. "We should go."

"See you later," Gav said with a small wave as he walked off with Jax to join Valerie.

Henry and I hopped onto the car's backseat and held hands as Max drove down the forest road. All was as it had been on our drive in with Malcolm until we exited the rich Quarters and I gasped. People filled the streets, dancing and cheering. "All hail The Liberator and The Vanquisher!" was the chant audible above all else.

The throng impeded our progress as citizens were slow to clear the road. Honking car horns mixed with the chant as other vehicles found themselves as stuck as us.

"It might take a while," Max said as our car crept onward, moving through the slivers of space between people.

"Let them celebrate. We're in no rush." Henry and I were going to my dad's house with no goals to accomplish or enemies to defeat. It felt strange, this lack of urgency, in a nice way.

I rested my head on Henry's shoulder, and his free hand stroked my hair as we moved through the dense crowd. The people became sparser and more spread out the closer we got to the Gates. Even now, few wanted to leave the City. I understood. It was home, and always would be for most of them. It had been mine once too, but there was no returning to that old apartment. That was another thing I didn't miss as much as my past self had expected. Time and saving the City had a funny way of giving perspective to what really mattered.

Max drove under the Car Gate, its massive slab of metal sliding into the wall when the sensor scanned the windshield pass. This was much better than overriding the lock and setting off the alarm.

I sat up as Dad's house came into view. Dad was outside, leaning against the door and tracking our approach.

Max stopped the car and unlocked the doors for Henry and me to exit. "I better get back," he said, his eyes meeting mine in the rear-view mirror. "I'll see you later."

"Bye, Max," I said as I followed Henry out of the car. "Thanks for everything."

He nodded as I closed the door. I heard him drive away as Henry and I walked up to Dad.

My dad stood up straight and met us halfway to the door. "I'm sure this isn't what either of you expected married life to be like," he said. "Welcome home anyway."

I flung my arms around him. He was the last person alive that I was related to and would always occupy a place in my heart. "I missed you, Dad."

He hugged me back with his strong and protective arms. His embrace was a comfort I treasured every time I had it. "Come inside. I have things of yours and Henry's to return."

My fingers twined with Henry's again when Dad and I broke our hug and the three of us went inside. On the small kitchen table, laid a familiar black, velvet box. Our jewelry was in there, and my heart leapt at the chance to show my ties to Henry again.

"The rest of your things are downstairs," Dad said, over my shoulder as I lifted the box. "I wanted to ensure you got this first."

"Thank you, Dad."

Henry placed his hand over mine. "You want to go change? I can't wear these clothes anymore."

"Definitely." Fresh clothes that hadn't been on me for eight days sounded like a perfect plan. "We'll be back in a few minutes, Dad," I said as Henry and I moved to the stairway door.

An earlier time when I'd traversed the staircase, blind to its location, flashed through my mind. This time I knew where to step and where the light cord was to illuminate the space.

Henry and I stepped into the wood panelled hallway and traversed down to my pink bedroom. Our bags and wedding clothes were on the bed, and I'd never been gladder to have my old backpack. The backpack of books was beside it, which I had to get back to Max.

The jewelry box and books were forgotten as a shower and cleaner outfit became my new priorities. Henry and I took turns showering and getting dressed. When I finished, Henry was holding the jewelry box. "It's all here," he said when he flipped the lid open.

I walked over and peeked. Our rings and his pin still laid in the middle of my bracelet with the ruby ring. With nimble fingers, I picked up Henry's pin and pinned it to his shirt. Then I lifted his ring and slid it onto his finger. "Now everyone will know you're mine."

He beamed, like my personal ray of sunshine. "I should return the favour," he said, putting all my jewelry into his hand.

I gave him my hand and wrist, and, when he finished placing the jewels, I felt complete. I'd been feigning a different version of myself, hiding the signs of my heart. It had been necessary, but showing the truth was a weight lifted from me.

"You're beautiful," Henry said.

"As are you," I said against his mouth as I closed the distance between our bodies.

He kissed me, only a short trip down the hall from where we'd had our first kiss. We both had changed in drastic ways since then, and this time I responded, and he didn't flee.

Maintaining our kiss, I grabbed his shirt and backed toward the bed until my legs bumped into the frame. The momentum sent me backward onto the mattress, and Henry caught himself on his elbows, distributing his weight above me. There was nowhere I'd have rather been.

"I love you," he breathed into my mouth between kisses.

"I love you too." I'd accomplished a lot since I'd fled the City. None of it felt as good as being with the boy my heart chose, and I wanted to feel this way forever.

The Epilogue

Eleven months later

Henry drove into the City. He did this daily, but today, instead of heading to the Archives, he went to the rich Quarters. The route to his dad's house was ingrained in his memory now; he didn't have to think about the directions.

Malcolm, no longer undercover or a member of the Government, had put time and money into restoring the house to its former glory. Grass and flowers, chosen with Valerie's help, covered the lawn. They'd also cleared the interior of dust, washed the windows until they shone, repainted the walls and bought a new set of furniture.

Henry had just parked on the street and opened his car door when his sister exited the house and sprinted to him. "You're here!" she squealed as she launched herself at Henry and hugged him.

Henry wiggled free from Valerie's arms and stood. "I said I would be." Like anything could have kept him from his sister's wedding.

Valerie deciding to move in with Malcolm and help restore the house had shocked Henry. But he hadn't been surprised when Max proposed. Henry was happy his sister had said yes. All he wanted for Valerie was happiness. She grinned and grabbed his hand, her pink topaz ring glittering on her finger. "I know."

When Valerie yanked on his hand to lead him to the house, Henry went without protest.

With the new laws, Valerie and Max hadn't encountered any obstacles in getting a Courtship. The new Courtship Reviewer approved everyone that wasn't related to their intended or already married to someone else. Henry and Molly had skipped that paperwork. Jack Birch, as interim leader for the six months leading up to the election, had legalized all unions made in the Colony. Henry had appreciated Molly's lack of disappointment at that.

They'd thought of themselves as married since their ceremony, even when it wasn't legal, but Henry had feared he'd robbed her of an elaborate City wedding. Molly had soothed that fear when he voiced it.

"I don't need a fancy wedding," she'd purred, her arms twined around him and her brilliant eyes on his. "I have you, and that's all I want."

"Henry." Valerie's voice brought him back to the present. "Did you hear me?"

Henry blinked, having no recollection of his sister saying anything.

She flashed him a lopsided smile. "I was asking if you're ready to help."

Henry gave his sister a mock bow. "I'll do my best."

A lot had changed since Henry shot Carl Wessin. As temporary leader, a position he needed much persuasion to take, my dad had enacted a slew of new laws. The one child per couple limit was increased to two full-term pregnancies per couple. It was no longer mandatory to abandon extra children born from those pregnancies – not that poor families didn't still give up kids they couldn't afford. And there were still orphans.

Driving past the End Camp sent bittersweet pangs through my chest. It was a hospital now, no longer a place for people waiting to die. The reforms ushered in by the new Leader and Council prohibited and criminalized poisonings of patients and made health care and medicine more affordable, but that couldn't bring back my mom or anyone else who'd met their end within those walls.

I'd enrolled in the new Justice and Equality Department training program to help ensure no one else would suffer mistreatment from corrupt landlords, the Government or other persons in authority. It felt like a way to honour my mom while continuing what the Rebel Cause stood for. The department was also responsible for recommending decriminalization of illegal acts such as fleeing the City. This helped lower the prison population, which was especially important since inmates weren't executed anymore.

Dad patted my knee as we drove toward the Car Gate, which opened as it scanned the pass on his windshield. Even with the freedom to move from the City, few people ventured south of the Outskirts. It was too warm, and the rugged, nocturnal lifestyle of the Colony didn't appeal to many people. More Colonists moved back to the City than those who did the opposite. "Traffic's light today," he said as he turned down the road leading to the rich Quarters.

"Valerie will be happy we're early."

Her wedding to Max would be a smaller, less extravagant event than mine was. She had chosen Malcolm's renovated back yard as her venue. It was large enough to accommodate the ceremony and small dance floor.

"Always better to be early," Dad replied. "Especially to important events."

Valerie and Malcolm thrust all the last-minute details on Henry. He didn't complain; he'd do anything for his sister. But the long to-do list was overwhelming. He was relieved when Juna and Jax came to help.

The three of them finished Valerie's list as Max's parents arrived with his friends from the Guard Corps. The guards had become less intimidating and corrupt under Malcolm's leadership and separation from Government control. Malcolm had offered Henry a position, which Henry had declined. Being a guard had never been his idea and held too many ties to and remembrances of Ben. Instead, he'd suggested his father ask Juna – who'd gladly accepted a position in the new gender-inclusive Guard Corps. Henry himself had acted on an idea Molly planted in his mind long ago, on a moonlit trek in the middle of nowhere, and joined the research and public education branch of the Archives.

His musings were interrupted when, over the fence, he saw a familiar car pull up and park on the street just past the driveway. Max's guests following Malcolm into the backyard went unnoticed as Henry jogged to the car. The passenger door opened, and Molly, wearing a sparkling red dress the exact shade of her rubies, stepped out.

Henry was at my side as I stepped out of Dad's car. The grey suit he wore matched Valerie's colour scheme and didn't clash with my dress. He was so attractive in it. I cupped his face and planted a kiss as my dad walked past us with a wave. I lowered my hands and clasped one of Henry's. "We shouldn't keep Valerie waiting."

Henry chuckled. We both knew there was plenty of time before the ceremony. "You look radiant."

I smirked. "Who knew store bought dresses were as nice as custom made ones?" I teased before changing my tone. "You look handsome. Maybe Valerie should choose all your clothes."

"Just what I need," Henry gave an exaggerated groan. "My sister's ego inflated." His twinkling eyes locked on me like there was nothing more captivating in the world.

"I see your romance hasn't fizzled out," Sage Parker said from behind me.

I tore my gaze from Henry and saw her standing on the street flanked by Peter and Evelyn. Neither Henry nor I had heard them approach.

"Hello, Sage," Henry said, his focus still on me. "Peter, Evelyn."

"Don't worry," Evelyn giggled. "We'll keep Molly company while you and Sage are busy." She sidled up to me, looped her arm around mine and pulled me from Henry.

I gave Henry a small wave as Peter approached the gate to the backyard. Because their parents were friends, Sage was Max's attendant, while Henry was Valerie's. Hopefully, Sage would behave during the ceremony.

Once on the other side of the gate, I shrugged free of Evelyn's grip and veered to a seat beside Juna and Jax. They were roommates in the City now. Juna was excelling in the Guard Corps, while Jax worked for the Government Electronics Agency, ensuring the stream and screens worked as did the Gates. It was ironic, I thought, that they'd put him in charge when he'd hacked both systems. Maybe that's why. Who better to make improvements than the one who knew their weak points best?

In the row behind, Peter and Evelyn sat next to Katie, who gave me a little wave. Her mom had died a couple months after my wedding, and she had returned to the City to become a nurse, which I knew she'd be great at after she completed her training.

The remaining guests arrived after I'd sat. Among them were the Moris and Gav. Over the past months, Gav and Henry and worked on repairing their friendship. With Carl Wessin dead, and the Ben and the Inner Circle members – except Malcolm – imprisoned and stripped of their wealth and positions, Gav had changed. He rented a small apartment and worked as a case worker at the Foster Centre to find loving families for the children, now that they weren't being sold.

Valerie and Max weren't close to Gav, but he and Jax had bonded during their short stint living together with the Moris. Still, I imagined his presence at the wedding was because of Henry. Gav glanced my way as he sat with the Moris in the backrow. I nodded in return. We'd made our peace, and I was grateful to be free of remorse and regret whenever I saw him.

As the last of the guests settled, the officiant walked to the front with Max and the music began.

Henry had Max's wedding ring in his pocket. The one missing part from his own wedding was a part of Valerie's, and she'd entrusted him with the gold band. It was on his mind as Sage, carrying Valerie's wedding ring, placed her hand on his arm and strode with him down the aisle. But that thought died when Valerie, glowing and resplendent, stepped into sight on Malcolm's arm.

Henry wasn't accustomed to his sister being glamourous, yet in her wedding ensemble she could've been a model from one of the magazines Eleanor had left around the apartment in his childhood. At his wedding, she'd looked nice, but Molly had been the focal point then. Now he had to admit that his sister was pretty, as weird as that was.

Molly was still dazzling. He spotted her in the front right row, glittering like his mother's gems on her finger and wrist. While everyone else focused on the bride, Molly glued her eyes on Henry, one corner of her mouth turned up.

I didn't absorb much of the ceremony. Valerie and Max made a handsome couple, but my attention was on Henry. Was his on me in return? That seemed unlikely, although he glanced my way between performing his attendant duties and during the meal immediately following.

I claimed a table with Peter and Evelyn and ate a plate of buffet food. Though I'd hardly cared when picking out my selection, it tasted alright when I ate it in forkfuls.

When the meal was over, Henry danced with Sage while Valerie danced with Max. I chuckled. Henry and Sage were cordial to each other, but no one would label them as friends. And I still found it difficult to read her.

"It was a beautiful ceremony, wasn't it?" Evelyn sniffled at my side.

"Yes." Weren't all weddings?

Peter laughed. "Really, Evelyn. Isn't it obvious she only watched Henry?"

My face warmed as blood rushed to my cheeks and coloured them pink.

Gav came up behind me and placed a hand on my shoulder. "You okay, Mol?"

I stood and spun to face him, his hand dropping as a I moved. "I'm fine."

While past versions of Gav would've been hurt by that brush off for an answer, the present version smirked and nudged me toward the dance floor. He could still see through me. "Then why are you standing here? The song changed."

I stumbled from the unexpected nudge. But I was quick to right myself, and I walked to Henry.

"I've been waiting all day to do this." He said as I neared, and he held my hands, leaned in and planted a kiss on my mouth.

My lips responded. I'd grown familiar with the taste of him – sweet and spicy like sugar mixed with the seasonings he liked to cook with. This time sweetness from the buffet desserts overpowered the spice. He still had sugar granules on his lips and moaned when I licked them off. "Was that worth the wait?"

Henry chortled, well used to my teasing. "Definitely."

I held tight to his hands. "I didn't take my eyes off you."

"Dance with me. Your dad can go home whenever he wants, and I'll drive you."

"Sounds like a plan. I'd rather ride with you anyway."

Henry's eyes sparkled as the song changed, and he led me onto the dance floor. He circled my waist in his arms, drawing our bodies together. My heart rate quickened and my hands, acting on autopilot, twined behind his neck. We swayed in time to the music, each captivated by the other.

Henry twirled me to the beat and dipped my torso back. He bent down, his mouth a hair's width from mine. I'd never craved his touch more. He straightened up, raising me with him and leaving my desire unfulfilled. My pulse raced, and I gulped down my nerves.

"Are you alright?"

I bobbed my head, my feet no longer moving to the music. "Yes."

Henry slid his hands from me and headed off the dance floor. "Let's get a drink."

I caught up to him at the refreshment table where he already held two glasses of punch. He pressed one into my hand. "I promised Val I'd pose for pictures with her and then help clean up. You don't mind waiting, do you?"

The weight of his eyes pressed on me, both expectant and hopeful. "I'd rather be somewhere else," I said as I sipped my punch and his face fell. "Alone with you," I continued. "But I can wait."

"Good." Henry chugged his punch, threw down the glass and grasped my hand. He led me over to where Valerie and Max, their families and friends and the photographer waited.

Valerie flung her arms around Henry while he still held Molly's hand. He returned the hug with his free hand. His sister was being uncharacteristically affectionate today, but it was her wedding.

"It took you long enough to get here," Sage said. "Valerie's impatient about the pictures."

At that remark, Valerie released Henry, turned and shot Sage a glare. This was the sister Henry had grown to know. "My brother has a right to dance with his wife, even if it means my makeup wears off a bit more."

"You're still beautiful," Max said, brushing his fingertips along Valerie's arm.

Valerie beamed at her husband, her face glowing. Henry had once felt jealous of Max, which had been misplaced and had vanished some time ago. His own wife looked at him the way Valerie was looking at Max.

"Yes," Malcolm said. "But we should take pictures while the light is good."

And so, it began. Valerie wanted pictures with every combination of her friends, family and Max's. Henry was content to observe his sister posing with Max, Malcolm, her in-laws and then Jax and Juna. It was the seemingly endless number of poses she wanted him to be in that wore him out. Later he'd be grateful to have pictures with his family, so he plastered a smile on his face and didn't complain. He bit back his protests even with he and Sage had to pose together.

It was bittersweet when, after she was finished with him, Valerie wanted to pose with Molly. Henry was glad he no longer had to maintain a picture-perfect expression, but watching his wife pose with his sister left him feeling excluded.

After the photographer snapped a final picture, Valerie leaned and whispered in Molly's ear. Henry watched her nod and press her lips together, her face serious. What was this about? He got his answer when Valerie skipped to his side and nudged him in Molly's direction. "Go on, little brother, pose with your wife."

Henry was bewildered when Valerie shoved him toward me. I covered my mouth to stifle my giggles. "Stay here," Valerie had whispered. It hadn't taken much effort to work out what she intended. Henry stopped at my side, and we both turned to gaze at each other.

The camera snapped and Valerie chuckled. "Happy anniversary!" she squealed. "I know it's not for a couple weeks, but I wanted to give my present early."

Only Valerie would give us a present on her wedding day. While his sister finished her sentence, Henry planted his lips on mine, and he dipped me as he had when we danced. The camera snapped another picture as I grasped his lapel where his family pin was, not caring if I creased the expensive material. We could always iron it later.

Henry and I posed for a few more, less candid, shots before the photographer's allotted time expired. Valerie and Max left to say goodbye to their guests, so Henry and I went with Malcolm to join the clean up crew.

Valerie departed Max's side and beelined to her brother. She grabbed his shoulders, turned him around and walked to the exit. "Take Molly home. It doesn't matter what you swore earlier."

Henry lips formed a small circle, and he launched a protest. "Val—"

"I don't mind staying to help clean up," I said as I jogged after them.

Valerie had a glint in her eye like she knew a secret. "Go home. Dad has enough help." Her tone left no room for argument.

Henry caved, as he usually did when his sister insisted on something. "Alright, we're going."

With Valerie appeased, Henry and I walked, hand-in-hand, past the couple and our dads. Mine shot us a knowing look, which I brushed off. He knew how little alone time we got.

Henry had bought a car when he turned eighteen. It was our means of escape from Dad's small house, though we usually ended up at Malcolm's. This time when Henry pulled out of his parking spot, he didn't navigate toward the Outskirts. It was late afternoon, giving us a few hours before the Gates locked at sundown. He headed down the road to Quarter 1. I leaned forward and peered out the windshield at the unfamiliar streets. Was this a detour? "Where are we going?"

"You'll see," Henry said, keeping his face neutral and his eyes on the road. "It's a surprise."

"The Gate—"

"Trust me. We have more time than if we'd stayed to help clean up."

I did trust him. And his words held a certain logic. Still. What could he have for me in the rich part of the City?

Henry drove into District A of Quarter 1 and stopped in front of house 7. This left me more confused. We knew no one living in this part of the City. He exited the car, walked around and opened my door. I placed my hand in his offered and accepted his help getting to my feet.

Someone had manicured the yard and planted neat rows of daffodils along the walkway. The house itself was empty. There were no curtains in the windows or furniture visible through them. I also saw no evidence of lights turned on. "Why are we looking at an abandoned house?"

Henry laughed and led me along the stone walkway. "It's not abandoned, only empty and waiting for the new owners."

New owners? I stopped walking. "Are we trespassing?" Henry wasn't this reckless. What was going on?

He gave me a small shake of his head. "No."

"I don't understand."

Henry clasped my hands and settled his eyes on me as he led me to the door. "This is our house. Unless you hate it, then I can halt the sale."

Our house? We couldn't afford an apartment, let alone anything this nice. His words left me in shock and unable to respond.

As I stared, my mouth open, he continued, clearly nervous. "I thought we needed our own place; an apartment is so small, and this is close to—"

"Henry," I cut in, having found my voice halfway through his sentence. "Stop."

Henry dropped my hands and used his to push his hair back. He was quick to think the worst. "You hate it."

I shrugged. "I don't know. You haven't shown me the inside."

"I'm about to." He pulled a key from his pocket and used it to unlock the door.

The interior was stunning, and I saw why Henry had chosen it. The rooms were spacious and bright, even without the lights turned on. I followed Henry through the halls and rooms, in awe at their size.

"What do you think?" Henry asked when we finished our informal tour.

"It's amazing. Did you really buy it? How'd you get the money?"

He blushed. "Our dads helped."

I should've guessed they were involved. It brought more clarity to the expression my dad had given me and why Valerie shooed us out. "I'll thank them later. When can we move in?"

"Whenever we sign the paperwork."

It was that simple. The next day, Henry and I inked our names on the deed, packed up our meagre belongings and claimed our new home. We sat on the makeshift bed we'd contrasted in the sparsely furnished master bedroom, both of us weary from moving and excited.

Henry leaned forward, the fading light casting his hair in gold, and planted a soft kiss on my lips. "Happy early anniversary, Molly. I love you."

"I love you too, Henry." I pushed him backward on the blankets we'd piled and returned his kiss. I was prepared and content to spend forever at his side regardless of where we lived. I would've followed him to the smallest, most run-down apartment. However, this time fate had other, better plans. I accepted my good fortune and allowed myself to be happy. Together we'd toppled the corrupt Government and freed the City. I knew those weren't the last of our accomplishments. Thinking about what we could achieve next sent excitement pulsing through my veins. I couldn't wait to find out.

The End.

Causes and Courtships: prequel to The Liberator

Coming in 2023

Acknowledgements

First, thank you to whoever is reading this for taking a chance on my books. I hope Molly's journey had an impact on at least one of you. Next, thank you to my friends Kayle for giving me the idea for Jax's last name, Ana for your support and letting me vent, and to Steven. Thank you to Lena Yang for the amazing cover. Once again, it turned out better than I imagined. And thanks to Hunter and Gus, my furbabies for your love and snuggles.

www.ingramcontent.com/pod-product-compliance
Lightning Source LLC
Chambersburg PA
CBHW020457310726
48979CB00016B/2697/J

* 9 7 8 1 7 7 7 6 1 7 4 4 8 *